# 英文寫作練習 365

國際語言中心委員會 / 著

# 用「3 行寫作」養成英文思考的習慣！

　　學了這麼久的英文，遇到需要回應自己的想法，或者回答寫作題目時，卻完全不知道怎麼表達嗎？這是因為，英文學習者大多停留在表面的知識學習，卻沒有養成習慣用英文思考、溝通的「英文腦」。

### ☑ 每天寫 3 行，練習用英文表達自己的想法

　　要克服無法表達的問題，每天練習「3 行寫作」就是最簡單的方法。每天只要用 3 行的篇幅，回答和自己的生活、觀念相關的問題，練習用英文思考、傳達自己的想法，就能改變學了英文卻不敢、不想、不會用的困境。

### ☑ 用最小的努力，養成長久的習慣，帶來巨大的成就

　　暢銷書《原子習慣》提到：「新習慣的開始應該要花不到 2 分鐘」。如果一開始就挑戰長篇寫作，很可能因為太困難而半途而廢。所以，從 2 分鐘就能完成的 3 行寫作開始，就很容易養成每天的習慣，用細微的改變累積出長遠的效果。

### ☑ 從最貼近自身的問題開始發想，更能激發寫作動力

　　本書與一般寫作練習書不同，是從最基本的日常主題開始，例如嗜好、飲食習慣、人際關係等等，因為從最切身相關的問題出發，才能激發表達的欲望。等到熟練之後，再進入比較進階的主題，就不會覺得困難了。

　　只要堅持每天書寫的習慣，久而久之，用英文寫作、表達就不再是陌生又令人害怕的事了！

# 找到適合自己的寫作練習方式

　　本書精選 52 個主題、365 個問題，讓讀者每天練習用 3 個句子回答。為了還不熟悉寫作的讀者，每個問題都提供 2 個「你可以這樣回答」的破題句範例，以及完整回答的例文。除了每天按照順序寫以外，讀者也可以依照自己的能力與喜好，決定適合自己的使用方式。

## ☑ 52 週的寫作主題：照順序寫，或者挑選有興趣的主題寫

　　書中提供 52 個寫作主題（包括 Prologue 與 Epilogue），每個主題都有 7 個問題，讓讀者以週為單位，每週進行一個主題的寫作。主題以從簡單到難的順序編排，除了照順序以外，也可以只選擇自己有興趣的主題進行寫作。

## ☑ 靠自己構思內容，或者參考句型寫出破題句

　　對自己英文能力有信心的人，可以直接開始作答。如果不知道該怎麼下筆，「你可以這樣回答」也提供開頭的句子可以使用的句型，或者可能的回答內容。讀者可以仿照這些句子，寫出破題的第一句後，接著完成後面的部分就不難了。

## ☑ 只寫一句話，或者抄寫例文……只要持續寫就沒關係！

　　如果真的想不出 3 個英文句子，那麼就算只是回答一句話，也沒有關係。最重要的是維持每天寫英文的習慣，不要輕易中斷，只要持續下去，就能逐漸累積實力而進步。或者也可以抄寫書中提供的例文，同時學習其中使用的詞彙與慣用表達方式。

# 「破題→說明→收尾」的 3 行寫作法則

即使只是寫 3 個句子，也可以寫出結構完整的敘述。最基本的「破題→說明→收尾」敘述結構如下：

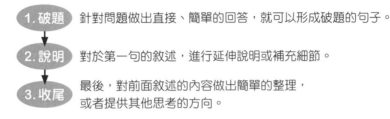

**1.破題** 針對問題做出直接、簡單的回答，就可以形成破題的句子。

**2.說明** 對於第一句的敘述，進行延伸說明或補充細節。

**3.收尾** 最後，對前面敘述的內容做出簡單的整理，或者提供其他思考的方向。

如果不知道怎麼收尾，或者覺得不需要的話，也可以用「破題→說明→說明」的模式來寫，也就是在簡單回答之後，只是提供說明，而不試圖下結論。

---

**範例**

**問題**

Are you growing plants? If not, would you like to give it a try?
你正在種植物嗎？如果沒有，你想試試看嗎？

**回答**

【破題】表達對於種仙人掌的興趣　　　【說明】解釋想要種仙人掌的原因

I'm considering growing a cactus. The main reason is its ability to survive in arid conditions, meaning it can still stay alive even if I forget to water it. Considering my poor gardening skills, a cactus seems like an ideal choice for me.

【收尾】表達因為前述的理由，而得到種仙人掌的結論

我正在考慮種仙人掌。主要的原因是它在乾旱的狀況存活的能力，意味著即使我忘記澆水，它也能夠存活。考慮到我糟糕的園藝技能，仙人掌似乎是對於我而言理想的選擇。

# 目 錄

## Prologue

未來一年計畫

## Q.1

# Have you ever set yearly goals? How effective do you think they are?

你曾經設定年度目標嗎？你認為它們效果如何？

....................

....................

....................

....................

Epilogue

**你可以這樣回答**

Yes, I find them quite effective.
是的，我覺得它們很有效。

No, I prefer to focus on shorter-term goals.
沒有，我比較喜歡聚焦在較短期的目標上。

**參考範例**

Yes, I do set my yearly goals, and I think they are very beneficial. Setting yearly goals helps me organize the upcoming year and keeps me motivated for a longer period. At the end of each year, these goals also help me go through what I have achieved.

是的，我會設定年度目標，而且我認為它們非常有益。設定年度目標幫助我安排接下來的一年，並且讓我在比較長的期間內保持動力。在每年的最後，這些目標也幫助我檢視一遍自己已經達成的事。

**詞彙**

beneficial 有益的

organize 組織，安排

upcoming 即將到來的

motivated
有動機的，有積極性的

go through 把…檢視一遍

**Q. 2**

# What do you want to learn in the upcoming year?

在接下來的一年，你想要學習什麼？

---

### 你可以這樣回答

I want to educate myself on how to use a professional camera.
我想要自學使用專業相機。

I am planning to develop my painting skills further.
我打算進一步發展我的繪畫技能。

### 參考範例

I want to learn Japanese because I am interested in Japanese culture. Luckily, I can take Japanese courses at the university without paying extra fees. I also plan to join the club of Japanese culture so that I can learn the language while making new friends.

我想要學日語，因為我對日本文化有興趣。幸運的是，我可以在大學修日語課而不用付額外的費用。我也打算加入日本文化社，這樣我就可以在交新朋友的同時學這個語言。

### 詞彙

luckily 幸運地

take a course 修一門課程

fee 費用

so (that) 好讓…，以便…

# What part of your life would you like to improve?

你想要改善自己生活中的什麼部分？

........................................................................................

........................................................................................

........................................................................................

........................................................................................

### 你可以這樣回答

I am looking to enhance my physical health.
我希望改善自己的身體健康。

Improving my communication skills is a priority for me.
改善溝通技能是我的一件優先事項。

### 參考範例

I would like to improve my time management. I find myself spending too much time on social media, making it hard to focus on things that matter more to my life. For example, I could use my screen time to do sports or learn new skills.

我想要改善我的時間管理。我覺得自己花太多時間在社交媒體上，讓我很難聚焦於對我的人生比較重要的事。舉例來說，我應該可以用我的螢幕時間來做運動或學習新的技能。

### 詞彙

time management
時間管理

social media 社交媒體

matter to 對於…而言重要

screen time
螢幕時間（看著電腦、電子設備等等的螢幕的時間）

# Q.4

# Where do you plan to travel in the following year?

在未來一年,你打算到哪裡旅行?

........................

........................

........................

........................

**你可以這樣回答**

I am planning a hiking trip to Patagonia.
我正在計畫到巴塔哥尼亞的登山健行之旅。

I am considering a trip around Taiwan.
我正在考慮台灣環島之旅。

**參考範例**

I am planning to go to Paris this summer with my family to see the well-known landmarks and enjoy the beautiful city. We are more than excited about the trip, and I believe it will be full of surprises, joyful moments, and unforgettable memories.

今年夏天我打算和家人去巴黎,看知名的地標並且享受這座美麗的城市。我們對於這趟旅行感到非常興奮,我也相信它會充滿驚喜、快樂的時刻以及難忘的回憶。

**詞彙**

well-known 知名的
landmark 地標
joyful 快樂的;使人高興的
unforgettable 難忘的

# What new habit would you like to build this year?

今年你想要培養什麼新習慣？

........................................................................

........................................................................

........................................................................

........................................................................

## 你可以這樣回答

I will start to read every day.
我會開始每天閱讀。

I plan to build a healthier sleep routine.
我打算建立比較健康的睡眠規律。

## 參考範例

I will begin commuting to work by bike. While I used to drive, I've recognized the negative impact on both the environment and my health. For the sake of myself and the planet, I think it is worthwhile to turn my commute into a workout.

我會開始騎單車通勤。我過去開車，但我認知到（開車）對於環境以及自身健康的負面影響。為了我自己和這個星球。我認為把我的通勤過程變成運動是值得的。

## 詞彙

commute
通勤（動詞或名詞）

recognize 認出

for the sake of 為了⋯

worthwhile 值得的

workout 運動

## Q.6

# What kind of people do you want to meet this year?

今年你想遇見怎樣的人？

......................................................................................................

......................................................................................................

......................................................................................................

......................................................................................................

**你可以這樣回答**

I'd love to connect with creative and artistic individuals.
我很想和有創意、有藝術氣質的人建立關係。

I hope to meet people who value family and relationships.
我希望遇見重視家庭與情感關係的人。

**參考範例**

I want to meet individuals who are open-minded, enthusiastic, and share similar interests with me. I think it would be meaningful to connect with people who have a positive outlook and a passion for the same hobbies. I am looking for connections that inspire me rather than drag me down.

我想要遇見心胸寬大、熱情，而且和我有類似興趣的人。我認為和有積極的展望、對同樣的嗜好有熱情的人建立關係，會很有意義。我在尋找能激勵我而不是把我拖垮的人際關係。

**詞彙**

open-minded 心胸寬大的

enthusiastic 熱情的

meaningful 有意義的

connect with
與…建立關係

outlook （對未來的）展望

inspire 激勵

# Think of something new you want to experience this year.

想一件你今年想要體驗的新事物。

........................................................

........................................................

........................................................

........................................................

### 你可以這樣回答

I've never run a marathon, but I want to try it this year.
我從來沒跑過馬拉松,但我今年想要嘗試。

I want to step out of my comfort zone by traveling solo.
我想要藉由獨自旅行來踏出舒適圈。

### 參考範例

I'd like to try something meaningful, such as volunteering at an animal shelter. I've always felt a deep sense of empathy toward animals, and I want to help surrendered and rescued pets find new homes. Making a difference in their lives would be incredibly rewarding.

我想要嘗試有意義的事,例如在動物收容所志願服務。我總是對動物有深深的同情,也想要幫助被放棄飼養與獲得救援的寵物找到新家。在他們的生命中做出改善會是非常值得的事。

### 詞彙

volunteer
志願服務,當志工

shelter 收容所

empathy 同感,同情

surrender 放棄

rewarding
有回報的,值得的

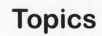

# Topics

# What's your favorite thing to do on weekends?

你週末最喜歡做的事情是什麼？

......................................................................................

......................................................................................

......................................................................................

......................................................................................

### 你可以這樣回答

I love spending my weekends Ving…
我喜歡做…來度過週末

My weekends are all about Ving…
我的週末都是用來做…

### 參考範例

My favorite thing to do on weekends is to go hiking in nature. I enjoy the tranquility nature brings. The spectacular views and fresh air make me forget about the hustle and bustle of city life.

在週末，我最喜歡做的事情是在自然中登山健行。我很喜歡自然帶來的寧靜。壯觀的景色和新鮮空氣，讓我忘記城市生活的喧囂擾攘。

### 詞彙

tranquility 寧靜

spectacular 壯觀的

hustle and bustle 喧囂擾攘

# Do you prefer outdoor or indoor activities?
你偏好戶外還是室內活動？

Prologue

1 嗜好

2 運動習慣

3 閱讀

4 音樂

5 影視娛樂

Epilogue

......................................................................

......................................................................

......................................................................

......................................................................

**你可以這樣回答**

I'm more of an outdoor/indoor person.
我比較算是喜愛戶外／室內活動的人。

… activities appeal to me.
…的活動對我有吸引力。

**參考範例**

I lean towards outdoor activities because I feel energized in the open air. When I engage in physical activities outside, such as jogging or biking, I become more cheerful than working out in a gym. Even walking on the street can make me feel better than staying at home.

我傾向於戶外活動，因為我在戶外感覺有活力。當我從事戶外的身體活動，例如慢跑或騎單車時，我比在健身房運動來得高興。就連在街上走路都能比待在家裡讓我感覺更好。

**詞彙**

lean towards 傾向於…
energized 感到有活力的
engage in 從事…
cheerful 高興的
work out 做運動，鍛鍊

# Is there a hobby you're thinking about starting these days?

你有什麼最近打算開始進行的嗜好嗎？

Prologue

1 嗜好

2 運動習慣

3 閱讀

4 音樂

5 影視娛樂

Epilogue

........................................................

........................................................

........................................................

........................................................

**你可以這樣回答**

I'm considering Ving…
我正在考慮做…

I feel like start Ving…
我想要開始做…

**參考範例**

Lately, I've been considering taking photos as a hobby. Having seen many captivating photos in online groups dedicated to photography, I started to learn how to use a camera. Through constant practice, I want to experiment with different techniques and develop my own unique style.

最近，我在考慮把拍照當作嗜好。因為在專門討論攝影的網路社團裡看到了許多迷人的照片，所以我開始學習如何使用相機。透過持續練習，我想要實驗各種不同的技巧，並且培養我自己獨特的風格。

**詞彙**

captivating 迷人的

dedicated to
專為某個目的的

constant 持續的

experiment with 實驗…

technique 技巧

Prologue

1 嗜好

2 運動習慣

3 閱讀

4 音樂

5 影視娛樂

Epilogue

# What's the most unique hobby you've ever heard of?

你聽過最獨特的嗜好是什麼？

........................................................

........................................................

........................................................

........................................................

**你可以這樣回答**

I know that some people are crazy about sand sculpting.
我知道有些人為做沙雕瘋狂。

There is a unique hobby called "noodling".
有一種叫做「徒手釣鯰魚」的獨特嗜好。

**參考範例**

I've heard about an extreme sport called "parkour". Jeremy, one of my closest friends, is very into it. Every Saturday, he and his partners film themselves conquering different terrains in the city. They can coordinate their limbs very well, and they all look very excited.

我聽過一種叫「跑酷」的極限運動。我一位最親近的朋友 Jeremy 非常喜歡這項運動。每週六，他和他的夥伴們會拍攝自己征服城市中各種不同地形的影片。他們可以把四肢協調得很好，而且他們看起來都非常興奮。

**詞彙**

be into 非常喜愛…
conquer 征服
terrain 地形
coordinate 協調
limb 肢（四肢）

# Do you prefer hobbies with or without social interaction involved?

你偏好有社交互動還是沒有社交互動的嗜好？

Prologue

1 嗜好

2 運動習慣

3 閱讀

4 音樂

5 影視娛樂

Epilogue

**你可以這樣回答**

As an extrovert/introvert, I prefer... 身為外向／內向的人，我偏好…
I tend to enjoy hobbies with/without social interaction.
我通常喜歡有／沒有社交互動的嗜好。

**參考範例**

As an extrovert, I enjoy social activities a lot. Compared to reading alone, I prefer discussing with others, so I joined a book club. Every week, we exchange ideas on a certain book, fiction or non-fiction, and I get the chance to engage in stimulating conversations with intellectually curious people.

身為外向的人，我很喜歡社交活動。和獨自閱讀比起來，我比較喜歡別人討論，所以我加入了讀書會。每星期我們都會針對一本特定的書交換想法，小說或非小說都有可能，而我有機會和智力層面渴望求知的人進行啟發人心的對話。

**詞彙**

extrovert 外向的人
exchange 交換
fiction 小說；虛構的事
stimulating 有啟發性的
intellectually 智力層面上
curious
好奇的，渴望求知的

19

Prologue

1 嗜好

2 運動習慣

3 閱讀

4 音樂

5 影視娛樂

Epilogue

# Is there any guilty pleasure you can't give up easily?

有什麼帶來罪惡感的快樂是你不容易戒掉的嗎？

................................................................................

................................................................................

................................................................................

................................................................................

### 你可以這樣回答

My guilty pleasure is N/Ving... 我罪惡的快樂是…

I can't resist N/Ving... 我無法抗拒…

Actually, I don't indulge too much in anything.
事實上，我不會太沉迷於什麼。

### 參考範例

I have a weakness for chocolate and ice cream, and I can't stop indulging in them. I know I should maintain a balanced and healthy diet, but I always end up giving in to the temptation. Maybe I should try replacing desserts with healthier alternatives, like fresh fruits.

我很難抗拒巧克力和冰淇淋，而且我無法停止沉迷於它們。我知道我應該維持均衡而健康的飲食，但結果總是屈服於誘惑。或許我應該嘗試用比較健康的代替品，像是新鮮水果來取代甜點。

### 詞彙

have a weakness for
難以抗拒（事物）

indulge in 沉迷於…

give in to 屈服於…

temptation 誘惑

alternative 替代的選擇

# Is there any hobby you've grown out of?

有什麼你長大後不再做的嗜好嗎？

Prologue

1 嗜好

2 運動習慣

3 閱讀

4 音樂

5 影視娛樂

Epilogue

........................................................................................

........................................................................................

........................................................................................

........................................................................................

### 你可以這樣回答

As I grew up, I stopped Ving…
隨著我長大，我不再做…

I don't have time to V… as an adult.
身為成年人，我沒有時間做…

### 參考範例

Yes, gaming is one of them. As a child, I used to rush home right after school to pick up the gamepad. RPG games like Zelda always made me lose track of time. However, as a grown-up, I have other distractions and don't have time for games anymore.

有，玩遊戲是其中之一。小時候，我經常在放學後衝回家拿起遊戲手把。薩爾達之類的角色扮演遊戲總是讓我忘記時間。不過，現在我是成年人，有了其他消遣，就再也沒時間玩遊戲了。

### 詞彙

gaming 玩電玩遊戲
gamepad 遊戲手把
lose track of
失去對…的掌握，忘記…
grown-up 成年人
distraction 消遣，娛樂

21

Prologue

1 嗜好

2 運動習慣

3 閱讀

4 音樂

5 影視娛樂

Epilogue

# How do you exercise, and how often do you do it?

你如何運動，多常運動？

.................................................................................................

.................................................................................................

.................................................................................................

.................................................................................................

## 你可以這樣回答

I ... on a weekly/daily basis.
我每週／每天…

I ... once/twice/X times a week.
我每週…一／二／X 次。

## 參考範例

I go to the gym twice a week for cardio exercises and strength training. If I can't make it to the gym before it closes, I do yoga at home. While my workout routine is diverse, I think I could increase the frequency to three or four days a week.

我每週去健身房兩次，做有氧運動和力量訓練。如果我無法在健身房關門前趕到，我就在家做瑜伽。雖然我的運動規劃很多元，但我想我可以把頻率增加到一週三或四天。

## 詞彙

cardio 有氧運動
（= cardiovascular exercise 心血管運動）

strength training
力量訓練

make it to 及時趕到…

routine 例行程序

diverse 多樣的

frequency 頻率

Q.16

# What is your favorite sport?
你最喜歡的（競賽）運動是什麼？

Prologue

1 嗜好

2 運動習慣

3 閱讀

4 音樂

5 影視娛樂

Epilogue

.................................................................

.................................................................

.................................................................

.................................................................

### 你可以這樣回答

I enjoy playing…
我喜歡打…（球類運動等）。

I love …, but I am more of a fan than a player.
我愛…，但我比較算是球迷而不是球員。

### 參考範例

My favorite sport is basketball. I love its fast-paced nature, the teamwork involved, and the thrill of competition. I've been playing basketball ever since I was seven, and I never get tired of it. Basketball has become a significant part of my life.

我最愛的競賽運動是籃球。我喜愛它節奏快的性質、其中牽涉的團隊合作，以及競爭的興奮感。我從 7 歲時就開始打籃球，而且從來不會厭倦。籃球已經成為我生活中很重要的一部分。

### 詞彙

fast-paced
步調（節奏）快的

nature 性質

teamwork 團隊合作

thrill 興奮感

competition 競爭

significant 重大的

23

Prologue

1
嗜好

2
運動習慣

3
閱讀

4
音樂

5
影視娛樂

Epilogue

# What sport or exercise would you like to try even though you don't have any experience?

什麼是你儘管沒經驗還是想試試看的運動？

........................................

........................................

........................................

........................................

你可以這樣回答

I've always been curious about…
我一直對…很好奇

I've never tried… before, but I'd like to give it a shot.
我從來沒試過…，但我想試一次。

參考範例

I would love to try rock climbing. Unlike other sports, rock climbing is more about challenging oneself than competition. When moving upwards, you have to stay mentally sharp and physically agile. I want to try it one day and test my limits.

我很想試試攀岩。不像其他運動，攀岩比較偏向自我挑戰而不是競爭。往上移動時，必須保持心智敏銳、身體敏捷。我有一天想要試試看，並且測試我的極限。

詞彙

competition 競爭
mentally 心智上
sharp （心智狀態）敏銳的
physically 身體上
agile 敏捷的

# What sport is the most popular among your friends?

什麼運動在你的朋友之間最受歡迎？

Prologue

1 嗜好

2 運動習慣

3 閱讀

4 音樂

5 影視娛樂

Epilogue

**你可以這樣回答**

A lot of my friends enjoy N/Ving…
我有許多朋友很喜歡…

Many of my friends are into N/Ving…
我有許多朋友非常喜歡…

**參考範例**

Among my friends, badminton is the most popular sport. It can be enjoyed by people of all physical abilities, making it inclusive and accessible to everyone. Many of my friends follow professional matches, and some of them even participate in badminton teams.

在我的朋友之間，羽毛球是最受歡迎的運動。各種身體能力的人都可以享受這種運動，使它能包容每個人、讓每個人都能接近。我有許多朋友追蹤職業比賽，其中有些人甚至參加羽毛球隊。

**詞彙**

physical 身體的
inclusive 包容的
accessible 可接近的

Prologue

1
嗜好

2
運動習慣

3
閱讀

4
音樂

5
影視娛樂

Epilogue

# Does exercise make you feel more positive?

運動讓你感覺更正面嗎？

........................................................................

........................................................................

........................................................................

........................................................................

你可以這樣回答

Exercise is a mood booster for me.
運動對我來說是能提振情緒的事。

I only feel exhausted when I exercise.
我運動時只覺得筋疲力盡。

參考範例

Sure! Exercise has a positive impact on my overall well-being. It boosts my mood, reduces anxiety, and increases my self-confidence. When I feel down, I put on my running shoes and go for a run. It always works!

當然！運動對我整體的身心健康有正面的影響。它提振我的心情、減少焦慮，並且增加我的自信。當我感到沮喪時，我就穿上我的跑步鞋去跑步。這樣總是會有效！

詞彙

overall 整體的
well-being 身心健康
boost 增進，提高
anxiety 焦慮
self-confidence 自信

# Do you enjoy team sports or individual sports more?

你比較喜歡團隊運動還是個人運動？

## 你可以這樣回答

Team/individual sports appeal to me because…
團隊／個人運動吸引我，因為…

I prefer team/individual sports.
我比較喜歡團隊／個人運動。

## 參考範例

I find team sports more enjoyable. I often play soccer with my friends, and the comradeship, shared goals, and collective effort give me a sense of belonging. Being part of a team makes victories more rewarding and memories more unforgettable.

我覺得團隊運動比較愉快。我經常和朋友踢足球，而同伴情誼、共同目標與集體努力讓我有歸屬感。身為隊伍的一員，讓成功感覺更有意義，回憶也更難忘。

## 詞彙

comradeship 同伴情誼

collective 集體的

sense of belonging 歸屬感

rewarding 有回報的，有意義的

unforgettable 難忘的

Prologue

1
嗜好

2
運動習慣

3
閱讀

4
音樂

5
影視娛樂

Epilogue

# Do you think e-sports are also sports?

你認為電競（電子競技）也是運動嗎？

........................................................

........................................................

........................................................

........................................................

### 你可以這樣回答

I believe e-sports should be considered sports.
我相信電競應該被認為是運動。

I think e-sports differ significantly from physical sports.
我認為電競和身體運動有很顯著的不同。

### 參考範例

Yes, I do consider e-sports to be a form of sport. Like all sports, e-sports require skill, strategy, and intense mental focus. Professional e-sports players also undergo rigorous training, where they must push their limits like all sportsmen do.

是的，我認為電競是一種運動的形式。就像所有運動一樣，電競需要技巧、策略與很強的心理專注力。職業電競選手也會接受嚴格的訓練，就像所有運動員一樣挑戰自己的極限。

### 詞彙

strategy 策略
intense 強烈的
rigorous 嚴格的

# Do you enjoy shopping for books in a physical bookstore?

你喜歡在實體書店選購書籍嗎？

Prologue

1 嗜好

2 運動習慣

3 閱讀

4 音樂

5 影視娛樂

Epilogue

**你可以這樣回答**

It is a delightful experience for me. 那對我來說是很愉快的經驗。

I find online bookstores more convenient.
我覺得網路書店比較便利。

**參考範例**

Absolutely! Walking in a bookstore allows me to browse books physically, experience the ambiance, and interact with the staff. Therefore, I can make better decisions when I shop there. Online shopping, on the other hand, lacks the same experience and immediate gratification of taking a book home instantly.

當然！走進書店讓我能實際瀏覽書籍、體驗書店的氛圍，並且和員工互動。所以，我在那裡購物時可以做出比較好的決定。至於網路購物，則是少了同樣的體驗，以及立刻帶一本書回家的立即滿足感。

**詞彙**

ambiance 氛圍

interact 互動

immediate gratification
立即滿足（相對於 delayed gratification〔延遲滿足〕的概念，表示立即獲得獎賞或享受，而不是等到未來）

# What is your favorite book genre?

你最喜愛的書籍類型是什麼？

Prologue

1 嗜好

2 運動習慣

3 閱讀

4 音樂

5 影視娛樂

Epilogue

............................................................

............................................................

............................................................

............................................................

你可以這樣回答

My favorite book genre is mystery.
我最喜歡的書籍類型是懸疑（推理）作品。

I'm drawn to science fiction.
科幻小說很吸引我。

參考範例

It's hard to pick just one favorite, but fantasy fiction is one I've been enjoying since childhood. Usually, I can finish a book in one sitting. The world of swords and magic is so captivating that I can't help imagining myself being part of it.

只挑一個最愛的很難，但奇幻小說是我從小就很喜歡的一種。通常我可以坐著一口氣讀完一本書。劍與魔法的世界很令我著迷，讓我忍不住想像自己是其中的一部分。

詞彙

**fantasy** 幻想，奇幻作品

**fiction** 小說（作為小說的總稱，不加 -s）

**in one sitting**
在坐著的期間一口氣…

**captivating** 令人著迷的

**cannot help Ving**
忍不住做…

# Do you prefer e-books, audiobooks, or printed books?

你比較喜歡電子書、有聲書還是紙本書？

.......................................................................................................

.......................................................................................................

.......................................................................................................

.......................................................................................................

Prologue

1 嗜好

2 運動習慣

3 閱讀

4 音樂

5 影視娛樂

Epilogue

### 你可以這樣回答

I prefer…　我偏好…

… are my favorite　…是我的最愛

… suit my lifestyle better　…比較適合我的生活型態

### 參考範例

I have a soft spot for printed books. There's something magical about flipping through actual pages and holding the weight of the story. Seeing my bookshelf filled with physical copies brings me a sense of fulfillment and reminds me of the worlds I have explored.

我對紙本書情有獨鍾。翻過實際的頁面並且拿著故事的重量，有一種奇妙的感覺。看到我放滿實體書的書架，帶給我一種滿足感，並且提醒我曾經探索過的（書的）世界。

### 詞彙

magical 魔法的，奇妙的

have a soft spot for
對…情有獨鍾

flip 翻動

copy 出版品的一份

fulfillment 滿足（感）

# When you were little, who was your favorite fairy tale character?

在你小的時候，誰是你最喜愛的童話故事角色？

Prologue
1 嗜好
2 運動習慣
3 閱讀
4 音樂
5 影視娛樂
Epilogue

........................................................................

........................................................................

........................................................................

........................................................................

### 你可以這樣回答

My favorite fairy tale character was Cinderella.
我當時最喜愛的童話故事角色是灰姑娘。

I adored Snow White when I was little.
我小時候很喜歡白雪公主。

### 參考範例

I would say the Little Mermaid. When I was little, I felt the world under the sea was mysterious yet intriguing. I was even convinced that mermaids actually exist because of the vivid depiction as seen in the animation.

我會說是小美人魚。當我很小的時候，我覺得海底世界神祕卻也吸引人。因為動畫裡看到的生動描繪，我甚至相信了人魚真的存在。

### 詞彙

mysterious 神祕的
intriguing 吸引人的
convinced 確信的
vivid 生動的
depiction 描繪
animation 動畫

# What is your most recent favorite book about?

你最近最喜歡的書是關於什麼？

Prologue

1 嗜好

2 運動習慣

3 閱讀

4 音樂

5 影視娛樂

Epilogue

.........................................................................................

.........................................................................................

.........................................................................................

.........................................................................................

### 你可以這樣回答

The book explores…
這本書探究…

It's a novel filled with…
它是充滿…的小說

### 參考範例

One of my recent favorites is a bestseller that relates fairy tale classics to popular psychology. This book helps people suffering from emotional distress overcome their fear of getting professional help. It makes me understand that I don't have to face my problems all by myself.

我最近最喜歡的其中一本書，是將經典童話故事和大眾心理學連結的暢銷書。這本書幫助遭受情緒痛苦的人克服對於尋求專業幫助的恐懼。它讓我明白我不必自己面對我的問題。

### 詞彙

bestseller
暢銷的東西，暢銷書

classic 經典作品

popular psychology
大眾心理學

distress 痛苦

overcome 克服

# What kind of setting do you find most suitable for reading?

你覺得怎樣的環境最適合閱讀？

........................................................................

........................................................................

........................................................................

........................................................................

Prologue

1 嗜好

2 運動習慣

3 閱讀

4 音樂

5 影視娛樂

Epilogue

### 你可以這樣回答

A peaceful setting is perfect for immersing myself in a book.
平靜的環境很適合讓我沉浸在書中。

I find cafés to be perfect for reading.
我覺得咖啡店很適合閱讀。

### 參考範例

When it comes to reading, I find sitting in a quiet corner with a warm cup of tea or coffee to be the most relaxing. It is also important for me not to be disturbed. To minimize distractions, I usually turn off my phone or switch to silent mode.

說到閱讀，我覺得坐在安靜的角落，伴隨一杯溫暖的茶或咖啡，是最讓人放鬆的。對我而言，不要被打擾也很重要。為了將分心的事物減到最少，我通常會關掉手機或切換到靜音模式。

### 詞彙

When it comes to 說到…

disturb 打擾

minimize
將…最小化、減到最少

distraction
令人分心的事物

silent mode
（手機）靜音模式

# Do you think children should start reading as early as possible?

你認為小孩應該儘早開始閱讀嗎？

Prologue

1 嗜好

2 運動習慣

3 閱讀

4 音樂

5 影視娛樂

Epilogue

........................................................................................

........................................................................................

........................................................................................

........................................................................................

## 你可以這樣回答

It depends on a child's interests.
這取決於一個小孩的興趣。

We cannot force children to read when they are not ready.
我們不能在小孩沒準備好的時候強迫他們閱讀。

## 參考範例

Of course. The sooner children start reading, the sooner they can learn to explore the world of their own accord. Plus, reading is a great way to improve their language skills. It also helps them stay focused, preparing them for success in school.

當然。小孩越早開始閱讀，就能越早學習自發地探索這個世界。而且，閱讀是增進他們語言能力的好方法。閱讀也能幫助他們保持專注，為他們在學校（學業）的成功做好準備。

## 詞彙

on one's own accord
主動地，自願地

focused 專注的

prepare someone for
讓某人為…做好準備

Prologue

1 嗜好

2 運動習慣

3 閱讀

4 音樂

5 影視娛樂

Epilogue

Q.29

# What is your favorite music genre?

你最喜愛的音樂類型是什麼？

.................................................................................

.................................................................................

.................................................................................

.................................................................................

### 你可以這樣回答

I'm a fan of electronic dance music.
我是電子舞曲（EDM）的樂迷。

I enjoy listening to indie pop.
我喜歡聽獨立流行音樂。

### 參考範例

I'm a fan of jazz. It's a genre with a rich history, and jazz musicians can convey their emotions through improvisation. Of course, I love the music itself: the smooth melodies and complex harmonies create a soothing atmosphere, which is captivating to me.

我是爵士樂迷。這是個有豐富歷史的音樂類型，而爵士樂手可以透過即興演奏來傳達自己的情緒。當然，我喜歡音樂本身：柔和的旋律和複雜的和聲，創造出舒緩的氣氛，這讓我很著迷。

### 詞彙

convey 傳達
improvisation 即興
harmony 和聲
soothing 撫慰的，舒緩的
captivating 令人著迷的

# Who is your favorite singer or band?

誰是你最喜歡的歌手或樂團？

........................................................................................

........................................................................................

........................................................................................

........................................................................................

Prologue
1 嗜好
2 運動習慣
3 閱讀
4 音樂
5 影視娛樂
Epilogue

### 你可以這樣回答

There aren't many singers that can sing/dance as well as…
沒有很多歌手唱歌／跳舞能像…一樣好

I listen to …'s songs every day.
我每天聽…的歌曲。

### 參考範例

My favorite band is Sodagreen. I especially love the vocalist's voice, which is flexible and expressive at the same time. I can really feel his emotions when I listen to their songs. They are also in a habit of rearranging their songs, making their live performances more interesting.

我最喜歡的樂團是蘇打綠。我特別喜愛主唱的聲音，靈活有彈性又富有表現力。我聽他們的歌的時候，真的可以感受到他的情緒。他們也習慣對自己的歌重新編曲，使他們的現場表演更加有趣。

### 詞彙

vocalist 歌手；主唱
flexible 有彈性的
expressive 富有表現力的
rearrange 重新編曲

# Do you listen to music when you work or study?

你工作或學習時會聽音樂嗎？

Prologue
1 嗜好
2 運動習慣
3 閱讀
4 音樂
5 影視娛樂
Epilogue

......

**你可以這樣回答**

Yes, I often listen to music while I work/study.
是的，我工作／學習時常常聽音樂。

No, I prefer to work/study in silence.
不，我比較喜歡在安靜的情況下工作／學習。

**參考範例**

No, listening to music often distracts me. When I study, I play white noise or ambient sounds instead to help myself focus. If I really want to listen to some music while studying, classical music is my go-to as it has no lyrics.

不會，聽音樂常常會讓我分心。當我學習的時候，我會改播放白噪音或環境音來幫助自己專注。如果我真的想在學習時聽點音樂，古典音樂是我的首選，因為它沒有歌詞。

**詞彙**

distract 使分心
white noise 白噪音
ambient 周遭的，環境的
classical 古典的
go-to （某種情況下的）首選

# Have you ever been to a classical or pop music concert?

你曾經去過古典音樂會或流行音樂演唱會嗎？

.................................................................

.................................................................

.................................................................

.................................................................

Prologue

1 嗜好

2 運動習慣

3 閱讀

4 音樂

5 影視娛樂

Epilogue

### 你可以這樣回答

I've been to… concerts.
我去過…音樂會／演唱會。

I haven't attended any concerts yet.
我從來沒去過任何音樂會／演唱會。

### 參考範例

I've been to quite a few pop music concerts. I remember attending a rock band's concert, where the audience sang along to every song. The crowd was so energetic and passionate that the band went all out. They really became one with their fans.

我曾經去過不少流行音樂演唱會。我記得去過一個搖滾樂團的演唱會，那裡的觀眾跟著唱每首歌。群眾很有活力而熱情，也讓樂團全力以赴。他們真的和歌迷融為一體了。

### 詞彙

quite a few 許多，不少
attend 出席，參加
energetic 有活力的
passionate 熱情的
go all out 全力以赴

# Do you listen to music while walking on the street? Why?

你走在路上時會聽音樂嗎？為什麼？

........................................

........................................

........................................

........................................

### 你可以這樣回答

No, I prefer to be aware of my surroundings and stay alert.
不，我比較喜歡察覺到周遭環境並且保持警覺。

It depends on my mood.
取決於我的心情。

### 參考範例

Yes, I love listening to music while walking on the street. Especially on my way to the office, I need some upbeat music to cheer myself up. Music always makes the walk more enjoyable and helps me tune out the noise around me.

是的，我很愛在走路時聽音樂。尤其是在往辦公室（公司）的路上，我需要一些歡快的音樂來提振我的心情。音樂總是讓走路比較愉快，並且讓我不會聽到周遭的噪音。

### 詞彙

especially 尤其

upbeat 歡快的

cheer up （使）高興起來

enjoyable 令人愉快的

tune out
不去聽⋯；不理會⋯

Prologue

1 嗜好

2 運動習慣

3 閱讀

4 音樂

5 影視娛樂

Epilogue

# Do you think vinyl records are worth having?

你認為黑膠唱片值得擁有嗎？

Prologue

1 嗜好

2 運動習慣

3 閱讀

4 音樂

5 影視娛樂

Epilogue

..................................................

..................................................

..................................................

..................................................

### 你可以這樣回答

Personally, I find vinyl records are worth collecting.
我個人覺得黑膠唱片值得收藏。

I don't see the appeal of vinyl records in the digital age.
我不明白黑膠唱片在數位時代的魅力。

### 參考範例

It depends. To hardcore music fans like me, vinyl records have a special charm. While they are not as convenient as streaming, they sound warmer and create a nostalgic experience. For others, however, vinyl records are just too pricey and take up a lot of space.

看情況。對於像我這樣的死忠樂迷，黑膠唱片有特別的魅力。雖然不像串流那麼便利，但它們聽起來比較溫暖，並且創造出懷舊的體驗。但對於其他人，黑膠唱片就是太貴了，而且很佔空間。

### 詞彙

hardcore 中堅的；堅定的

charm 魅力

steaming （影音的）串流

nostalgic 懷舊的

pricey 昂貴的

Prologue

1 嗜好

2 運動習慣

3 閱讀

4 音樂

5 影視娛樂

Epilogue

# Do you enjoy karaoke? Why or why not?

你喜歡唱卡拉 OK 嗎？為什麼？

......

......

......

......

## 你可以這樣回答

I enjoy karaoke with friends.
我喜歡和朋友唱卡拉 OK。

Karaoke is not my thing.
我不喜歡／不擅長唱卡拉 OK。

## 參考範例

As a typical Taiwanese, I definitely enjoy karaoke. To me, karaoke is all about having fun and singing your heart out with friends. Even if you don't have the best singing voice, you can relax and enjoy the moment without worrying about judgment.

身為典型的台灣人，我當然喜歡唱卡拉 OK。對我而言，卡拉 OK 就是要玩得開心，並且和朋友一起熱情地唱。就算你沒有最好的歌聲，也可以放鬆並享受這一刻，而不用擔心（別人的）評判。

## 詞彙

typical 典型的

definitely 當然

sing one's heart out
熱情地唱

judgment 評判

# Do you prefer movies or TV series?
你比較喜歡電影還是電視影集？

................................................

................................................

................................................

................................................

### 你可以這樣回答

I enjoy both, but I tend to V... 我兩個都喜歡，但我傾向於…

I love TV series because I can immerse myself in the story for an extended period.
我愛電視影集，因為我可以長時間沉浸在故事中。

### 參考範例

I prefer movies to TV series. Movies can encapsulate a complete narrative within a limited time frame, and they can be artistic in their expression. TV series, on the other hand, consist of multiple episodes, so they demand considerable investment of time, making it exhausting to keep up with the storylines.

我喜歡電影勝過電視影集。電影可以在有限的時間範圍內包含一個完整的敘事，而且它們的表達可以是藝術性的。至於電視影集，則包含許多集數，所以需要投資許多時間，使得跟上故事情節變得很累人。

### 詞彙

encapsulate
（精煉地）包括，概括
narrative 敘事
time frame 時間範圍
artistic 藝術性的
consist of 由…構成
storyline 故事情節

# What kind of movie do you like best?

你最喜歡哪種電影？

Prologue

1 嗜好

2 運動習慣

3 閱讀

4 音樂

5 影視娛樂

Epilogue

.......................................................................................

.......................................................................................

.......................................................................................

### 你可以這樣回答

My favorite genre is science fiction.
我最愛的類型是科幻（電影）。

I'm a big fan of horror movies.
我非常喜歡恐怖片。

### 參考範例

I enjoy romantic comedies the most. I find love to be a timeless topic that I never get tired of, and love stories can always make me cry and smile. I am captivated by the emotions that romantic comedies evoke, so I think they are perfect for a movie night.

我最喜歡浪漫喜劇。我覺得愛情是我永遠不會厭倦的經典主題，而愛情故事總是能讓我又哭又笑。我為浪漫喜劇引起的情緒而著迷，所以我認為它們非常適合看電影的夜晚。

### 詞彙

romantic comedy
浪漫喜劇

timeless 永恆的，不朽的

captivate 使著迷

emotion 情緒

evoke 喚起，引起

# Do you prefer watching movies at home or going to the theater?

你比較喜歡在家看電影還是去電影院？

Prologue

1 嗜好

2 運動習慣

3 閱讀

4 音樂

5 影視娛樂

Epilogue

........................................................................

........................................................................

........................................................................

........................................................................

**你可以這樣回答**

Ving … is my favorite.
…是我最喜歡的。

I like the comfort of watching movies at home.
我喜歡在家看電影的舒適。

**參考範例**

While the comfort at home is appealing, I still think that the theater experience always makes a movie better. The surround sound, stunning visuals, and the shared excitement with other people in the audience all elevate the experience and make a movie more memorable.

雖然家裡的舒適很吸引人，但我仍然認為電影院的體驗總是會讓電影更好。環繞音效、令人驚豔的視覺效果，以及和其他觀眾共同的興奮感，都會提升體驗，並且讓電影更加難忘。

**詞彙**

appealing 吸引人的
surround sound 環繞音效
stunning 令人驚豔的
elevate 提升
memorable 難忘的

# Which actor/actress is your all-time favorite?

哪位演員是你一直以來最喜歡的？

....................................................................

....................................................................

....................................................................

....................................................................

你可以這樣回答

I have a special admiration for…
我特別仰慕…

… is my top pick.
…是我的第一選擇。

參考範例

Steven Yeun, who is well-known for his role in the series *The Walking Dead*, is my all-time favorite. He has a knack for bringing characters to life and always delivers convincing performances. As an Asian American, he has a special place in the industry, yet he remains underrated.

以在《陰屍路》中的角色知名的史蒂芬．連，是我一直以來最喜歡的演員。他有本事讓角色變得生動，而且總是帶來有說服力的表演。身為亞裔美國人，他在業界有特別的地位，然而他（的演技等等）還是被低估了。

詞彙

have a knack for
有…的本事

bring… to life
使…有生氣、變得生動

deliver 遞送，給出

convincing 有說服力的

underrated
（相對於實力、表現）被低估的，評價過低的

# Which fictional character do you have the most empathy towards?

你對哪個虛構的角色最能感同身受？

........................................

........................................

........................................

........................................

Prologue

1 嗜好

2 運動習慣

3 閱讀

4 音樂

5 影視娛樂

Epilogue

**你可以這樣回答**

… is the character I empathize with the most.
…是我最能感同身受的角色。

I feel the most empathy towards…
我對…最能感同身受

**參考範例**

I would say Severus Snape from the *Harry Potter* series. He is one of the most misunderstood and complex characters in the series. His story is filled with sacrifice and unrequited love. I tear up every time I think about all he has been through.

我會說是《哈利波特》系列的賽佛勒斯·石內卜。他是這個系列裡最被誤解而複雜的角色之一。他的故事充滿犧牲與沒有回報的愛。每次我想到他經歷的一切就會眼裡含淚。

**詞彙**

misunderstood 被誤解的
character 角色
sacrifice 犧牲
unrequited
（愛情）沒有回報的
tear up 眼裡含淚

# Do you eat anything when watching movies?

你（用家裡的螢幕）看電影的時候會吃東西嗎？

Prologue

1 嗜好

2 運動習慣

3 閱讀

4 音樂

5 影視娛樂

Epilogue

### 你可以這樣回答

I enjoy having some chips as a movie treat.
我喜歡吃洋芋片當作看電影的點心。

I try not to eat during movies.
我看電影時儘量不吃東西。

### 參考範例

Yes, especially when I'm enjoying a movie with my family. Normally, we order pizzas and prepare tubs of ice cream. Sharing these delicious treats adds to the fun and creates comforting movie-watching moments together.

會，尤其是我和家人一起看電影的時候。通常我們會點披薩，並且準備幾桶冰淇淋。共享這些美味的點心會增添樂趣，並且讓一起觀看電影成為撫慰人心的時刻。

### 詞彙

tub 裝冰淇淋的紙桶

treat 點心

comforting 撫慰人心的

# Do you have a favorite series you wish had more seasons?

你有希望出更多季的最愛影集嗎？

Prologue

1 嗜好

2 運動習慣

3 閱讀

4 音樂

5 影視娛樂

Epilogue

........................................

........................................

........................................

........................................

### 你可以這樣回答

I wish… had more seasons.
我希望…有更多季。

… is my favorite, and I think it has a lot of potential for further development.
…是我的最愛，我認為它有許多進一步發展的潛力。

### 參考範例

I wish there were more seasons of *Modern Family*. Having been with the characters for over 100 episodes, it felt like leaving my real family when the finale aired. I remember myself crying so hard because I was not ready to say goodbye to the lovable big family.

我希望《摩登家庭》有更多季。陪伴了那些角色超過一百集，當結局播出時，感覺就像是離開我真正的家人。我記得自己哭得很厲害，因為我還沒準備好跟這個可愛的大家庭說再見。

### 詞彙

episode （節目的）一集
finale 最後一幕，結局
air （節目）播出
lovable 可愛的

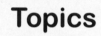

# Topics

# Do you enjoy visiting art museums?

你喜歡去美術館嗎？

....................................................

....................................................

....................................................

....................................................

Prologue

6 藝術與手工藝

7 食物

8 飲料

9 購物與消費

10 財務規劃

Epilogue

**你可以這樣回答**

I find visiting art museums incredibly enriching.
我覺得去美術館讓我感到很充實。

Art museums aren't really my thing.
我不怎麼喜歡（去）美術館。

**參考範例**

Yes, I really enjoy visiting art museums. It's so much fun to see works of art and learn about different artists' techniques and inspirations. Also, there are usually some experimental works that challenge me to appreciate them in unconventional ways.

是的，我真的很喜歡去美術館。看藝術作品並且了解不同藝術家的技法與靈感來源，真的很有趣。還有，通常也會有一些實驗性的作品，挑戰我用不尋常的方式來欣賞它們。

**詞彙**

work of art 藝術作品

technique 技術

inspiration
帶來靈感的人或事物

experimental 實驗性的

unconventional
不因循守舊的，不尋常的

# Do you prefer classical or modern art?

你比較喜歡古典藝術還是現代藝術？

Prologue

6 藝術與手工藝

7 食物

8 飲料

9 購物與消費

10 財務規劃

Epilogue

### 你可以這樣回答

I am drawn to classical art because it tells stories from the past.
我受到古典藝術的吸引，因為它述說過去的故事。

Modern art appeals to me more because it feels more relatable.
現代藝術比較吸引我，因為它比較讓人能感同身受。

### 參考範例

I appreciate both for different reasons. The timeless beauty and historical background of classical art often take me to different eras. On the other hand, modern art's experimental and thought-provoking nature inspires me to see the world in new ways.

我因為不同的理由而同時欣賞這兩者。古典藝術超越時代的美與歷史背景，常常把我帶到不同的時代。另一方面，現代藝術實驗性與發人省思的性質，則是激勵我用不同的方式看世界。

### 詞彙

timeless 不受時間影響的，永不過時的

historical 歷史的

era 時代

thought-provoking 引人深思的

inspire 激勵，激發靈感

# Are you good at painting or drawing things?
你擅長（用顏料）繪畫或（用筆畫線）描畫東西嗎？

Prologue

6 藝術與手工藝

7 食物

8 飲料

9 購物與消費

10 財務規劃

Epilogue

........

**你可以這樣回答**

I wouldn't say I'm a professional, but I enjoy painting and drawing.
我不會說自己是專業的人，但我很喜歡繪畫和描畫。

I'm not very skilled at painting or drawing.
我不怎麼擅長繪畫和描畫。

**參考範例**

I have dedicated a lot of time to improving my skills of painting and drawing, so I can say I am good at both. It is rewarding to see my progress over time. It has become natural to turn my image in mind into pictures while conveying my emotions.

我投注了很多時間來改善我繪畫和描畫的技巧，所以我可以說我兩者都擅長。看到我隨著時間進步，感覺很值得。把我心中的影像變成圖畫，同時傳達我的情緒，已經變成一件自然的事。

**詞彙**

dedicate 獻出

rewarding 有回報的，值得的

progress 進展，進步

convey 傳達

emotion 情緒

# Have you ever thought about becoming an artist?

你曾經想過要當藝術家嗎？

Prologue

6 藝術與手工藝

7 食物

8 飲料

9 購物與消費

10 財務規劃

Epilogue

........................................................

........................................................

........................................................

........................................................

你可以這樣回答

I've (never) thought about pursuing a career as an artist.
我想過（從來沒想過）要當藝術家作為職業。

It has (never) crossed my mind to become an artist.
我曾經（從來不曾）有過當藝術家的想法。

參考範例

I love being creative and expressing myself through different media, so there was a time that I dreamed of making a living as an artist. However, as I knew more about some artists' real life, I realized that it could be challenging to pursue art as a career.

我喜歡有創意（發揮創意）並且透過多種不同媒介來表達自己，所以我曾經夢想以藝術家的身分賺錢謀生。不過，隨著我對於一些藝術家的真實生活了解更多，我了解到把藝術當成職業可能是很困難的事。

詞彙

media
媒介（medium 的複數）

dream of Ving 夢想做…

make a living 賺錢謀生

challenging
有挑戰性的，困難的

pursue … as a career
尋求…作為職業

# Do you have great manual dexterity when making handcrafts?

做手工藝時，你的手很靈巧嗎？

## 你可以這樣回答

I have some manual dexterity, but there's still room for improvement.
我算是手巧，但還有進步空間。

I am not very skilled when it comes to handcrafts.
說到手工藝，我的技能並不是很好。

## 參考範例

I am quite proficient with my hands, particularly when it comes to delicate embroidery. It demands precision and meticulous work, and I take pride in my ability to execute them with skill and efficiency. It's satisfying to work with my hands and see my craftsmanship come to life.

我運用手很熟練，尤其是說到纖細的刺繡。它需要精準度與一絲不苟的做工，而我對於自己以技術和效率執行這些事情的能力感到驕傲。運用我的手並且看到我的技藝實現出來（成為作品），是很讓我滿足的事。

## 詞彙

proficient 熟練的

delicate
纖弱的，精美的，纖細的

embroidery 刺繡

meticulous 一絲不苟的，非常注意細節的

take pride in 以⋯自豪

craftsmanship
工藝，技藝

Prologue

6 藝術與手工藝

7 食物

8 飲料

9 購物與消費

10 財務規劃

Epilogue

# Do you think art is an important part of our life?

你認為藝術是我們生活中重要的一部分嗎？

.................................................................................................

.................................................................................................

.................................................................................................

.................................................................................................

### 你可以這樣回答

Art is always a central part of human culture.
藝術永遠都是人類文化的中心部分。

I don't think people pay much attention to art in their daily life.
我不認為人們在日常生活中很注重藝術。

### 參考範例

I believe art is an indispensable part of our life. We should explore the art of today as it reflects the latest trends in creativity and thought. While I may not create art myself, I can still be an appreciator and be connected with the world through art.

我相信藝術是我們生活中不可或缺的一部分。我們應該探索今日的藝術，因為它反映創意與思想的最新趨勢。雖然我自己可能不會創造藝術，但我仍然可以當個欣賞者，並且透過藝術和世界連結。

### 詞彙

indispensable
不可或缺的

explore 探索

reflect 反映

creativity 創造力，創造性

appreciator 欣賞者

# Q.49

## Do you think human artists will be replaced by AI?

你認為人類藝術家會被人工智慧（AI）取代嗎？

.................................................................................................

.................................................................................................

.................................................................................................

.................................................................................................

### 你可以這樣回答

The role of artists may evolve with the integration of AI.
藉由整合 AI，藝術家的角色可能會演變。

Yes, AI is already proving its capacity to create impressive art.
是的，AI 已經證明自己有能力創造令人印象深刻的藝術。

### 參考範例

While AI has made advancements in various fields, I don't think human artists will be completely replaced by AI. Art is deeply connected to human experiences. While AI can assist artists in creating impressive works, the unique human touch will always be valued.

雖然 AI 在各種領域取得了進展，但我不認為人類藝術家會完全被 AI 取代。藝術和人類經驗有很深的連結。雖然 AI 可以協助藝術家創造令人印象深刻的作品，但獨特的人類氣息總是會得到重視。

### 詞彙

advancement 進展

assist 協助

impressive
令人印象深刻的

touch 風格；潤色，修飾

value 重視

Q.50

# What is your favorite style of food?
你最愛的食物風格是什麼？

...................................................

...................................................

...................................................

...................................................

你可以這樣回答

I am a fan of Thai food.
我熱愛泰式料理。

I would say American-style comfort food is my favorite.
我會說美式安慰食物（難過時感覺可以提振心情的食物）是我的最愛。

參考範例

My favorite style of food is Italian. Italian cuisine, such as pasta and pizza, are rich in their flavor, thanks to the variety of spices used. I'm also a fan of gelato, which is usually fruitier and less airy than American ice cream.

我最愛的食物風格是義大利風。義大利食物，例如義大利麵和披薩，口味很豐富，這是因為其中使用的香料的多樣性。我也是義式冰淇淋的愛好者，跟美式冰淇淋比起來，它通常比較有水果的風味，而且質地不那麼膨鬆。

詞彙

cuisine 料理，烹飪菜式

spice 香料

be a fan of 熱愛⋯

gelato 義式冰淇淋

fruity 水果的，果味的

airy 空氣的（在這裡指冰淇淋質地中帶有空氣）

# What is your favorite Taiwanese street food? You can write its name in Chinese.

你最愛的台灣街頭食物是什麼？你可以用中文寫出它的名字。

........................................................................

........................................................................

........................................................................

........................................................................

Prologue

6 藝術與手工藝

7 食物

8 飲料

9 購物與消費

10 財務規劃

Epilogue

### 你可以這樣回答

Oyster Omelette (蚵仔煎) is my favorite.
蚵仔煎是我的最愛。

I can't get enough of Taiwanese Fried Chicken (鹽酥雞).
鹽酥雞我怎麼吃都吃不膩。

### 參考範例

My favorite Taiwanese street food is bubble tea (珍珠奶茶). Honestly, I never leave a night market without a cup of it in my hand. I really enjoy the combination of sweet milk tea and chewy tapioca pearls, which weirdly always goes well with any street food!

我最愛的台灣街頭食物是珍珠奶茶。老實說，我離開夜市時總是會帶一杯在手上。我真的很喜歡甜甜的奶茶和有嚼勁的珍珠粉圓的組合，而奇怪的是，這（個組合）總是和任何街頭食物都很搭！

### 詞彙

combination 組合
chewy 有嚼勁的
tapioca pearl 珍珠粉圓
weirdly 奇怪地
go well with 和⋯很搭

# Do you enjoy fast food?

你喜歡（吃）速食嗎？

......................................................................

......................................................................

......................................................................

......................................................................

### 你可以這樣回答

I often crave for fast food.
我常常很渴望（吃）速食。

Fast food is not my thing.
我不愛速食。

### 參考範例

I enjoy eating fast food once in a while.
Among all kinds of fast food, I especially
love French fries that are crispy outside
while soft inside. Even though fast food
tends to be unhealthy, I think it's fine to
eat as long as we keep our overall diet
balanced.

我喜歡偶爾吃速食。在各種速食中，我特別
愛外脆內軟的薯條。儘管速食通常不健康，
但我認為只要我們保持整體的飲食均衡，那
麼吃速食是沒有關係的。

### 詞彙

especially 特別，尤其
crispy 脆的
tend to V 傾向於…
as long as 只要…
overall 整體的

# Do you usually eat with your family?

你通常和家人一起吃飯嗎？

Prologue

6 藝術與手工藝

7 食物

8 飲料

9 購物與消費

10 財務規劃

Epilogue

#### 你可以這樣回答

We have a tradition of eating together every day.
我們有每天一起吃飯的傳統（習慣）。

Due to our different routines, we don't eat together very often.
由於我們不同的日常作息，所以我們不是很常一起吃飯。

#### 參考範例

I have several dinners a week together with my family. We would talk about our daily life and plan our weekends at the table. During these family dinners, we also share our aspirations and support each other in pursuing our individual goals.

我每週和家人吃幾次晚餐。我們會在桌邊談日常生活，並且計劃我們的週末。在這些家庭晚餐中，我們也會分享自己的志向，並且支持彼此追求個人的目標。

#### 詞彙

aspiration 志向

pursue 追求

individual 個人的

Prologue

6
藝術與手工藝

7
食物

8
飲料

9
購物與消費

10
財務規劃

Epilogue

# What's your favorite comfort food when you're under pressure?

在壓力狀態下，你最愛的安慰食物（能提振心情，通常富含碳水或油脂的食物）是什麼？

.................................................

.................................................

.................................................

.................................................

### 你可以這樣回答

I eat… when I need comfort.
當我需要安慰的時候，我吃…

I often opt for herbal tea instead of so-called comfort food.
我通常選擇草本茶而不是所謂的安慰食物。

### 參考範例

I crave for macaroni and cheese when I'm under pressure. It's warm, cheesy, soothing, and more importantly, it's very easy to make. It brings me a sense of comfort and helps me relax when I'm feeling stressed.

當我在壓力狀態下，我渴望（吃）起司通心麵。它溫暖、充滿起司味、撫慰人心，而且更重要的是，它非常容易製作。它帶給我安慰的感覺，而且在我感到有壓力的時候幫助我放鬆。

### 詞彙

crave for 渴望…

macaroni 通心麵

cheesy 起司（味）的

soothing 撫慰的

stressed 感到有壓力的

# Do you think it is worth it to eat at an upscale restaurant?

你認為在高檔餐廳用餐值得嗎？

Prologue

6 藝術與手工藝

7 食物

8 飲料

9 購物與消費

10 財務規劃

Epilogue

........................

........................

........................

........................

### 你可以這樣回答

I believe it's worth it when you're looking for a memorable dining experience.
在你想尋求難忘的用餐體驗時，我認為是值得的。

I don't find upscale dining worth the expense.
我不覺得高檔餐飲值得那樣的花費。

### 參考範例

Even though dining at an upscale restaurant could be unforgettable, it's not always worth the hefty prices. It seems to me that people who are willing to pay that much for a meal are either seeking culinary artistry or simply enjoying the atmosphere. I am neither of them.

儘管在高檔餐廳用餐可能令人難忘，但並不一定值得高昂的價格。在我看來，願意付那麼多錢吃一餐的人如果不是追求烹飪的藝術性，就是享受氣氛而已。我兩者都不是。

### 詞彙

unforgettable 令人難忘的
hefty （數額等）很大的
culinary 烹飪的
artistry 藝術性
atmosphere 氣氛

Prologue

6 藝術與手工藝

7 食物

8 飲料

9 購物與消費

10 財務規劃

Epilogue

# Do you cook or bake? Why?

你煮菜或烘焙嗎？為什麼？

........................................................................

........................................................................

........................................................................

........................................................................

你可以這樣回答

I cook/bake because…
我煮菜／烘焙，因為…

I don't cook or bake because I lack the necessary skills.
我不煮菜也不烘焙，因為我缺乏必要的技巧。

參考範例

I like to do some baking during my leisure time. Creating something from scratch and seeing the joy on people's faces when they take a bite gives me a great sense of achievement. The process of experimenting with recipes and trying different formulas also inspires my creativity.

我喜歡在閒暇時間做些烘焙。從頭開始創造東西，並且在人們一口咬下的時候看見他們臉上的快樂，帶給我很大的成就感。實驗食譜並嘗試不同配方的過程，也激發我的創意。

詞彙

leisure 閒暇
from scratch 從頭開始
take a bite 咬一口
experiment with 實驗…
formula 配方

# Do you find it hard to fall asleep after drinking coffee or tea?

你覺得喝了咖啡或茶之後很難入睡嗎？

Prologue

6 藝術與手工藝

7 食物

8 飲料

9 購物與消費

10 財務規劃

Epilogue

### 你可以這樣回答

I find it hard to fall asleep after drinking coffee, but not so much when I drink tea. 我覺得喝咖啡後很難入睡，但喝茶的時候就不太會。

I am not sensitive to caffeine, so I can drink them even before sleep. 我對咖啡因不敏感，所以即使在睡前我也可以喝。

### 參考範例

Coffee and tea can greatly hinder my sleep. While they work wonders in helping me stay awake and alert, if I drink them before bedtime, I often end up having a restless night. Therefore, I avoid drinking coffee or tea during and after dinner to ensure a restful night's sleep.

咖啡和茶會嚴重妨礙我的睡眠。雖然它們在幫助我保持清醒與警覺方面效果很好，但如果我在睡前喝，最後我常常會夜不成眠。所以，我避免在晚餐和之後的時間喝咖啡或茶，以確保晚上睡覺得到充分的休息。

### 詞彙

**hinder** 妨礙

**work wonders** 產生神奇的效果

**alert** 警覺的

**restless** 焦躁不安的，得不到休息的

**restful** 給人充分休息的

# Do you think drinking wine is good for one's health?

你認為喝酒對健康有益嗎？

---

### 你可以這樣回答

I kind of believe red wine can benefit heart health.
我有點相信紅酒有益心臟健康。

I believe refraining from drinking is the best way to protect my health.
我相信避免喝酒是保護自己健康最好的方法。

### 參考範例

While some research suggests that a glass of wine before sleep can be good for health, I still believe one can easily drink too much and end up damaging their own health. Instead of convincing ourselves that it's harmless, I think we are better off not to drink in the first place.

雖然某些研究暗示睡前一杯紅酒可能有益健康，但我仍然相信人很容易喝太多，最終損害自己的健康。與其說服自己喝酒無害，我認為我們不如一開始就不要喝酒還比較好。

### 詞彙

end up Ving
結果、最終…

convince 說服

harmless 無害的

better off 情況比較好的

in the first place 一開始

# Do you avoid sugared beverages? Why?

你會避免（喝）加糖的飲料嗎？為什麼？

Prologue

6 藝術與手工藝

7 食物

8 飲料

9 購物與消費

10 財務規劃

Epilogue

........................................................................

........................................................................

........................................................................

........................................................................

## 你可以這樣回答

Even though sugared beverages are not good for health, I still enjoy them occasionally.
儘管加糖的飲料對健康不好，我偶爾還是會享受這些飲料。

I prefer not to consume sugared beverages.
我傾向於不喝加糖飲料。

## 參考範例

I avoid sugared beverages in my daily life. I've learned that excessive added sugars can lead to issues such as weight gain and tooth decay, so I simply drink water most of the time. Besides, unlike sugared beverages, water truly quenches my thirst and keeps me hydrated.

我在日常生活中避免加糖的飲料。我已經了解過量的添加糖可能導致體重增加和蛀牙之類的問題，所以我大多只是喝水。而且，不像加糖的飲料，水真的能解我的渴，並且讓我保持水分。

## 詞彙

excessive 過度的

weight gain 體重增加

tooth decay 蛀牙

quench one's thirst
為某人解渴

hydrated 含水的

# What is your favorite drink in hot summer?

在炎熱的夏天，你最愛的飲料是什麼？

Prologue

6 藝術與手工藝

7 食物

8 飲料

9 購物與消費

10 財務規劃

Epilogue

........................................................................

........................................................................

........................................................................

........................................................................

### 你可以這樣回答

I enjoy iced tea in the summertime.
在夏天，我喜歡喝冰紅茶。

I love drinking cold brew coffee when it's hot outside.
外面很熱的時候，我愛喝冷萃咖啡。

### 參考範例

My favorite drink in hot summer is cold and refreshing lemonade. When a lemonade strikes a good balance between sweetness and sourness, it's not only delicious but also appetizing. This alone makes it the perfect drink in hot weather.

在炎熱的夏天，我最愛的飲料是冰涼又清爽的檸檬水。當一杯檸檬水達到甜味與酸味之間很好的平衡時，它不但美味而且開胃。光這一點就讓它成為炎熱天氣的完美飲料。

### 詞彙

refreshing 使人涼爽的

lemonade 檸檬水

strike a balance between
達到⋯之間的平衡

appetizing
刺激食慾的，開胃的

# Do you think expensive coffee tastes better?

你認為貴的咖啡比較好喝嗎？

Prologue

6 藝術與手工藝

7 食物

8 飲料

9 購物與消費

10 財務規劃

Epilogue

....................................................

....................................................

....................................................

....................................................

### 你可以這樣回答

I think expensive coffee generally has a better taste.
我認為貴的咖啡通常比較好喝。

Expensive coffee is not a guarantee of better taste.
貴的咖啡並不是比較好喝的保證。

### 參考範例

While expensive coffee may be better in their sourcing and roasting techniques, it doesn't necessarily result in great taste for everyone. For instance, I dislike any light roast coffee due to its sourness, regardless of its quality. In my opinion, coffee taste is largely a matter of personal preference.

雖然貴的咖啡在採購（從產地獲取）和烘焙技術方面可能比較好，但結果並不一定是每個人都覺得好的味道。舉例來說，因為酸味的關係，所以我不喜歡任何淺焙咖啡，不論品質如何。在我看來，咖啡的口味大部分取決於個人偏好。

### 詞彙

sourcing （咖啡的）採購
（從產地取得咖啡豆）

technique 技術

light roast coffee
淺焙咖啡

regardless of
不管，不論…

preference 偏好

# Do you have iced drinks in winter?

冬天你喝冷飲嗎？

Prologue

6 藝術與手工藝

7 食物

8 飲料

9 購物與消費

10 財務規劃

Epilogue

......................................................................

......................................................................

......................................................................

......................................................................

## 你可以這樣回答

I enjoy iced drinks even when it's cold outside.
就算外面很冷，我也喜歡喝冷飲。

I avoid iced drinks in winter because I have a fear of the cold.
我在冬天避免冷飲，因為我怕冷。

## 參考範例

Even though I tend to have hot drinks in winter to keep myself warm, sometimes I do have iced coffee to help me stay sharp. Cold weather can sometimes make me feel drowsy, and the chill of iced coffee helps wake me up.

儘管我冬天通常喝熱的飲料讓自己保持溫暖，但有時候我會喝冰咖啡來讓自己保持精神敏銳。冷天氣有時候會讓我覺得想睡，而冰咖啡的冷有助於讓我清醒。

## 詞彙

tend to V 傾向於⋯

sharp 敏銳的

drowsy 想睡的

chill 寒冷

# At a banquet, would you choose to drink alcohol or juice?

在宴會上，你會選擇喝酒精飲料還是果汁？

........................................................................................................

........................................................................................................

........................................................................................................

........................................................................................................

Prologue

6 藝術與手工藝

7 食物

8 飲料

9 購物與消費

10 財務規劃

Epilogue

**你可以這樣回答**

For celebratory banquets, I usually choose alcohol.
對於慶祝的宴會，我通常選擇酒精飲料。

I prioritize my health, so I often choose juice at banquets.
我優先看待自己的健康，所以在宴會上我常選擇果汁。

**參考範例**

It depends on what's more appropriate for that specific occasion. If it's OK to let my hair down, I will go for alcohol. However, sometimes I don't want to risk losing self-control. That's when I tend to choose non-alcoholic beverages like juice to stay refreshed.

取決於對於那個特定場合而言（喝）什麼比較適當。如果可以不拘禮節而放鬆的話，我會選擇酒精飲料。不過，有時候我不想冒失去自我控制的風險。這時候我通常會選擇果汁之類的無酒精飲料來保持精神清醒。

**詞彙**

appropriate 適當的
let one's hair down
不拘禮節，放開自我
risk Ving 冒…的風險
self-control 自我控制
refreshed 精神振作的

# Do you prefer shopping online or offline?

你偏好線上還是線下購物？

Prologue

6 藝術與手工藝

7 食物

8 飲料

9 購物與消費

10 財務規劃

Epilogue

### 你可以這樣回答

I prefer online shopping because it's simply more convenient.
我偏好線上購物，因為它就是比較便利。

I choose offline shopping for the in-person experience.
因為有親身進行購物的體驗，所以我選擇線下購物。

### 參考範例

Personally, I prefer online shopping to offline shopping. Online shopping offers convenience and a wide range of options. With it, I can compare prices among different stores without visiting each store in person. Also, the review system also helps make the whole experience more transparent.

我個人偏好線上購物勝過線下購物。線上購物提供便利與大範圍的選擇。靠著線上購物，我可以比較不同商店的價格，而不用親自到每間店。另外，評論系統也有助於使整個體驗更加透明。

### 詞彙

convenience 便利

a wide range of 廣範圍的，種類多的…

in person 親自，當面

transparent 透明的

# Do you go window shopping on weekends?

週末你會進行只看不買的逛街（櫥窗購物）嗎？

Prologue

6 藝術與手工藝

7 食物

8 飲料

9 購物與消費

10 財務規劃

Epilogue

．．．．．．．．．．．．．．．．．．．．．．．．．．．．．．．．．．．．．．．．．．．．．．．．．．．．．．．．．．．．．．

．．．．．．．．．．．．．．．．．．．．．．．．．．．．．．．．．．．．．．．．．．．．．．．．．．．．．．．．．．．．．．

．．．．．．．．．．．．．．．．．．．．．．．．．．．．．．．．．．．．．．．．．．．．．．．．．．．．．．．．．．．．．．

．．．．．．．．．．．．．．．．．．．．．．．．．．．．．．．．．．．．．．．．．．．．．．．．．．．．．．．．．．．．．．

**你可以這樣回答**

Yes, I think window shopping is a relaxing way to spend my free time.
是的，我認為只看不買是很放鬆的度過空閒時間方式。

To me, shopping without buying anything feels pointless.
對我來說，逛街而不買任何東西感覺沒有意義。

**參考範例**

Yes, I enjoy going window shopping on weekends. It is fun to browse through stores, see new trends, and get inspiration. To be honest, I do make purchases occasionally, but most of the time I just buy nothing and enjoy the experience of exploring itself.

是的，我喜歡在週末進行只看不買的逛街。瀏覽商店、看看新的潮流並且獲得靈感，是很好玩的事。老實說，我偶爾會買東西，但我大多什麼也不買，並且享受探索的經驗本身。

**詞彙**

browse through 瀏覽…

trend 趨勢，潮流

inspiration 靈感

occasionally 偶爾

explore 探索

Prologue

6 藝術與手工藝

7 食物

8 飲料

9 購物與消費

10 財務規劃

Epilogue

# Have you ever returned anything you have bought?

你曾經退過你買的東西嗎？

........................................

........................................

........................................

........................................

你可以這樣回答

I once returned … because …
我有一次退過…因為…

No, I would resell or gift an item if I am not satisfied with it.
沒有，如果我對一個物品不滿意，我會轉賣或者送給別人。

參考範例

I have returned clothes that didn't fit and home appliances that failed to meet my expectation. Some may be reluctant to return items because they don't want to cause trouble for others, but for me it's actually a chance to exchange for items that better satisfy me.

我曾經退過不合身的衣服，還有沒達到我的期望的家電。有些人可能不願意退東西，因為不想造成別人的麻煩，但對我而言這其實是換成比較能滿足我的東西的機會。

詞彙

home appliance 家電

expectation 期望

reluctant 不情願的

cause trouble for others 給別人添麻煩

exchange for 交換成…

# How much do you spend a month on non-essential shopping?

你每個月花費多少在非必要的購物上？

Prologue

6 藝術與手工藝

7 食物

8 飲料

9 購物與消費

10 財務規劃

Epilogue

### 你可以這樣回答

I allocate about... a month for non-essential shopping.
我分配每月大約…在在非必要的購物上。

I spend around …% of my monthly income on non-essential shopping.
我把每月收入的…%花在非必要的購物上。

### 參考範例

On average, I spend about NT$10,000 a month on non-essential shopping, usually buying clothes and books. Even though I can do without them, I still think they are worthwhile investments. Clothes boost my self-confidence, while books contribute to my personal growth.

我平均每個月花大約一萬台幣在非必要的購物上，通常是買衣服和書。儘管我沒有這些也行，但我仍然認為它們是值得的投資。衣服提升我的自信，而書促成我的自我成長。

### 詞彙

on average 平均
do without 沒有…也行
worthwhile 值得的
boost 增加，提高
contribute to 促成…

75

Prologue

6 藝術與手工藝

7 食物

8 飲料

9 購物與消費

10 財務規劃

Epilogue

## Q.68

# What is your latest impulse purchase?

你最近的衝動購物是什麼？

你可以這樣回答

Recently, I bought… on impulse.
最近我衝動買下了…

I impulsively purchased…
我衝動買下了…

參考範例

My latest impulse purchase was a small decorative rug. I saw it while strolling past a home decor store and believed it would enhance the ambiance of my room. I bought the rug on impulse, but I don't regret it because I feel happy every time I see it.

我最近的衝動購物是張小小的裝飾地毯。我在散步經過一間家飾品店時看到它，並且相信它會提升我房間的氣氛。我在衝動下買了這張地毯，但我不後悔，因為每次我看到它都覺得滿足。

詞彙

decorative 裝飾的

stroll 散步

home decor 家飾品

ambiance 氣氛，格調

on impulse 衝動地

# Do you prefer to pay in cash or through mobile payment?

你偏好現金支付還是行動支付？

........................................................

........................................................

........................................................

........................................................

Prologue

6 藝術與手工藝

7 食物

8 飲料

9 購物與消費

10 財務規劃

Epilogue

### 你可以這樣回答

I prefer to pay in cash / through mobile payment.
我偏好現金支付／行動支付。

I prefer using cash / mobile payment methods.
我偏好使用現金／行動支付方式。

### 參考範例

I generally prefer mobile payment when making a purchase. It's convenient and secure, and it eliminates the need to carry cash. Additionally, I find that mobile payment simplifies financial management since each purchase is automatically recorded in the app.

購買東西的時候，我通常偏好行動支付。它既方便又安全，而且免除攜帶現金的必要。此外，我覺得行動支付能簡化財務管理，因為每次購買都自動記錄在 app 裡。

### 詞彙

generally 一般，通常
eliminate 排除
simplify 簡化
financial management 財務管理
automatically 自動地

Prologue

6 藝術與手工藝

7 食物

8 飲料

9 購物與消費

10 財務規劃

Epilogue

## Q.70

# Are you saving up for a big purchase? What is it?

你正在為一項高額的購買存錢嗎？要買的是什麼？

........................................................................................

........................................................................................

........................................................................................

........................................................................................

### 你可以這樣回答

Yes, I am saving up for a…
是的，我正在為了（買）…存錢。

I am saving for a down payment on a house.
我正在為了房子的頭期款存錢。

### 參考範例

I am saving up for a laptop. I'll be a college student this year, so I need a laptop to do research and write assignments. For this goal, I've created a dedicated virtual account, and I've also cut back on non-essential expenses, such as dining out and entertainment.

我正在為了買筆記型電腦存錢。我今年即將成為大學生，所以我需要筆記型電腦來做研究以及寫作業。為了這個目標，我開了專用的虛擬帳戶，也大幅削減了非必要的開銷，像是外食和娛樂。

### 詞彙

save up for
為（目標）儲備金錢

assignment 分派的作業

dedicated 專用的

virtual 虛擬的

cut back on 大量削減…

# Are you more of a buyer, a saver, or a mix of both?

你比較會花錢還是存錢，或者是兩者之間？

Prologue

6 藝術與手工藝

7 食物

8 飲料

9 購物與消費

10 財務規劃

Epilogue

........................................................

........................................................

........................................................

........................................................

### 你可以這樣回答

I am more of a buyer/saver.
我比較偏向會花錢／存錢。

I enjoy spending more than saving.
我喜歡花錢勝過存錢。

### 參考範例

I consider myself a mix of both. I enjoy making purchases for things that appeal to me or bring me joy, but I also recognize the importance of saving money for future goals and financial security. It is necessary to strike a balance between the two.

我認為自己是兩者之間。我喜歡購買吸引我或者帶給我快樂的東西，但我也認知到為將來的目標與財務安全存錢的重要性。在兩者之間取得平衡是必要的。

### 詞彙

appeal to 吸引…

recognize 認出，承認

financial security
財務安全

strike a balance 取得平衡

# Do you have any savings goals for the next ten years?

你對於未來十年有任何儲蓄計畫嗎？

Prologue

6 藝術與手工藝

7 食物

8 飲料

9 購物與消費

10 財務規劃

Epilogue

---

### 你可以這樣回答

I plan to save for a new car and a home renovation.
我打算為新車和房屋翻修儲蓄。

I don't plan too far ahead financially.
我在財務方面不會做太長遠的規劃。

### 參考範例

I plan to pursue an MBA overseas and aim to save NT$1 million. It is a lot of money, but considering rising prices, I believe it's a reasonable goal to strive for. After all, it has to cover not only tuition fees but also living expenses and travel costs.

我打算在海外唸 MBA（企業管理碩士），並且以存台幣 100 萬元為目標。這是很大一筆錢，但考慮到上漲中的物價，我相信這是需要努力的合理目標。畢竟，這筆錢不止要付學費，還有生活開銷和旅費。

### 詞彙

pursue 追求
aim to V 以做…為目標
reasonable 合理的
strive for 為…努力
cover （足夠）支付…

# Do you want to buy real estate in the future?

未來你想購買不動產嗎？

Prologue

6 藝術與手工藝

7 食物

8 飲料

9 購物與消費

10 財務規劃

Epilogue

........................

........................

........................

........................

### 你可以這樣回答

Yes, I'm planning to invest in real estate.
是的，我正打算投資不動產。

I don't see it as a possible goal with my income.
考慮我的收入，我不認為那是可能實現的目標。

### 參考範例

No, I don't have an interest in buying real estate. While real estate can provide stability and potential investment returns, I prefer the flexibility of not being tied to a specific location. I actually enjoy the idea of relocating and exploring new places every two or three years.

不，我對於購買不動產沒有興趣。雖然不動產可以提供穩定以及潛在的投資收益，但我比較喜歡不被特定地點綁住的彈性。其實我喜歡每兩三年搬遷並且探索新地方的想法。

### 詞彙

stability 穩定
potential 潛在的
returns 收益
flexibility 彈性
relocate 搬遷

Prologue

6 藝術與手工藝

7 食物

8 飲料

9 購物與消費

10 財務規劃

Epilogue

## Q.74

# If you were given NT$10 million, what would you do?

如果有人給你台幣 1000 萬元，你會做什麼？

........................................................................

........................................................................

........................................................................

........................................................................

你可以這樣回答

I would start my own business with that money.
我會用這筆錢創立自己的事業。

I would quit my job and pursue my dream of becoming a musician.
我會辭掉工作，並且追逐成為音樂人的夢想。

參考範例

I would use that money to invest in myself. I've always wanted to study abroad, so I would probably take the opportunity to finance my own education. Without worries about financial security, I would be able to focus on my studies.

我會用這筆錢投資自己。我一直想要出國留學，所以我可能會利用這個機會，為自己的教育提供資金。沒有對於財務安全的擔憂，我就能專注在學習上。

詞彙

invest in 投資⋯

opportunity 機會

finance 為⋯提供資金

financial security
財務安全

focus on 專注於⋯

# Are you currently stressed about your own finances?

你目前對於自己的財務狀況感覺有壓力嗎？

................................................................

................................................................

................................................................

................................................................

Prologue

6 藝術與手工藝

7 食物

8 飲料

9 購物與消費

10 財務規劃

Epilogue

### 你可以這樣回答

Yes, I've been feeling some financial pressure lately.
是的，我最近感覺到一些財務壓力。

Fortunately, I am doing well financially.
幸好，我目前財務狀況良好。

### 參考範例

Thankfully, I am not troubled by financial stress. I have a steady income that allows me to pay for my expenses and save for the future. I've also made it a habit to make monthly budgets and track my expenses, so I seldom overspend.

幸好，我並沒有財務壓力的困擾。我擁有讓我能支付開銷並且為未來儲蓄的穩定收入。我也養成了制定每月預算和追蹤開銷的習慣，所以我很少超支。

### 詞彙

trouble 使煩惱，困擾
steady 穩定的
make it a habit to V
養成…的習慣
track 追蹤
overspend 超支

Prologue

6 藝術與手工藝

7 食物

8 飲料

9 購物與消費

10 財務規劃

Epilogue

# How have your parents affected the way you deal with money?

你的父母如何影響了你處理錢的方式？

...................................................................................

...................................................................................

...................................................................................

...................................................................................

### 你可以這樣回答

My parents' have shown me the value of investing and planning for the future. 我的父母向我展示了投資以及規劃未來的價值。

I've witnessed my parents' tendency of overspending, so I became cautious about using money.
我見證了父母超支的傾向，所以我對於用錢變得小心。

### 參考範例

My parents were both brought up in less well-off families, so they've always been careful about making unnecessary purchases. I've never seen them buy things they end up regretting. As I grew up, I became mindful of shopping, and I consider it a legacy of my parents.

我的父母都是在比較不富裕的家庭長大，所以他們總是對於進行不必要的購買很謹慎。我從來沒看過他們買最終後悔的東西。隨著我長大，我對於購物變得小心而覺察，我認為這是父母留給我的（習性）。

### 詞彙

well-off 富裕的
unnecessary 不必要的
end up 結果，最終
mindful 小心的，覺察的
legacy 遺留給後人的東西

# Do you think it is worthwhile to pursue so-called financial freedom?

你認為追求所謂的財富自由是值得做的事嗎？

Prologue

6 藝術與手工藝

7 食物

8 飲料

9 購物與消費

10 財務規劃

Epilogue

---

**你可以這樣回答**

Financial freedom is important, but I don't think it's the ultimate goal.
財富自由很重要，但我不認為那是終極目標。

I think the idea of financial freedom is over-exaggerated.
我認為財富自由的概念被過度誇大了。

**參考範例**

Yes, I like the concept of eliminating anxiety over money through financial planning. Pursuing financial freedom not only provides peace of mind but also allows us to pursue our own passions. I believe it is possible to achieve financial freedom by consistently saving and making wise investments.

是的，我喜歡透過財務規劃消除金錢焦慮的概念。追求財富自由不僅帶來心靈平靜，也讓我們能追求自己熱愛的事物。我相信透過持續儲蓄與聰明投資達成財富自由是有可能的。

**詞彙**

eliminate 排除，消除
anxiety 焦慮
peace of mind 心靈平靜
passion 熱愛的事物
consistently 一貫地

# Topics

# Do you review after studying? Why?

你學習後會複習嗎？為什麼？

Prologue

11 學習

12 語言能力

13 健康狀況

14 養生方法

15 家族關係

Epilogue

......................................................................

......................................................................

......................................................................

......................................................................

### 你可以這樣回答

I (don't) review after studying because... 我學習後（不）會複習，因為…
Reviewing is an essential part of my study routine.
複習是我日常學習流程中必不可少的一部分。

### 參考範例

I've read that going through my notes after each class helps me retain information more effectively, and that's why I started to review after studying. I think it's a chance to identify what I haven't fully grasped. Thanks to this practice, I've noticed significant improvements in my academic performance.

我曾經讀到，在每堂課後複習筆記能幫助我更有效地記住資訊，而那就是我開始在學習後複習的原因。我想這是讓我找出還沒完全掌握的東西的機會。多虧了我這樣做，我注意到自己的學業表現有顯著的改善。

### 詞彙

go through 仔細檢視
retain 保持；記住
identify 發現，認出
grasp 掌握
academic performance 學業表現

Prologue

11 學習

12 語言能力

13 健康狀況

14 養生方法

15 家族關係

Epilogue

# What will you do when facing something you don't understand?

面對你不懂的東西，你會怎麼做？

..................................................................................................

..................................................................................................

..................................................................................................

..................................................................................................

### 你可以這樣回答

If I encounter something I don't understand, I will…
如果我遇到不懂的東西，我會…

My approach is to V…
我的方法是…

### 參考範例

When facing something I don't understand, my first approach is to conduct research on the Internet to figure it out. If that proves insufficient, I seek assistance from my classmates or teachers to clarify the concept. Additionally, I believe discussions can also help in the problem-solving process.

面對我不懂的東西時，我的第一個方法是在網路上進行研究來把它搞懂。如果結果證明還不夠，我會向同學或老師尋求幫助以釐清概念。另外，我也相信討論可以在解決問題的過程中幫上忙。

### 詞彙

approach 方法
conduct 進行…
figure out 理解，搞懂…
insufficient 不足的
assistance 協助
clarify 澄清，釐清

Prologue

11
學習

12
語言能力

13
健康狀況

14
養生方法

15
家族關係

Epilogue

## Q.80

# What is the worst learning experience at school you've had?

你在學校有過最差的學習經驗是什麼？

.........................................................................................

.........................................................................................

.........................................................................................

.........................................................................................

### 你可以這樣回答

My worst learning experience was in high school when I…
我最糟糕的學習經驗是高中的時候，我…

During my elementary years, I…
在國小的時候，我…

### 參考範例

It happened when I was a second grader. My math teacher was teaching basic mathematical operations, and he asked each person a question of multiplication. He slapped my cheek when I gave a wrong answer, and I started crying. This incident made me hate math afterwards.

那發生在我國小二年級的時候。我的數學老師在教基本的數學四則運算，他問了每個人一個乘法問題。我答錯的時候，他打了我巴掌，我就開始哭了。這件事讓我之後很討厭數學。

### 詞彙

second grader
小學二年級生

mathematical operations
四則運算

multiplication 乘法

slap 打耳光

incident 事件

Prologue

11 學習

12 語言能力

13 健康狀況

14 養生方法

15 家族關係

Epilogue

# Do you think it's important to embrace lifelong learning?

你認為擁抱終身學習很重要嗎？

........................................................................................

........................................................................................

........................................................................................

........................................................................................

### 你可以這樣回答

Yes, lifelong learning can bring us many benefits.
是的，終身學習可以帶給我們許多好處。

I don't think it is a must for everyone. 我不認為每個人都必須終身學習。

### 參考範例

I believe lifelong learning is crucial for the elderly as it enhances their quality of life in many ways. By engaging in learning, seniors can stay mentally active, improve cognitive abilities, and remain socially connected. Therefore, it's a way to help us live a happier retired life.

我相信終身學習對於老年人而言是至關重要的，因為它能在許多方面提升他們的生活品質。藉由參與學習，老年人可以保持心智活躍、改善認知能力，並且保持和社會的連結。所以，這是幫助我們過更快樂的退休生活的方法。

### 詞彙

crucial 至關重要的

engage in 從事，參與⋯

mentally 在心智方面

cognitive 認知的

retired 退休的

# Are you good at learning new things?

你擅長學習新事物嗎？

Prologue

11 學習

12 語言能力

13 健康狀況

14 養生方法

15 家族關係

Epilogue

**你可以這樣回答**

I (don't) think I am a fast learner.
我（不）認為自己是學習很快的人。

I am (not) good at learning new things.
我（不）擅長學習新事物。

**參考範例**

I consider myself unable to learn new things quickly. For instance, when I was little, I had a hard time learning to play piano and guitar. No matter how much time I invest in practicing, I just couldn't seem to get the knack of it.

我認為自己不能很快學習新事物。舉例來說，在我小時候，我學鋼琴和吉他感覺很困難。不管我投入多少時間練習，我好像就是無法掌握訣竅。

**詞彙**

have a hard time Ving
做…很困難

invest 投資
（在這裡指投入時間）

get the knack of
掌握…的訣竅

# What would you like to learn if you have plenty of free time?

如果你有很多空閒時間，你想學什麼？

Prologue

11 學習

12 語言能力

13 健康狀況

14 養生方法

15 家族關係

Epilogue

............................................................................

............................................................................

............................................................................

............................................................................

**你可以這樣回答**

If I have a lot of free time, I would like to learn N/Ving
如果我有很多空閒時間，我想學…

I've always wanted to learn N/Ving
我一直想學…

**參考範例**

If I have a lot of free time, I would like to learn photography. When I was little, my parents would take me to art museums, and photographic works were especially refreshing to me. Therefore, it is always my dream to pursue photography and capture the world through my lens.

如果我有很多空閒時間，我想學攝影。在我小的時候，我的父母會帶我去美術館，而攝影作品特別令我耳目一新。所以，從事攝影並且用鏡頭捕捉這個世界，一直是我的夢想。

**詞彙**

photographic 攝影的

refreshing
令人耳目一新的

pursue 追求，從事

capture 捕捉

lens
鏡片，（相機的）鏡頭

# Which do you prefer, online courses or classes in person?

你比較喜歡哪個，是線上課程還是當面教學的課？

Prologue

11 學習

12 語言能力

13 健康狀況

14 養生方法

15 家族關係

Epilogue

........................................................................

........................................................................

........................................................................

........................................................................

### 你可以這樣回答

I like… more than…
我喜歡…勝過於…

For me, … work better.
對我而言，…比較有效。

### 參考範例

I prefer online courses, especially those allowing self-paced learning, as they allow me to adjust the schedule of learning so it suits me best. In addition, online courses are often more affordable because they eliminate the need for facility expenses associated with in-person classes.

我比較喜歡線上課程，尤其是容許按照自己步調學習的，因為它們讓我能調整學習的時間表，讓它變得最適合我。另外，線上課程通常比較便宜，因為它們排除對於當面上課相關設施花費的需求。

### 詞彙

self-paced
自己決定步調的

affordable
可負擔的，買得起的

eliminate 排除

expense 花費

associated 關聯的

# Do you think you speak English well?

你認為自己英語說得好嗎？

Prologue

11 學習

12 語言能力

13 健康狀況

14 養生方法

15 家族關係

Epilogue

........................................................................................

........................................................................................

........................................................................................

........................................................................................

### 你可以這樣回答

I think I am good at speaking English.
我認為自己擅長說英語。

I am not a good English speaker.
我英語說得不好。

### 參考範例

Yes, I think I speak English well. Besides taking English classes, I also regularly converse with native speakers to improve my speaking and listening abilities. This has enabled me to confidently engage in both casual conversations and more formal settings, such as presentations and professional interactions.

是的，我認為自己英語說得好。除了上英語課以外，我也定期和母語人士對話，藉此增進我的聽說能力。這樣讓我能有信心地參與日常對話和比較正式的情境，例如發表簡報和專業互動。

### 詞彙

converse with 和…對話

confidently 有信心地

casual 非正式的，隨意的

formal 正式的

presentation
（發表報告等的）簡報

# Do you find English useful in your daily life?

你認為英語在你的日常生活中有用嗎？

**你可以這樣回答**

Yes, I find English an essential tool in my daily life.
是的，我認為英語是我日常生活中必要的工具。

No, I don't think English ability does me any good.
不，我不認為英語能力對我有什麼好處。

**參考範例**

Yes, I think English is very useful in my daily life. For instance, I have been interviewed by some international companies recently. Being able to speak in English fluently helped me a lot in the interviews, and it also made me an outstanding candidate over other interviewees.

是的，我認為英語在我的日常生活中非常有用。舉例來說，最近我接受了一些國際公司的面試。能夠流暢地說英語，在面試中幫了我很大的忙，也讓我成為突出於其他接受面試者的人選。

**詞彙**

interview 面試（某人）
fluently 流暢地
outstanding 突出的
candidate 人選
interviewee 接受面試者

Prologue

11 學習

12 語言能力

13 健康狀況

14 養生方法

15 家族關係

Epilogue

# Besides English, are you learning any other foreign languages? Why?

除了英語以外，你在學其他任何外語嗎？為什麼？

### 你可以這樣回答

… is my focus of learning right now.
…是我現在的學習重點。

No, but I'm interested in learning…
沒有，但我有興趣學…

### 參考範例

Besides English, I am learning Spanish. I am planning to travel to South America, and I want to communicate with the locals in their native language. Therefore, I am dedicating time to mastering Spanish for a more enriching travel experience.

除了英語以外，我在學西班牙語。我正打算到南美洲旅遊，而我想要用當地人的語言和他們溝通。所以，我正把時間投注在精通西班牙語上，藉此獲得更令我感到充實的旅行經驗。

### 詞彙

local 當地人

native 本土的，本國的

dedicate 獻出

master 精通

enrich 使豐富、充實

# What do you think are the benefits of being multilingual?

你認為有多種語言能力的好處是什麼？

Prologue

11 學習

12 語言能力

13 健康狀況

14 養生方法

15 家族關係

Epilogue

................................................................

................................................................

................................................................

................................................................

### 你可以這樣回答

Multilingual individuals can enjoy literature in its original language.
有多種語言能力的人可以用原始語言享受文學。

Multilingual people often have a greater appreciation for diversity.
有多種語言能力的人通常更能尊重多樣性。

### 參考範例

Multilingual people can communicate with a wider range of individuals, and this ability can enhance their cultural understanding. Also, it can be a competitive advantage in the job market, especially in the era of globalization. Nowadays, it feels like a limitation if one cannot speak any foreign language.

會說多種語言的人可以和更廣範圍的人溝通，而這個能力可以提升他們在文化方面的了解。而且，這在就業市場可能是一項競爭優勢，尤其在全球化的年代。現在，如果一個人不會說任何外語，感覺就像是一種限制。

### 詞彙

cultural 文化的
competitive 競爭的
advantage 優勢
globalization 全球化
limitation 限制

Prologue

11 學習

12 語言能力

13 健康狀況

14 養生方法

15 家族關係

Epilogue

# Do you think it is necessary to take a language proficiency test?

你認為有必要接受語言能力測驗嗎？

你可以這樣回答

Taking a language proficiency test can enhance our credibility in the job market. 接受語言能力測驗可以提升我們在就業市場的可信度。

I don't think it is worth the time and money to take a language proficiency test. 我不認為值得花時間和金錢去接受語言能力測驗。

參考範例

I think it is a must for language learners. By taking a language proficiency test, we can accurately know our levels of language skills and show others how competent we are in the language. Moreover, language proficiency tests provide a tangible goal to strive for in our language learning journey.

我認為它對於語言學習者而言是必要的。藉由接受語言能力測驗，我們可以精確知道自己的語言能力水平，並且向他人展示我們的語言程度多高。而且，語言能力測驗也在我們的語言學習之旅中提供一個具體的努力目標。

詞彙

proficiency 精通，熟練

accurately 精確地

competent 有能力的

tangible
可觸知的，實際的

strive for 為…而努力

# What do you think is the best way to learn a language?

你認為學語言最好的方法是什麼？

Prologue

11 學習

12 語言能力

13 健康狀況

14 養生方法

15 家族關係

Epilogue

......................................................................

......................................................................

......................................................................

......................................................................

**你可以這樣回答**

In my opinion, the best way to learn a language is through immersion.
我的意見是，學語言最好的方法是透過沉浸（在環境中）學習。

I think using language-learning apps can be helpful.
我認為使用語言學習 app 可能有幫助。

**參考範例**

I think language learners must practice regularly. It helps to not only retain but also reinforce what has been learned. It is important to practice by talking with others rather than solely relying on textbooks because only by immersing themselves in real-life conversations can learners use a language naturally.

我認為學習語言的人必須規律練習。它不但有助於維持學過的東西，還能加以強化。藉由和別人交談練習而不是只靠課本，是很重要的，因為只有靠著沉浸在真實生活的對話中，學習者才能自然地使用語言。

**詞彙**

retain 保持，保留
reinforce 強化
solely 單獨地，僅僅
rely 依靠
immerse 使沉浸

Prologue

11 學習

12 語言能力

13 健康狀況

14 養生方法

15 家族關係

Epilogue

# Do you think grammar is important when learning a foreign language?

你認為在學外語的時候,文法很重要嗎?

........................................................................

........................................................................

........................................................................

........................................................................

你可以這樣回答

I believe grammar is vital when learning a foreign language.
我認為學外語時文法很重要。

In my view, focusing solely on grammar can hinder language learning.
我認為只著重於文法可能妨礙語言學習。

參考範例

In my opinion, grammar is a crucial component of learning a foreign language. Without a solid understanding of grammar rules, it is difficult to communicate effectively and convey meaning accurately. Therefore, I believe grammar should be given proper attention in language-learning programs.

我的意見是,文法是學習外語不可或缺的一部分。沒有對文法規則的確實了解,就很難有效溝通、準確傳達意義。所以,我相信文法在語言學習的課程中應該得到適度的關注。

詞彙

crucial 至關重要的
component 構成要素
solid 堅實的
effectively 有效地
convey 傳達
accurately 準確地

# Do you easily get a cold when the seasons change?

季節變換時，你容易感冒嗎？

Prologue

11 學習

12 語言能力

13 健康狀況

14 養生方法

15 家族關係

Epilogue

### 你可以這樣回答

When the seasons shift, I tend to catch a cold.
季節變換時，我容易感冒。

It's rare for me to catch a cold during seasonal changes.
我很少在季節變換時感冒。

### 參考範例

Yes, I've noticed that I easily get a cold when the seasons change. My immune system becomes more vulnerable when autumn turns into winter or winter turns into spring. For example, I'll start to sniffle and sneeze constantly. In severe cases, I even have a high fever.

是的，我注意到自己在季節變換時容易感冒。我的免疫系統在秋天轉變為冬天，或者冬天變成春天的時候變得比較脆弱。舉例來說，我會開始一直吸鼻涕並且打噴嚏。嚴重的時候，我甚至會發高燒。

### 詞彙

immune system 免疫系統
vulnerable 脆弱的
sniffle （用鼻子）吸鼻涕
sneeze 打噴嚏

Prologue

11
學習

12
語言能力

13
健康狀況

14
養生方法

15
家族關係

Epilogue

# When you have a cold, do you see a doctor or purchase medicine on your own?

當你感冒時,你會看醫生還是自己買藥?

...................................................................................

...................................................................................

...................................................................................

...................................................................................

### 你可以這樣回答

I usually see a doctor when I have a cold.
我感冒時通常會看醫生。

I prefer to purchase medicine on my own for a common cold.
對於普通感冒,我偏好自己買藥。

### 參考範例

It depends on the symptoms I have. If I have mild ones such as a mild cough, sneezing, or runny nose, I'll choose to buy over-the-counter medications in a pharmacy. However, if the cold symptoms persist or worsen, I'll seek medical attention promptly.

取決於我的症狀。如果我的症狀輕微,例如輕微咳嗽、打噴嚏或流鼻水,我會選擇在藥局買非處方藥物。不過,如果感冒症狀持續或者惡化,我會立即尋求醫療。

### 詞彙

symptom 症狀

mild 溫和的,輕微的

runny nose
流鼻水(的鼻子)

over-the-counter
medication (在藥局櫃台直接購買的)非處方藥物

medical attention 醫療

# Have you ever undergone surgery or accompanied someone who has?

你曾經接受手術，或者陪伴接受手術的人嗎？

......................................................................................

......................................................................................

......................................................................................

......................................................................................

Prologue

11 學習

12 語言能力

13 健康狀況

14 養生方法

15 家族關係

Epilogue

### 你可以這樣回答

I have personally undergone surgery in the past.
我自己以前接受過手術。

I have accompanied a close friend during his/her surgery.
我曾經在一位親近的朋友手術期間陪伴他／她。

### 參考範例

I have once accompanied my best friend for cosmetic surgery aimed at enhancing her nose. The procedure lasted a couple of hours, and I also accompanied her during the recovery process. I helped her to keep her head elevated and to take the prescribed medications.

我曾經陪我最好的朋友動改善她鼻子（外型）的美容整型手術。過程持續大約兩小時，而我也在恢復過程中陪伴她。我幫忙她保持頭部抬高（有點斜躺而不是平躺）以及服用處方藥物。

### 詞彙

cosmetic surgery
美容整型手術

procedure 程序

a couple of
兩個（或者幾個）

recovery 恢復

elevate 抬起

prescribe 開（藥方）

Prologue

11 學習

12 語言能力

13 健康狀況

14 養生方法

15 家族關係

Epilogue

Q. 95

# Do you think that you need to gain or lose weight?

你認為自己需要增重或減重嗎？

你可以這樣回答

My BMI is too high/low, so I need to lose/gain weight.
我的 BMI（身體質量指數）太高／低，所以我需要減／增重。

I believe my weight is fine as it is.
我相信我現在的體重就不錯了。

參考範例

I believe it's important for me to achieve a healthy weight gain due to my thin appearance. I plan to gradually increase my calorie intake in a balanced manner, which includes incorporating more lean protein and fresh fruits into my diet. Additionally, I'll also engage in some strength training.

由於我很瘦的外型，我相信達成健康的增重對我而言是很重要的。我打算用均衡的方式逐漸增加我的卡路里攝取，其中包括在我的飲食中納入更多精益蛋白質和新鮮水果。此外，我也會進行一些力量訓練。

詞彙

gradually 逐漸

calorie 卡路里

intake 攝取

incorporate 包含，納入

lean protein （低脂、低卡的）精益蛋白質（食物）

# Is there any aspect of your health that you feel you could improve upon?

你覺得自己的健康有哪方面可以改進嗎？

.................................................................................

.................................................................................

.................................................................................

.................................................................................

Prologue

11 學習

12 語言能力

13 健康狀況

14 養生方法

15 家族關係

Epilogue

**你可以這樣回答**

I would like to boost my energy levels and digestion.
我想要增進我的精力與消化能力。

I am aiming to improve my mental health.
我正在試圖改善我的心理健康。

**參考範例**

After discovering that my cholesterol levels were high during a recent medical check-up, I became aware of the need to lower them and prevent cardiovascular diseases. Therefore, I've started making mindful dietary choices, eating more heart-healthy foods such as fruits and vegetables.

在最近的健康檢查發現我的膽固醇水平很高後，我就意識到降低膽固醇與預防心血管疾病的必要。所以，我開始做謹慎的飲食選擇，吃更多對心臟健康的食物，例如水果和蔬菜。

**詞彙**

cholesterol 膽固醇

medical check-up
（醫學的）健康檢查

cardiovascular
心臟與血管的

mindful 留心的

dietary 飲食的

Prologue

11 學習

12 語言能力

13 健康狀況

14 養生方法

15 家族關係

Epilogue

# Do you feel that you are sacrificing your health for work or school?

你覺得自己正為了工作或學業而犧牲健康嗎？

.........................................................................................

.........................................................................................

.........................................................................................

.........................................................................................

### 你可以這樣回答

I find myself prioritizing work/school over my well-being.
我覺得自己重視工作／學業更優先於健康。

I've worked hard to strike a balance between my health and the demands of work/school. 我很努力在健康與工作／學業的要求之間達成平衡。

### 參考範例

I believe my dedication to work is taking a toll on my health. I am making an all-out effort, hoping to get promoted someday. However, the extended work hours and irregular meal times have already negatively affected my metabolism. It has become hard for me to lose weight now.

我認為自己對工作的奉獻正在傷害我的健康。我竭盡全力，希望有一天獲得升遷。然而，過長的工作時數和不規律的用餐時間，已經對我的新陳代謝造成了負面影響。現在我已經很難減重了。

### 詞彙

dedication 奉獻

take a toll on
對…造成傷害

make an all-out effort
竭盡全力

promote 使…升遷

extended
延長了的，超過長度的

metabolism 新陳代謝

# Has anything ever caused you difficulty falling asleep?

有什麼原因曾經造成你難以入眠嗎？

Prologue

11 學習

12 語言能力

13 健康狀況

14 養生方法

15 家族關係

Epilogue

.....................................................................................................

.....................................................................................................

.....................................................................................................

.....................................................................................................

### 你可以這樣回答

Using electronic devices before bed has caused me issues with falling asleep.
睡前用電子設備造成了我難以入睡的問題。

Fortunately, sleep hasn't been a major concern for me.
幸好睡眠對我而言不曾是個重大的問題。

### 參考範例

During my time at a technology company two years ago, the stress and anxiety made it difficult for me to fall asleep. What is worse, I had developed a habit of relying on coffee to boost my mood during work hours, aggravating my sleeping problem.

當我兩年前在科技公司工作的時候，壓力與焦慮讓我很難入睡。更糟的是，我養成了在工作時間依賴咖啡提振心情的習慣，讓我的睡眠問題更加嚴重。

### 詞彙

anxiety 焦慮

develop a habit 養成習慣

rely 依靠，依賴

boost one's mood
提振心情

aggravate 使惡化

Prologue

11 學習

12 語言能力

13 健康狀況

14 養生方法

15 家族關係

Epilogue

## Q.99

# What do you do to keep yourself healthy?

你做什麼事來保持健康？

.....................................................................................................

.....................................................................................................

.....................................................................................................

.....................................................................................................

### 你可以這樣回答

To stay healthy, I eat healthily and exercise consistently.
為了保持健康，我吃得健康而且持續運動。

I maintain a healthy lifestyle through nutritious diet and regular physical activity.
我透過營養的飲食與規律的身體活動來維持健康的生活型態。

### 參考範例

I try to maintain good health by eating a balanced diet, which includes plenty of fruits, vegetables, and healthy fats. Additionally, I integrate regular exercise into my daily routine, doing both aerobic exercise and weight training to achieve well-rounded physical fitness.

我試圖藉由均衡飲食來維持健康，其中包括許多水果、蔬菜和健康的脂肪。此外，我也把規律運動整合在每天例行事項中，藉由做有氧運動與重量訓練來達成全面的體適能。

### 詞彙

integrate 使融入，整合

aerobic exercise
有氧運動

weight training 重量訓練

well-rounded 全面的

physical fitness 體適能

Prologue

11 學習

12 語言能力

13 健康狀況

14 養生方法

15 家族關係

Epilogue

# Q.100

## Do you take supplements? Why or why not?

你吃營養補給品嗎？為什麼？

....................
....................
....................
....................

### 你可以這樣回答

Yes, I take supplements as a precaution.
是的，我吃營養補給品作為一種預防措施。

No, I prefer not to rely on supplements.
不，我比較希望不要依賴營養補給品。

### 參考範例

Taking supplements has become a habit of mine. This shift is primarily due to the fact that my strength and vitality have declined after age 30. To enhance my overall well-being, I make sure to supplement my diet with essential nutrients such as vitamin C, calcium, and iron.

吃營養補給品已經成為我的習慣。這個轉變主要是因為我的體力和活力在 30 歲後下降的事實。為了提升我的整體健康，我都會用維生素 C、鈣、鐵之類的必要營養素來對我的飲食進行補充。

### 詞彙

supplement
補給品（n.）；補充（v.）

vitality 活力

decline 下降，減少

enhance 提升

make sure to V 務必…

109

Prologue

11 學習

12 語言能力

13 健康狀況

14 養生方法

15 家族關係

Epilogue

# Do you think you have a healthy diet? Why?

你認為自己的飲食健康嗎？為什麼？

.................................................................

.................................................................

.................................................................

.................................................................

你可以這樣回答

I consider my diet healthy.
我認為自己的飲食很健康。

My diet isn't as healthy as I'd like.
我的飲食不如我所希望的健康。

參考範例

No, I don't think I have a healthy diet. Due to my busy schedule with schoolwork and a part-time job, I've been eating fast food and processed snacks almost every day. Having no time to eat well, I've noticed a decline in my energy levels and a gradual weight gain.

不，我認為自己的飲食不健康。由於我因為學校功課與兼職工作而忙碌的行程，我幾乎每天都在吃速食和加工零食。因為沒時間吃得好，我注意到自己精力衰退，而且逐漸變胖。

詞彙

schoolwork 學校功課
processed 經加工處理的
gradual 逐漸的
weight gain 體重增加

# Do you check nutrition information before you eat something?

你在吃東西之前會查看營養資訊嗎？

Prologue

11 學習

12 語言能力

13 健康狀況

14 養生方法

15 家族關係

Epilogue

........................................................................

........................................................................

........................................................................

........................................................................

### 你可以這樣回答

Yes, I make it a habit to check nutrition labels before eating anything.
是的，我在吃任何東西之前習慣查看營養標示。

No, I tend to just eat what I feel like.
不，我通常就是吃我想吃的東西。

### 參考範例

I always examine nutrition information prior to consuming any food. This practice serves a dual purpose: firstly, it enables me to track my calorie intake; secondly, it helps me identify the presence of added preservatives or artificial ingredients. I believe informed choices will lead to better health.

我在吃或喝東西之前總是會檢視營養資訊。這樣做有雙重目的：首先，是讓我可以追蹤自己的卡路里攝取；第二，是幫助我發現外加防腐劑或人工原料的存在。我相信知情的選擇將會改善健康。

### 詞彙

consume 消耗，吃或喝
dual 雙重的
identify 發現，認出
presence 存在，在場
preservative 防腐劑
informed 知情的，有根據的

111

Prologue

11 學習

12 語言能力

13 健康狀況

14 養生方法

15 家族關係

Epilogue

## Q.103

# Do you have regular medical checkups? Why or why not?

你定期接受健康檢查嗎？為什麼？

..........................................................................................

..........................................................................................

..........................................................................................

..........................................................................................

### 你可以這樣回答

I undergo medical checkups to ensure that I'm in good health.
我接受健康檢查來確保自己處在健康的狀態。

I find medical checkups too costly for me.
我覺得健康檢查對我而言太貴了。

### 參考範例

Yes, I have a medical checkup every year. It not only allows me to monitor my health but also indicates underlying health issues that need to be addressed. For instance, during one of my checkups, the doctor identified an elevated cholesterol level, so I could work on it early.

是的，我每年接受健康檢查。這不但能讓我監控我的健康，還會指出需要處理的潛藏健康問題。例如，在一次檢查中，醫生發現了過高的膽固醇水平，讓我能夠及早改善。

### 詞彙

monitor 監控

underlying 潛藏的

address 處理（問題等）

elevated 偏高的

work on 處理…，
（付出時間或心力）改善…

# Do you think you are getting enough sleep?

你認為自己睡眠充足嗎？

Prologue

11 學習

12 語言能力

13 健康狀況

14 養生方法

15 家族關係

Epilogue

### 你可以這樣回答

No, I often struggle to get adequate sleep due to…
不，我經常因為…而很難獲得充足的睡眠。

Yes, I get around seven hours of sleep regularly.
是的，我通常有七個小時的睡眠。

### 參考範例

No, I only sleep four hours a day on average. Lately, I've been feeling exhausted, and I find myself yawning constantly during meetings or working on daily tasks. Besides, I get irritable and anxious over minor reasons, which might also result from a lack of sleep.

不，我平均每天只睡四個小時。最近我感覺精疲力盡，而且我發現自己在會議中或者進行日常工作時不斷打呵欠。此外，我也會因為細微的原因而易怒、焦慮，這也可能是缺乏睡眠的結果。

### 詞彙

on average 平均

constantly 不斷地

irritable 易怒的

minor 較小的，不重要的

result from 起因於…

# What coping strategy do you employ when you feel depressed?

當你感到沮喪時，你採用什麼應對的方法？

**你可以這樣回答**

Cooking can lift my mood when I'm feeling down.
當我感到沮喪時，烹飪可以提振我的心情。

Spending time outdoors is my strategy to combat depression.
花時間在戶外是我戰勝憂鬱的方式。

**參考範例**

First, I'll seek support from my family, friends, or therapists and talk about my feelings. This can bring me a sense of relief and comfort. Additionally, I might engage in various forms of physical activities like jogging, swimming, or practicing yoga.

首先，我會尋求家人、朋友或治療師的協助，並且談談我的感受。這樣可以為我帶來如釋重負的感覺與安慰。另外，我可能也會進行各種形式的身體活動，像是慢跑、游泳或者做瑜伽。

**詞彙**

therapist
（身體或心理的）治療師
relief
（痛苦的）減輕，解脫
comfort 安慰；舒適
engage in 從事⋯
practice yoga 做瑜伽

# Do you spend much time with your family? What do you usually do together?

你花很多時間和家人在一起嗎？你們通常一起做什麼？

........................................................................

........................................................................

........................................................................

........................................................................

Prologue

11 學習

12 語言能力

13 健康狀況

14 養生方法

15 家族關係

Epilogue

### 你可以這樣回答

I try to spend as much time as possible with my family.
我儘可能多花時間和家人在一起。

I don't have much time to spend with my family.
我沒有很多時間可以和家人共處。

### 參考範例

Usually, I spend a lot of time with my family in the evening. We have dinner together and share interesting things. After dinner, we sit on the sofa watching TV. We make comments on the latest news or watch variety shows for entertainment.

通常我晚上會花很多時間和家人在一起。我們一起吃晚餐，並且分享有趣的事。晚餐後，我們坐在沙發上看電視。我們會對最近的新聞發表評論，或者看綜藝節目作為娛樂。

### 詞彙

make a comment on
評論…

latest 最近的，最新的

variety show 綜藝節目

entertainment 娛樂

Prologue

11 學習

12 語言能力

13 健康狀況

14 養生方法

15 家族關係

Epilogue

# How would you describe the atmosphere in your family?

你會怎樣形容你家的氣氛？

........................................................................................................

........................................................................................................

........................................................................................................

........................................................................................................

### 你可以這樣回答

In my family, we have a ADJ atmosphere.
在我家，我們有⋯的氣氛。

We maintain a ADJ atmosphere.
我們維持⋯的氣氛。

### 參考範例

The atmosphere in my family is warm and supportive. We feel comfortable sharing our thoughts because we respect each other and encourage open dialogue. We also do our best to make everyone feel valued, such as by celebrating achievements and offering a helping hand during challenges.

我家的氣氛既溫暖又能給予支持。我們對於分享想法感到很自在，因為我們尊重彼此並鼓勵公開對話。我們也盡量讓每個人都感覺受到重視，例如藉由慶祝成就，以及在困難時伸出援手。

### 詞彙

supportive 給予支持的
open dialogue 公開對話
value 重視
achievement 成就
offer a helping hand
伸出援手

# Do you have a good relationship with your family?

你和家人關係好嗎？

Prologue

11 學習

12 語言能力

13 健康狀況

14 養生方法

15 家族關係

Epilogue

........................................................................

........................................................................

........................................................................

........................................................................

### 你可以這樣回答

Yes, I get along with my family.
是的，我和我的家人相處融洽。

No, I have an awful relationship with my family.
不，我和家人的關係很糟糕。

### 參考範例

Yes, I have a robust and positive relationship with my family. I talk about my work with them every day, and we go on weekend hikes once in a while. Our open conversations and shared activities create a strong understanding among us, giving me a deep sense of belonging.

是的，我和我的家人有健康而正面的關係。我每天和他們談論我的工作，我們也偶爾會在週末去登山健行。我們的公開對話和共同的活動，創造出我們之間很深的互相了解，讓我有很強烈的歸屬感。

### 詞彙

robust 強健的
positive 正面的
hike 登山健行
shared 共同的
sense of belonging
歸屬感

# What do you think are some advantages or disadvantages of growing up in a large family?

你認為在大家庭長大有什麼優點或缺點？

Prologue

11 學習

12 語言能力

13 健康狀況

14 養生方法

15 家族關係

Epilogue

........................................................................

........................................................................

........................................................................

........................................................................

### 你可以這樣回答

Growing up in a large family can enhance your social skills.
在大家庭長大可以提升你的社交技能。

In a large family, finding personal space and privacy can be challenging.
在大家庭，要找到個人空間和隱私可能很難。

### 參考範例

On the positive side, there is always someone to spend time with and talk to. Whether it is playing games, sharing stories, or seeking advice, the presence of siblings and cousins provides constant companionship. However, it is also true that disagreements over trivial matters can arise more frequently.

從正面來看，（在大家庭）總是有人可以共度時光以及講話。不管是玩遊戲、分享故事或者尋求建議，兄弟姊妹與堂表兄弟姊妹的存在都提供持續的情誼。不過，因為小事而起的爭執可能更常發生也是事實。

### 詞彙

presence 在場，存在

sibling(s) 兄弟姊妹

companionship（陪伴的）情誼

disagreement 爭執，意見不合

trivial 瑣碎的，微不足道的

# What's a favorite memory you have with your family?

在你和家人的回憶中，你最愛的其中之一是什麼？

................................................................

................................................................

................................................................

................................................................

Prologue

11 學習

12 語言能力

13 健康狀況

14 養生方法

15 家族關係

Epilogue

## 你可以這樣回答

One of my favorite memories with my family was when we…
和家人的回憶中，我最愛的其中之一是我們…的時候。

Ving… together is a memory I hold dear.
一起…是我很珍惜的回憶。

## 參考範例

I vividly recall when I was fifteen, my family went on a trip to Japan. It was my first time going abroad, and the visit to Disneyland added a magical touch to the experience. We tried to communicate with locals even though we couldn't speak Japanese, making the trip even more memorable.

我生動地記得 15 歲的時候，我家去日本旅行。那是我第一次出國，而參觀迪士尼樂園為這次經驗增添了一點魔幻的色彩。儘管我們不會說日語，還是努力和當地人溝通，讓這次旅行更加難忘。

## 詞彙

vividly 生動地

recall 回憶，回想

magical 魔法的

add a ADJ touch to
為…增添一點…的色彩

memorable 難忘的

Prologue

11 學習

12 語言能力

13 健康狀況

14 養生方法

15 家族關係

Epilogue

# Are you more like your mother or father in your personality?

你的個性比較像媽媽還是爸爸？

..................................................................................

..................................................................................

..................................................................................

..................................................................................

### 你可以這樣回答

I am more like… in my personality.
我在個性方面比較像…

I have a mix of both my parents' personalities.
我的個性是父母的綜合。

### 參考範例

I find my personality similar to my father's, as we both possess a great sense of humor. His resolute determination has been passed down to me as well. In addition to these strengths, we also share a few shortcomings. We are both impatient and have a quick temper.

我覺得我的個性和我爸爸（的個性）類似，因為我們都很有幽默感。他堅定的決心也遺傳到我身上。除了這些優點以外，我們也有一些共同的缺點。我們都沒耐心，而且容易發脾氣。

### 詞彙

resolute 堅決的
determination 決心
pass down to 遺傳到…
shortcoming 缺點
impatient 沒耐心的
quick temper 易怒的脾氣

# What is your parents' philosophy of parenting?

你的父母養育子女的哲學是什麼？

Prologue

11 學習

12 語言能力

13 健康狀況

14 養生方法

15 家族關係

Epilogue

........................................................................

........................................................................

........................................................................

........................................................................

### 你可以這樣回答

My parents believe in nurturing our passions.
我的父母相信要培養我們的興趣／愛好。

Building self-confidence is paramount for my parents.
建立自信對我的父母而言是最重要的。

### 參考範例

My parents believe in showing love and fostering independence. Besides providing emotional support, they also encourage me and my sister to make decisions by ourselves. This approach has nurtured strong bonds and shaped us into confident and capable individuals.

我父母相信要表現愛並且培養獨立能力。除了提供情緒方面的支持以外，他們也鼓勵我和我的妹妹自己做決定。這樣的方式培養了（家人之間）堅定的關係，並且將我們形塑成自信而且能幹的人。

### 詞彙

foster 養育，培養
independence 獨立
nurture 養育，培養
bond 聯繫，關係
capable 有能力的，能幹的

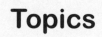

# Topics

# What activities do you usually do when you hang out with your friends?

你和朋友在一起的時候，通常會做什麼活動？

Prologue

16 人際關係

17 感情狀況

18 寵物與動物

19 植物與園藝

20 居家環境

Epilogue

........................................

........................................

........................................

........................................

### 你可以這樣回答

We usually go shopping when we get together.
我們在一起的時候通常會去購物。

We enjoy attending concerts and festivals.
我們喜歡參加演唱會和節慶活動／音樂節。

### 參考範例

My friends and I usually hang out at our favorite coffee shop to enjoy desserts and drinks. In addition to discussing interesting school topics, we also talk about the latest trends and fashion. When we have an upcoming exam to prepare for, we may also study together there.

我的朋友和我通常待在我們最愛的咖啡店，享受甜點和飲料。除了討論有趣的學校話題以外，我們也談論最近的趨勢和流行。當我們有即將到來的考試要準備時，我們也有可能一起在那裡念書。

### 詞彙

hang out
（和某人）一起打發時間

in addition to
除了…以外（還有）

trend 趨勢

upcoming 即將到來的

# How do you maintain a good friendship?

你如何維持良好的友誼？

Prologue

16 人際關係

17 感情狀況

18 寵物與動物

19 植物與園藝

20 居家環境

Epilogue

.......................................................................................

.......................................................................................

.......................................................................................

.......................................................................................

### 你可以這樣回答

I make it a habit to express my gratitude for my friends.
我把對朋友表示感謝變成習慣。

My friends and I often engage in activities we all enjoy.
我和我的朋友們常常進行我們都喜歡的活動。

### 參考範例

I consider communication the most important element for maintaining a good friendship. By openly expressing our thoughts about what our friends say and do, we allow them to gain a deeper insight into our feelings. In this way, our interactions can become more meaningful and affectionate.

我認為溝通是維持良好友誼最重要的要素。藉由坦率表達我們對朋友言行舉止的想法，我們讓朋友能對我們的感受有更深的了解。如此一來，我們的互動就能變得更有意義而充滿感情。

### 詞彙

element 要素

openly 公開地，坦率地

insight 洞見，深刻的了解

interaction 互動

affectionate 充滿深情的

# Do you prefer to have many friends or just a few close friends?

你偏好有許多朋友,還是只有少數親近的朋友?

Prologue

16 人際關係

17 感情狀況

18 寵物與動物

19 植物與園藝

20 居家環境

Epilogue

### 你可以這樣回答

I prefer having many friends / a few close friends.
我偏好有許多朋友/少數親近的朋友。

I think it's ideal to have a wide network of friends.
我認為有廣闊的朋友(人際)網路是理想的。

### 參考範例

I believe it's better to build a small circle of close and genuine friends than deal with a lot of acquaintances. Close friends provide us with comfort and unwavering emotional support. On the other hand, acquaintances may offer casual interactions, but they are rarely connected with us emotionally.

我相信建立一小群親近而真誠的朋友圈,比跟一大堆泛泛之交打交道來得好。親近的朋友提供我們安慰與堅定的情感支持。另一方面,泛泛之交可能會帶來輕鬆隨意的互動,卻很少在情感上和我們有所連結。

### 詞彙

genuine 真正的,真誠的

acquaintance
只是認識的人,泛泛之交

unwavering 堅定不移的

casual 輕鬆隨意的

rarely 很少

Prologue

16
人際關係

17
感情狀況

18
寵物與動物

19
植物與園藝

20
居家環境

Epilogue

# Do you prefer to stay alone or with your friends?

你偏好一個人還是和朋友在一起？

......................................................................

......................................................................

......................................................................

......................................................................

### 你可以這樣回答

I love being alone / around friends.
我很喜歡一個人／和朋友在一起。

While I enjoy socializing, there are moments when I need to be alone.
雖然我喜歡社交，但有時候我需要一個人。

### 參考範例

I prefer to stay alone than spend time with friends. When I'm alone, I have the freedom to engage in activities I truly enjoy without the need to compromise. Additionally, solitary moments offer me the opportunity to focus on self-development and inner peace.

我偏好一個人，勝過和朋友一起度過時間。當我一個人的時候，我有從事自己真正喜愛的活動的自由，而不需要妥協。另外，一個人的時光帶給我專注於自我成長與內在平靜的機會。

### 詞彙

engage in 從事（活動）

compromise 妥協

solitary 單獨的，獨自的

self-development
自我成長（自我發展）

inner 內在的

# Do you think the Internet is a good way to make new friends?

你認為網路是交新朋友的好方法嗎？

........................................................

........................................................

........................................................

........................................................

Prologue

16 人際關係

17 感情狀況

18 寵物與動物

19 植物與園藝

20 居家環境

Epilogue

### 你可以這樣回答

I think it is efficient/enjoyable/risky to make new friends online.
我認為在網路上交新朋友是有效率的／愉快的／風險高的。

I am cautious about making friends online.
我對於在網路上交朋友很謹慎。

### 參考範例

I think it's convenient to use the Internet to start a friendship. By joining online communities, we can easily meet people with similar hobbies, while in the real world we need to go to different occasions to do so. Through the Internet, we can even make friends from foreign countries.

我認為用網路開始一段友誼很方便。藉由加入網路社群，我們可以很容易遇到有類似嗜好的人，而在真實世界我們必須去各種不同的場合才能做到。透過網路，我們甚至可以交來自外國的朋友。

### 詞彙

friendship 友誼
hobby 嗜好
community 社群
occasion 場合

Prologue

16
人際關係

17
感情狀況

18
寵物與動物

19
植物與園藝

20
居家環境

Epilogue

# Do your friends and you share the same interests?

你的朋友和你有相同的興趣嗎？

........................................................................................

........................................................................................

........................................................................................

........................................................................................

**你可以這樣回答**

We have many/some shared interests.
我們有許多／一些共通的興趣。

Our interests are quite different, but this diversity often leads to new experiences.
我們的興趣相當不同，但這種多樣性經常讓我們得到新的經驗。

**參考範例**

Yes, we all enjoy going camping. We frequently invite each other to camp at various campsites. Staying in tents is the most common way we camp, but occasionally, we rent recreational vehicles or go glamping to refresh our bodies and minds.

是的，我們都很喜歡去露營。我們經常邀請彼此去各種營地露營。住在帳篷裡是我們最常用的露營方式，但偶爾我們會租露營車（RV）或者進行豪華露營來讓身心恢復活力。

**詞彙**

campsite 營地
occasionally 偶爾
recreational vehicle 露營車，RV（「娛樂性的車輛」）
glamping 豪華露營
refresh 使恢復活力

# Have you ever betrayed your friend or vice versa?

你曾經背叛過朋友,或者相反(被朋友背叛)嗎?

........................................

........................................

........................................

........................................

Prologue

16
人際關係

17
感情狀況

18
寵物與動物

19
植物與園藝

20
居家環境

Epilogue

### 你可以這樣回答

I have betrayed a friend / experienced a friend's betrayal.
我曾經背叛朋友/遭遇過朋友的背叛。

Fortunately, there hasn't been betrayal between my friends and me.
很幸運,我和朋友之間從來沒有過背叛。

### 參考範例

I regret to say that I have betrayed a friend. Once before an exam, I asked her to assist me in cheating due to my lack of preparation. Unfortunately, we were caught, and I shifted the blame to my friend by saying it was her idea to cheat.

我很遺憾地說,我曾經背叛過一位朋友。有一次在考試前,因為我準備不足,所以我要她協助我作弊。不幸的是,我們被逮到了,而我把責任推給朋友,說作弊是她的主意。

### 詞彙

regret to say 很遺憾地說

betray 背叛

assist 協助

preparation 準備

shift the blame
把做錯事的責任推給別人

# Do you believe in love at first sight?

你相信一見鍾情嗎？

Prologue

16 人際關係

17 感情狀況

18 寵物與動物

19 植物與園藝

20 居家環境

Epilogue

**你可以這樣回答**

I think it is possible for people to fall in love at first sight.
我相信一見鍾情是有可能的。

I am skeptical about love at first sight.
我對一見鍾情持懷疑的態度。

**參考範例**

I think love at first sight is just a strong crush. In most cases, relationships take time to develop, going through stages such as physical attraction, mutual understanding, and emotional connection. Many people who initially believed in love at first sight often come to realize that it's not true love.

我認為一見鍾情只是強烈的迷戀而已。在大部分的情況下，感情關係需要時間發展，會經歷身體／外表上的吸引、彼此了解、情感連結等等的階段。許多一開始相信一見鍾情的人，後來常常會開始了解那不是真正的愛情。

**詞彙**

crush 迷戀

physical 身體的，肉體的

mutual 互相的

emotional 情感的

come to V 開始…

# Do you think getting married means giving up freedom and ideals?

你認為結婚意味著放棄自由和理想嗎？

**你可以這樣回答**

Marriage involves some compromises, but I don't think it means giving up freedom entirely.
婚姻涉及一些妥協，但我不認為這意味著完全放棄自由。

Getting married does not necessarily mean giving up one's free will.
結婚並不一定意味著放棄自由意志。

**參考範例**

I think marriage inevitably requires some sacrifice. This is primarily because getting married means becoming an inseparable part of someone else's life. In a marriage, one cannot make decisions without considering the other. As a result, personal freedom and ideals can easily be given up.

我認為婚姻免不了需要一些犧牲。這主要是因為，結婚意味著成為另一個人生命中不可分的一部分。在婚姻中，做決定時無法不考慮另一個人。結果，個人的自由和理想就很容易被放棄。

**詞彙**

inevitably 不可避免地
require 需要，要求
sacrifice 犧牲
primarily 主要
inseparable 不可分的

Prologue

16 人際關係

17 感情狀況

18 寵物與動物

19 植物與園藝

20 居家環境

Epilogue

# Do you have any experience with online dating?

你有網路約會（在網路上和可能的對象交流）的經驗嗎？

### 你可以這樣回答

I've had some great/interesting/frustrating experiences with online dating.

我有過一些很好的／有趣的／令人洩氣的網路約會經驗。

I haven't tried online dating yet.

我還沒嘗試過網路約會。

### 參考範例

I've had some pleasant experiences with online dating through dating apps. The most unforgettable one was when I met a girl who shared some interests and hobbies with me. We both like cats and enjoy rock music. I always felt at ease when chatting with her.

我有過一些透過約會 app 進行網路約會的愉快經驗。最難忘的是我遇見了一個和我有一些相同興趣與嗜好的女孩。我們都喜歡貓和搖滾音樂。和她聊天時我總是覺得很自在。

### 詞彙

pleasant 令人愉快的

unforgettable 難忘的

at ease （感覺）自在

132

# Do you think it is cheating to text and flirt with someone else?

你覺得和別人傳訊息打情罵俏算是出軌嗎？

Prologue

16 人際關係

17 感情狀況

18 寵物與動物

19 植物與園藝

20 居家環境

Epilogue

## 你可以這樣回答

I consider it a form of emotional cheating.
我認為這是一種情感上出軌的形式。

Some couples may accept it as long as no physical contact is involved.
只要沒有身體接觸，有些情侶可能會接受。

## 參考範例

I think flirting with someone else could be regarded as emotional infidelity. If I caught my partner texting and flirting with someone else, I would feel betrayed and hurt, even though there is no physical relationship involved.

我認為和別人打情罵俏可以被認為是情感上的不忠。如果我逮到自己的伴侶跟別人傳訊息打情罵俏，我會覺得遭到背叛而且受傷，儘管並沒有發生肉體上的關係。

## 詞彙

flirt 調情，打情罵俏

emotional 情緒的，情感的

infidelity 不忠

betray 背叛

physical 身體的，肉體的

# When it comes to finding a partner, what qualities do you consider the most important?

說到尋找伴侶，你認為什麼特質是最重要的？

........................................................

........................................................

........................................................

........................................................

Prologue

16 人際關係

17 感情狀況

18 寵物與動物

19 植物與園藝

20 居家環境

Epilogue

### 你可以這樣回答

I value honesty/empathy/independence highly.
我很重視誠實／同理心／獨立。

It's important to me that my partner be responsible/considerate/romantic.
伴侶負責任／體貼／浪漫對我很重要。

### 參考範例

I prioritize trustworthiness above all. It's like the foundation of a relationship. If I find it hard to trust my partner, it will be impossible for me to build strong emotional connection with him. Also, I hope he has a sense of humor and good emotional intelligence.

我最優先考慮值得信任這一點。它就像是關係的基礎。如果我覺得很難相信我的伴侶，我就不可能和他建立強烈的情感連結。還有，我希望他有幽默感和良好的情商（EQ）。

### 詞彙

prioritize 優先考慮

trustworthiness
值得信任，可靠（的特質）

foundation 基礎

sense of humor 幽默感

emotional intelligence
情緒智力，情商（EQ）

Prologue

16 人際關係

17 感情狀況

18 寵物與動物

19 植物與園藝

20 居家環境

Epilogue

# Q.125

## Would you continue to date someone your parents don't like?

你會持續跟父母不喜歡的人談戀愛嗎？

..................................................

..................................................

..................................................

..................................................

### 你可以這樣回答

I will follow my heart and keep dating.
我會跟從自己的心，並且繼續談戀愛。

I'll consider my parents' concern and decide to continue dating or not.
我會考慮父母的擔心，並且決定要不要繼續談戀愛。

### 參考範例

I'll stick to my choice of partner. While it can be challenging under my parents' pressure, I believe they will eventually accept her if I keep communicating with them. After all, love is a matter between two people, and it should not be influenced by external judgments.

我會堅持自己選擇的伴侶。雖然在我父母的壓力之下可能很困難，但我相信如果持續和他們溝通的話，他們最終會接受她。畢竟愛情是兩個人之間的事，不應該受到外界的看法影響。

### 詞彙

stick to 堅持…

eventually 最終

influence 影響

external 外部的，外界的

judgment
判斷，意見，看法

# Do you think dating is a waste of time?

你認為談戀愛是浪費時間嗎？

Prologue

16 人際關係

17 感情狀況

18 寵物與動物

19 植物與園藝

20 居家環境

Epilogue

........................................................................

........................................................................

........................................................................

........................................................................

### 你可以這樣回答

I see dating as an important part of my life journey.
我把談戀愛視為人生旅程中重要的一部分。

I don't think dating is necessary.
我不認為談戀愛是必要的。

### 參考範例

I don't think dating is a waste of time. Actually, I find it an enjoyable and fulfilling experience, and I think meaningful relationships can only be achieved through this process. It allows individuals to know each other better and build connections.

我不認為談戀愛是浪費時間。事實上，我覺得它是愉快而令人滿足的經驗，而且我認為只有經過這個過程，才能達成有意義的關係。它讓人能夠更了解彼此，並且建立（情感上的）連結。

### 詞彙

enjoyable 令人愉快的
fulfilling 令人滿足的
meaningful 有意義的
achieve 達成
individual 個人

# Do you have a pet? If not, do you want to have one?

你有寵物嗎？如果沒有的話，你想養嗎？

Prologue

16 人際關係

17 感情狀況

18 寵物與動物

19 植物與園藝

20 居家環境

Epilogue

................................................................

................................................................

................................................................

................................................................

**你可以這樣回答**

Yes, I have a dog/cat/rabbit called…
是的，我有一隻叫…的狗／貓／兔子

No, and my current lifestyle doesn't allow for a pet.
沒有，而且我目前的生活型態不容許養寵物。

**參考範例**

I would like to keep a cat if I could. Sometimes I feel lonely when I return to an empty home, and that's when I imagine the company of a cat. Its purring and playful behavior could give me comfort and alleviate my loneliness.

如果可以的話，我想養一隻貓。有時候我回到空無一人的家會感覺寂寞，這時候我就會想像貓的陪伴。牠的呼嚕聲和愛玩的行為可以帶給我安慰，並且緩解我的寂寞。

**詞彙**

company 陪伴
purring （貓的）呼嚕聲
playful 愛玩的
alleviate 緩解
loneliness 寂寞

Prologue

16 人際關係

17 感情狀況

18 寵物與動物

19 植物與園藝

20 居家環境

Epilogue

# What do you think is the main reason for people to keep pets?

你認為人們養寵物主要的原因是什麼？

................................................................

................................................................

................................................................

................................................................

**你可以這樣回答**

Many people keep pets because they help reduce stress.
許多人養寵物是因為牠們有助於減少壓力。

Pets' loyalty and affection make us feel valued.
寵物的忠誠和愛情讓我們感覺受到重視。

**參考範例**

I think people keep pets mainly for the emotional support they could provide. It takes some time to feed and groom them regularly, but seeing them curling up beside us with complete trust makes all the effort worthwhile. The emotional connection between pets and us can improve our well-being, too.

我認為人們主要是為了寵物能提供的情感支持而養牠們。定時餵養並梳洗寵物會花一些時間，但看到牠們全然信任地蜷臥在我們身邊，這些努力就全都值得了。寵物與我們之間的情感連結，也能改善我們的身心健康。

**詞彙**

feed 餵

groom 刷洗，梳理（動物的毛皮）

curl up 蜷坐，蜷臥

worthwhile 值得的

well-being 身心健康

# Do you think cats and dogs can understand what humans say?

你認為貓狗聽得懂人說的話嗎？

.................................................................................

.................................................................................

.................................................................................

.................................................................................

Prologue

16 人際關係

17 感情狀況

18 寵物與動物

19 植物與園藝

20 居家環境

Epilogue

### 你可以這樣回答

I think they can get our intentions by observing our tone of voice and body language.
我認為牠們可以藉由觀察我們的語調和身體語言而了解我們的意圖。

I don't think they can grasp the abstract concepts in our language.
我不認為牠們能掌握我們語言中的抽象概念。

### 參考範例

I think cats and dogs only have limited understanding of human language. While they may learn to recognize certain commands such as "sit", "stay", or "come" through repeated training, they cannot comprehend the complexity of human conversation beyond those cues.

我認為貓狗對於人類語言只有有限的了解。雖然牠們可能透過反覆訓練學會認出「坐下」、「不要動」、「過來」等特定指令，但牠們無法理解人類語言在這些提示之外的複雜性。

### 詞彙

command 命令
repeated 反覆的
comprehend 理解
complexity 複雜性
cue 提示

Prologue

16
人際關係

17
感情狀況

18
寵物與動物

19
植物與園藝

20
居家環境

Epilogue

# Are you a dog person or a cat person? Why?

你是狗派還是貓派（比較喜歡哪種動物）？為什麼？

......................................................................

......................................................................

......................................................................

......................................................................

**你可以這樣回答**

I am more of a dog/cat person.
我比較算是狗派／貓派。

I prefer dogs/cats because…
我比較喜歡狗／貓，因為…

**參考範例**

I consider myself a dog person. I prefer dogs because of their loyalty. Dogs stay close to us under any circumstances, offering support without reservation. There is also something comforting about their presence, especially when I feel stressed or overwhelmed.

我認為自己是狗派。我偏好狗是因為牠們的忠誠。狗在任何情況下都待在我們身邊，毫無保留地提供支持。牠們的存在也有一種撫慰人心的感覺，尤其在我感覺有壓力或者不堪負荷的時候。

**詞彙**

loyalty 忠誠

circumstance 情況

without reservation
沒有保留地

presence 在場，存在

overwhelmed
感到不堪負荷的

# What is your favorite wild animal?

你最喜歡的野生動物是什麼？

....................................................................................

....................................................................................

....................................................................................

....................................................................................

Prologue

16 人際關係

17 感情狀況

18 寵物與動物

19 植物與園藝

20 居家環境

Epilogue

## 你可以這樣回答

Lions/Dolphins/Koalas are my favorite wild animals.
獅子／海豚／無尾熊是我最愛的野生動物。

I am fascinated by penguins/kangaroos/wolves.
企鵝／袋鼠／狼很吸引我。

## 參考範例

My favorite wild animal is the elephant. Although their sizes are massive, the way they move is graceful and powerful at the same time. Besides, I am fascinated by their complex social structures and strong family bonds, which I learned about when watching a documentary on elephants.

我最喜歡的野生動物是大象。雖然牠們的體型很巨大，但牠們移動的樣子既優雅又強而有力。而且，我也受到牠們複雜的社會結構與堅定的家庭關係吸引，這是我在看關於大象的紀錄片時知道的。

## 詞彙

massive 巨大的

graceful 優雅的

fascinate
迷住，（強烈地）吸引

bond
（人際間緊密的）關係

documentary 紀錄片

141

# Do you think it is appropriate to keep wild animals in a zoo or aquarium?

你認為把野生動物養在動物園或水族館是恰當的嗎？

Prologue

16 人際關係

17 感情狀況

18 寵物與動物

19 植物與園藝

20 居家環境

Epilogue

### 你可以這樣回答

I think zoos and aquariums play an important role in education and conservation.
我認為動物園和水族館在教育和保育方面扮演重要角色。

I think it is against animal welfare to keep wild animals in captivity.
我認為囚禁野生動物違反動物福利。

### 參考範例

I think it is inappropriate to do so. No matter how well-designed a zoo or aquarium is, it cannot truly replicate natural environments. Moreover, the animals in such facilities are deprived of the autonomy they could have in the wild.

我認為這是不恰當的。不管動物園或水族館設計得多好，都不能真正複製自然環境。而且，在這種設施中的動物被剝奪了在野外可以擁有的自主權。

### 詞彙

inappropriate 不恰當的

replicate 複製

be deprived of 被剝奪…

autonomy 自主權

in the wild 在野外

# Are you afraid of any animals? Why?

你有任何害怕的動物嗎？為什麼？

Prologue

16 人際關係

17 感情狀況

18 寵物與動物

19 植物與園藝

20 居家環境

Epilogue

.................................................................................

.................................................................................

.................................................................................

.................................................................................

### 你可以這樣回答

I am scared of dogs/spiders/cockroaches.
我怕狗／蜘蛛／蟑螂。

I don't have any particular fear of animals.
我不害怕任何特定的動物。

### 參考範例

I'm afraid of snakes. While I understand that snakes rarely attack human beings voluntarily, the sight of one still sends shivers down my spine. I guess it's the sleek way they move that makes me nervous. That's why I don't like hiking, especially in grassy areas.

我怕蛇。雖然我了解蛇很少主動攻擊人類，但看到蛇還是會讓我脊背發涼。我猜是他們滑溜的移動方式讓我緊張。那就是我不喜歡登山健行的原因，尤其在長滿草的地區。

### 詞彙

voluntarily
自願地，自動自發地

send shivers down one's spine 讓某人脊背發涼

sleek 光滑的，滑溜的

grassy 長滿草的

Prologue

16 人際關係

17 感情狀況

18 寵物與動物

19 植物與園藝

20 居家環境

Epilogue

# Do you have a green thumb?

你擅長栽培植物嗎？

..................................................................
..................................................................
..................................................................
..................................................................

### 你可以這樣回答

I think I have a bit of a green thumb.
我認為我有點擅長栽培植物。

I haven't tried gardening before.
我沒有嘗試過園藝。

### 參考範例

I don't have a talent for gardening. Despite my best efforts, I struggle to keep my plants alive. Even if they start strong, they tend to wither away over time. It's so frustrating that I've already given up the idea of having a lush garden.

我沒有園藝的才能。儘管付出最大的努力，我還是很難讓我的植物活下來。就算一開始很茁壯，它們通常會隨著時間過去而枯萎。這很令人洩氣，所以我已經放棄擁有一座茂盛花園的想法了。

### 詞彙

talent 天賦，才能
gardening 園藝
struggle to V 艱難地做…
wither away 枯萎
lush 茂盛的，蔥翠的

# Are you growing plants? If not, would you like to give it a try?

你正在種植物嗎？如果沒有，你想試試看嗎？

Prologue

16 人際關係

17 感情狀況

18 寵物與動物

19 植物與園藝

20 居家環境

Epilogue

**你可以這樣回答**

Yes, I have a few plants at home.
是的，我家裡有一些植物。

Gardening is not my thing, so I haven't considered growing plants.
我對園藝沒興趣，所以我沒考慮過種植物。

**參考範例**

I'm considering growing a cactus. The main reason is its ability to survive in arid conditions, meaning it can stay alive even if I forget to water it. Considering my poor gardening skills, a cactus seems like an ideal choice for me.

我正在考慮種仙人掌。主要的原因是它在乾旱的狀況存活的能力，意味著即使我忘記澆水，它也能夠存活。考慮到我糟糕的園藝技能，仙人掌似乎是對於我而言理想的選擇。

**詞彙**

survive
（在困難的狀況下）存活

arid 乾旱的

water 澆水

Prologue

16 人際關係

17 感情狀況

18 寵物與動物

19 植物與園藝

20 居家環境

Epilogue

# Do you prefer to have plants in your room or not?

你比較希望自己房間裡有植物還是沒有？

### 你可以這樣回答

Yes, I love having plants in my room.
是的，我喜歡自己房間裡有植物。

No, I think they take up too much space / are hard to maintain.
不，我認為它們太佔空間／很難維護。

### 參考範例

I would like to have plants in my room if possible. They not only create a calming and refreshing atmosphere, but also help purify the air. In addition, the fact that plants are living things will make me feel responsible for taking care of them.

如果可能的話，我希望自己房間裡有植物。它們不但創造出讓人平靜又有新鮮感的氣氛，也有助於淨化空氣。另外，植物有生命的事實也會讓我感覺有責任照顧它們。

### 詞彙

refreshing 帶來新鮮感的

atmosphere 氣氛

purify 淨化

# Do you think it is a good idea to have fake plants instead of real ones?

你認為擁有人造（假的）植物而非真的植物是個好主意嗎？

Prologue

16 人際關係

17 感情狀況

18 寵物與動物

19 植物與園藝

20 居家環境

Epilogue

### 你可以這樣回答

Fake plants can be convenient for those who don't have a green thumb.
對於不擅長栽培植物的人，人造植物可能是很方便的。

In my opinion, the natural beauty of real plants is irreplaceable.
在我看來，真實植物的自然美是無可取代的。

### 參考範例

I think it's always better to have real plants whenever possible. While fake plants seem like an easy way out, they lack the many benefits that real plants offer. For instance, fake plants do not help remove toxins in the air. What's worse, they collect more dust over time.

我認為只要可能的話，擁有真的植物總是比較好。雖然人造植物看似是個省事的解決辦法，但它們缺少真實植物提供的許多好處。舉例來說，人造植物不會幫助去除空氣中的毒素。更糟的是，隨著時間過去，它們會聚積比較多的灰塵。

### 詞彙

**whenever possible**
只要可能的話

**easy way out** （困難情況下）省事的解決辦法

**toxin** 毒素

Prologue

16 人際關係

17 感情狀況

18 寵物與動物

19 植物與園藝

20 居家環境

Epilogue

# Do you like to receive flowers as a gift? Why?

你喜歡收到花當禮物嗎？為什麼？

.............................................................

.............................................................

.............................................................

.............................................................

### 你可以這樣回答

Yes, receiving flowers is a delightful experience for me.
是的，收到花對我而言是愉快的經驗。

No, flowers as gifts don't resonate with me.
不，我對送花當禮物沒有感覺（不能引起我的共鳴）。

### 參考範例

I will be disappointed if I receive flowers as a gift. The main reason is that flowers have a short lifespan. Flowers look stunning in full bloom, but they will eventually wither and need to be discarded in a few days, leaving no lasting value in the end.

如果我收到花當禮物，我會很失望。主要原因是花的壽命很短。花盛開的時候看起來很迷人，但最終會在幾天後枯萎而必須丟棄，結果不會剩下任何持久的價值。

### 詞彙

lifespan 壽命
stunning 非常迷人的
in full bloom 盛開
eventually 最終
discard 丟棄

# Do you think it is worthwhile to grow edible plants on a balcony?

你認為在陽台種可食用的植物是值得做的事嗎？

Prologue

16 人際關係

17 感情狀況

18 寵物與動物

19 植物與園藝

20 居家環境

Epilogue

### 你可以這樣回答

I think growing edible plants on a balcony is a great idea.
我認為在陽台種可食用的植物是很好的主意。

I don't see it as a better choice than buying from stores.
我不認為那是比從店裡買更好的選擇。

### 參考範例

I believe that growing edible plants is worthwhile because it allows us to have easy access to fresh homegrown produce. Among such plants, I think ginger and scallion are especially easy to grow, and they don't take up too much space.

我認為種可食用的植物是值得的，因為這讓我們能夠很容易取得新鮮的自家種植作物。在這類（可食用的）植物中，我認為薑和蔥特別容易種，而且不會佔用太多空間。

### 詞彙

edible 可食用的

have access to
可以接近／利用…

homegrown 自家種植的

produce 農產品

scallion 蔥

Prologue

16
人際關係

17
感情狀況

18
寵物與動物

19
植物與園藝

20
居家環境

Epilogue

# Would you be interested in learning about flower arranging?

你會有興趣學插花嗎？

你可以這樣回答

I think it could be a fascinating skill to learn.
我想那可能會是很棒（值得學習）的技能。

I don't think I have the artistic skills needed for it.
我不認為我有插花所需要的藝術技能。

參考範例

Yes, I've been dreaming of adding more beauty to my life by decorating with flowers. Flower arrangement seems like a wonderful way to beautify my home while using my creativity. It can also reflect my personal style, making my home look more unique.

是的，我一直夢想藉由用花朵裝飾來為我的生活增添美麗。插花似乎是在運用創意的同時又美化我家的好方法。它也能反映我的個人風格，讓我的家看起來更獨特。

詞彙

**flower arrangement**
插花，花藝設計

**beautify** 美化

**creativity** 創意

**reflect** 反映

# Would you describe your room as neat and tidy or more on the cluttered side?

你會形容自己的房間是整潔有條理，還是偏雜亂？

Prologue

16
人際關係

17
感情狀況

18
寵物與動物

19
植物與園藝

20
居家環境

Epilogue

### 你可以這樣回答

I make an effort to keep my room neat and tidy.
我努力保持自己的房間整潔有條理。

I must admit my room is a bit cluttered.
我必須承認自己的房間有點雜亂。

### 參考範例

I would say my room is neat because everything in my room has its designated place. There are no obstacles hindering my movement. In addition, I regularly clean up my room and vacuum the floor to maintain cleanliness.

我會說我的房間很整潔，因為房間裡的每樣東西都有指定的位置。沒有障礙物妨礙我的移動。而且，我定期打掃我的房間並且用吸塵器吸地板來維持清潔。

### 詞彙

designate 指定
obstacle 障礙物
hinder 妨礙
vacuum 用吸塵器清理
cleanliness 清潔

Prologue

16 人際關係

17 感情狀況

18 寵物與動物

19 植物與園藝

20 居家環境

Epilogue

# Do you clean up your room regularly?

你定期打掃自己的房間嗎？

.................................................

.................................................

.................................................

.................................................

### 你可以這樣回答

I usually clean up my room once a week.
我通常一週打掃一次房間。

I tend to neglect cleaning my room.
我通常會疏忽打掃房間這件事。

### 參考範例

Due to my busy work schedule and engagements, I don't always have time to clean up my room. As a result, my room can be quite messy due to my negligence. Despite the occasional mess, it seems to me that the atmosphere is still comforting.

由於我忙碌的工作排程與（社交）約會，我不是隨時都有時間打掃我的房間。結果，我的房間有可能因為疏忽而變得很髒亂。儘管偶爾髒亂，但在我看來氣氛還是很令人舒適。

### 詞彙

engagement
社交上的約會

messy 髒亂的

negligence 疏忽

occasional 偶爾的

comforting 令人舒適的

# Do you find it helpful to organize your home by decluttering?

你覺得藉由斷捨離來整理你的家是有幫助的嗎？

Prologue

16 人際關係

17 感情狀況

18 寵物與動物

19 植物與園藝

20 居家環境

Epilogue

### 你可以這樣回答

Yes, decluttering greatly improves the tidiness of my home.
是的，斷捨離大幅改善我家裡的整潔。

Decluttering doesn't seem to be very helpful for me.
斷捨離對我而言似乎不是很有幫助。

### 參考範例

Yes, I think it is helpful to let go of unused items. Decluttering not only helps me get rid of excessive items but also makes my essential items more accessible when I need them. Through this process, I also become more conscious of what each item really means to me.

是的，我認為捨棄不用的東西很有幫助。斷捨離不但幫助我擺脫過多的物品，也讓我必要的物品在需要時更容易取用。透過這個過程，我也對於每個物品對於我真正的意義更有覺知。

### 詞彙

unused 沒有使用的

declutter
斷捨離（清除不需要的多餘物品，減少空間的雜亂）

get rid of 擺脫…

excessive
過度的，過多的

accessible
可接近的，可取用的

153

Prologue

16
人際關係

17
感情狀況

18
寵物與動物

19
植物與園藝

20
居家環境

Epilogue

# Q.144

# When it comes to interior style, do you prefer it to be cozy or modern?
說到室內風格,你偏好溫馨舒適還是現代風?

........................................................................................................

........................................................................................................

........................................................................................................

........................................................................................................

你可以這樣回答

I'm more drawn to cozy/modern interior styles.
溫馨舒適/現代風的室內風格比較吸引我。

I prefer a balance between cozy and modern.
我偏好溫馨舒適與現代風之間的平衡。

參考範例

I prefer the interior style to be modern. I like the clean lines of minimalist designs, which clearly reflect the personality of a homeowner. The color schemes of modern interior designs are also to my liking: the use of neutral colors along with white and gray creates an airy feel.

我偏好現代風的室內風格。我喜歡極簡主義設計的乾淨線條,清楚地反映房屋主人的個性。現代風室內設計的配色也是我喜歡的:中性色和白與灰的使用,創造出寬敞明亮的感覺。

詞彙

minimalist 極簡主義的
homeowner 房屋主人
color scheme
配色,整體的色彩搭配
neutral
中性的,(顏色)低彩度的
airy (空間)寬敞明亮的

# How do you personalize your living space to reflect your taste?

你如何個人化居住空間來反映自己的品味？

......................................................................

......................................................................

......................................................................

......................................................................

### 你可以這樣回答

I grow indoor plants to show my love for nature.
我種植室內植物來展現我對自然的喜愛。

I've placed some designer lamps in my home to make it more stylish.
我在家裡擺放了一些設計師燈款，讓家感覺更時尚。

### 參考範例

I like to display photographs, travel souvenirs, and nostalgic items to personalize my living place. These items represent my precious memories and experiences I had with family and friends. They also create a welcoming environment that makes me feel at home.

我喜歡展示照片、旅行紀念品和懷舊的物品來個人化我的居住空間。這些物品代表我珍貴的回憶，以及和家人與朋友共同的體驗。它們也創造出讓我感到自在的溫馨環境。

### 詞彙

souvenir 紀念品
nostalgic 懷舊的
personalize 個人化
precious 珍貴的
welcoming 歡迎的，友好的，（氣氛）溫馨的

# Do you use any fragrances to change the atmosphere of your room?

你會用香氣改變房間的氣氛嗎？

Prologue

16 人際關係

17 感情狀況

18 寵物與動物

19 植物與園藝

20 居家環境

Epilogue

........................................................................................

........................................................................................

........................................................................................

........................................................................................

### 你可以這樣回答

I use incense sticks / room sprays / essential oils to change the atmosphere.
我用線香／室內芳香噴霧／精油來改變氣氛。

I am sensitive to scents, so I avoid using scented products.
我對香味很敏感，所以我避免使用有香味的產品。

### 參考範例

I light a lavender-scented candle when I get back home. The gentle scent of lavender creates a soothing atmosphere. This allows me to relax my muscles and release tension from my body after a long and tiring day at work.

我回家的時候會點薰衣草香味的蠟燭。薰衣草溫和的香氣會創造出撫慰人心的氣氛。這讓我在漫長又疲勞的一天工作之後，能放鬆肌肉並且釋放身體的緊繃。

### 詞彙

lavender 薰衣草
scented 有香味的
scent 香氣
soothing 撫慰的
tension 緊繃，緊張

# Which part of your home do you feel could be improved?

你覺得自己家裡的哪個部分可以改善？

........................................................................................................

........................................................................................................

........................................................................................................

........................................................................................................

Prologue
16 人際關係
17 感情狀況
18 寵物與動物
19 植物與園藝
20 居家環境
Epilogue

### 你可以這樣回答

I think my kitchen/bathroom/backyard could use some improvements.
我覺得我的廚房／浴室／後院可能需要做點改善。

I'm quite happy with my home as it is, so I don't see any immediate need for improvements.
我很滿意我家現在的樣子，所以我認為目前不需要改善。

### 參考範例

I would like to improve the storage space of my home because I often struggle to find items when I need them. For example, my closets are overflowing, so I have to spend extra time searching for specific clothing items in the morning.

我想要改善我家的儲藏空間，因為我需要的時候很難找到東西。舉例來說，我的衣櫃滿出來了，所以我早上必須花額外的時間尋找特定的衣物。

### 詞彙

storage 儲存

struggle to V 很艱難地…

overflow 溢出，滿出來

clothing item
（一件）衣物

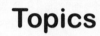

# Topics

# What do you like about your neighborhood?
你喜歡你家周遭地區的什麼方面？

Prologue

21 在地生活

22 天氣

23 我的個性

24 穿著風格

25 兒時回憶

Epilogue

......

## 你可以這樣回答

One of the things I like most about my neighborhood is how safe it feels.
我最喜歡我家附近的其中一點是安全的感覺。

The tranquility of the area is something I cherish.
這個地區的寧靜是我珍惜的地方。

## 參考範例

I like the convenience of my neighborhood. For instance, the convenience store is just a minute away from my home, making quick errands a breeze. Additionally, the local park provides a peaceful retreat for relaxation and outdoor activities, also within walking distance.

我喜歡我家周遭的便利性。例如，便利商店就在離我家一分鐘的地方，讓快速的跑腿（買東西）變得很簡單。另外，當地的公園提供放鬆與戶外活動的僻靜場所，同樣在走路可以到的距離內。

## 詞彙

errand 跑腿，差事
breeze 很簡單的事
retreat 僻靜處
relaxation 放鬆
within walking distance
在走路可到的距離內

159

Prologue

21 在地生活

22 天氣

23 我的個性

24 穿著風格

25 兒時回憶

Epilogue

# Where is your go-to in your neighborhood?

在你家周遭的地區，什麼是你一定會去的地方？

.................................................................

.................................................................

.................................................................

.................................................................

**你可以這樣回答**

My go-to spot is the bookstore a few blocks away.
我必去的地點是幾個街區外的書店。

You can always find me at the French bakery.
你總是可以在法式烘焙坊找到我。

**參考範例**

The cozy little coffee shop called Ann's Café holds a special place in my heart. I usually sit in one of its window-side chairs, observing the lively street and passersby. What's more, the exquisite coffee it serves never fails to provide me with a serene moment of relaxation.

名叫「Ann's Café」的溫馨小咖啡店在我心中有特別的地位。我通常會坐在窗邊的椅子，觀察充滿活力的街道與路過行人。而且，這家店供應的精緻咖啡總是帶給我寧靜的放鬆片刻。

**詞彙**

cozy （空間比較小而讓人感覺）溫馨的，舒適的

passer(s)by 路過行人

exquisite 精緻的

serene 寧靜的

never fail to V 總是（能）…

# Would you prefer to live in the downtown area or a less populated area?

你會比較想住在市中心還是比較少人居住的地區？

Prologue

21 在地生活

22 天氣

23 我的個性

24 穿著風格

25 兒時回憶

Epilogue

........................................................................

........................................................................

........................................................................

........................................................................

### 你可以這樣回答

I'd rather live in the downtown area / a less populated area.
我比較想住在市中心／比較少人居住的地區。

The downtown/suburban/rustic lifestyle suits me better.
市中心／郊區／鄉村的生活型態比較適合我。

### 參考範例

I prefer the urban lifestyle. The vibrant energy of the downtown area always excites and invigorates me. Moreover, the convenience is unmatched. With easily accessible public transportation, exploring every corner of the downtown area becomes effortless.

我比較喜歡城市的生活型態。市中心區充滿生氣的能量，總是讓我興奮並且振奮我的精神。而且，市中心的便利是無可匹敵的。因為有容易利用的大眾運輸，所以探索市中心區的每個角落變得毫不費力。

### 詞彙

urban 城市的

vibrant 充滿生氣的

invigorate 使…精神振奮

unmatched 無與倫比的

accessible
容易到達的，可利用的

# If you have a choice, will you live in your hometown or elsewhere?

如果你有選擇的話,你會住在故鄉還是別的地方?

Prologue

21 在地生活

22 天氣

23 我的個性

24 穿著風格

25 兒時回憶

Epilogue

......................................................................

......................................................................

......................................................................

......................................................................

### 你可以這樣回答

I would choose to stay in my hometown / live elsewhere.
我會選擇留在故鄉/住在別的地方。

I am more inclined to live in my hometown / elsewhere.
我比較想住在故鄉/別的地方。

### 參考範例

If I have a choice, I will live somewhere other than my hometown. It's not that my hometown isn't good enough, but I want to seize fresh opportunities and broaden my horizons. By relocating, I can build new relationships and develop a sense of independence.

如果我有選擇的話,我會住在故鄉以外的地方。並不是因為我的故鄉不夠好,而是我想要抓住新的機會並擴展視野。藉由搬遷,我可以建立新的關係,並且發展獨立感。

### 詞彙

hometown 故鄉

seize 抓住

broaden one's horizons
擴展視野

relocate 搬遷

independence 獨立

# How connected do you feel to the local community?

你覺得自己跟當地社群的關係有多緊密？

Prologue

21 在地生活

22 天氣

23 我的個性

24 穿著風格

25 兒時回憶

Epilogue

........................................................................

........................................................................

........................................................................

........................................................................

### 你可以這樣回答

I feel deeply connected to the local community.
我覺得自己和當地社群的關係很緊密。

I feel moderately/minimally connected to the local community.
我覺得自己和當地社群的關係中等／很不緊密。

### 參考範例

I feel I'm not very connected to the local community. Due to my busy work schedule and unfamiliarity with the area, while I exchange polite greetings with some neighbors, I haven't had the opportunity to engage in deeper conversations or establish strong connections with them.

我覺得自己跟當地社群的關係不是很緊密。因為我忙碌的工作時程，以及對於那個地區的不熟悉，所以雖然我和一些鄰居禮貌地打招呼，但我從來沒有機會和他們進行比較深入的對話，或者建立很強的連結。

### 詞彙

connected 有關聯的

unfamiliarity 不熟悉

exchange greetings 打招呼

engage in 從事於…

Prologue

21
在地生活

22
天氣

23
我的個性

24
穿著風格

25
兒時回憶

Epilogue

# Do you get along with your neighbors?

你和鄰居相處得好嗎？

........

........

........

........

你可以這樣回答

I am on friendly terms with my neighbors.
我和鄰居是友好的關係。

I am not very familiar with my neighbors at the moment.
我目前跟鄰居不是很熟。

參考範例

Yes, I get along well with my neighbors, especially the boy living next door. We frequently have friendly chats over the fence, hang out together in the front yard, or simply enjoy weekend barbecues. Our connection has grown beyond the realm of mere acquaintances.

是的，我和鄰居相處得很好，尤其是住在隔壁的男生。我們經常隔著圍欄做友善的交談、在前院一起消磨時間，或者只是享受週末的烤肉。我們的關係已經超過了只是認識的人的領域。

詞彙

**get along with**
和…相處良好

**hang out**
出去玩，消磨時間

**realm** 領域

**acquaintance**
認識（但不熟）的人

164

# Have you ever had to resolve any conflicts with your neighbors?

你曾經不得不解決和鄰居發生的衝突嗎？

Prologue

21 在地生活

22 天氣

23 我的個性

24 穿著風格

25 兒時回憶

Epilogue

...................

...................

...................

...................

### 你可以這樣回答

Yes, I've experienced conflicts with neighbors on a couple of occasions.
是的，我經歷過和鄰居的幾次衝突。

Thankfully, I've never faced conflicts with my neighbors.
幸好，我從來沒遇過和鄰居的衝突。

### 參考範例

Yes, I had a conflict with the Chens next door regarding our shared property boundary. To prevent the situation from escalating, we invited some other neighbors to help mediate the conflict. Fortunately, the dispute transformed into an opportunity for improved communication, and we successfully resolved the problem.

是的，我和隔壁陳家人曾經有過關於我們土地界線的衝突。為了避免情況惡化，我們邀請了其他一些鄰居來協助調解衝突。幸運的是，爭論轉變成改善溝通的機會，而我們成功解決了問題。

### 詞彙

property 房地產

boundary 界線

escalate
（情況）逐步上升，惡化

mediate 調解

dispute 爭論

# What is your favorite season? Why?

你最愛的季節是什麼？為什麼？

Prologue

21 在地生活

22 天氣

23 我的個性

24 穿著風格

25 兒時回憶

Epilogue

................................................................

................................................................

................................................................

................................................................

**你可以這樣回答**

My favorite season is…
我最愛的季節是…

I love all seasons, but I'm particularly drawn to…
我愛所有季節，但…特別吸引我。

**參考範例**

My favorite season is winter. I love watching snowflakes falling, but snow is rare in Taiwan, so I often travel to snowy destinations, such as Hokkaido. Besides simply seeing snow, I also enjoy staying in winter cabins after skiing all day.

我最愛的季節是冬天。我愛看雪花飄落，但雪在台灣很少見，所以我常常到有雪的目的地旅行，例如北海道。除了只是看雪以外，我也喜歡在滑雪一整天以後住在冬季（雪地）木屋。

**詞彙**

snowflake 雪花
rare 罕見的
snowy 下雪的
destination 目的地
cabin 小木屋

# What is the weather like in your hometown?

你的故鄉的天氣怎麼樣？

Prologue

21 在地生活

22 天氣

23 我的個性

24 穿著風格

25 兒時回憶

Epilogue

........................................................................

........................................................................

........................................................................

........................................................................

**你可以這樣回答**

My hometown has a subtropical climate.
我的故鄉是亞熱帶氣候。

The weather in my hometown is characterized by frequent rain.
我故鄉的天氣特色是很常下雨。

**參考範例**

In my hometown, Kaohsiung, the humidity and temperature remain relatively high throughout the year, so it can be too sultry for those who can't stand the heat. Even though there are occasional cold surges during winter, it's safe to say it is generally sunny and warm in Kaohsiung.

在我的故鄉高雄，一整年的濕度和溫度都維持相對較高，所以對於受不了炎熱的人可能太悶熱了。儘管冬天偶爾有寒流，但還是可以說高雄的天氣大致上晴朗而溫暖。

**詞彙**

humidity 濕度
relatively 相對地
sultry 悶熱的
occasional 偶爾的
cold surge 寒流

# Do you think the weather can influence one's mood?

你認為天氣能影響一個人的情緒嗎？

........................................................................................................

........................................................................................................

........................................................................................................

........................................................................................................

Prologue

21 在地生活

22 天氣

23 我的個性

24 穿著風格

25 兒時回憶

Epilogue

### 你可以這樣回答

I believe the weather can have a significant impact on one's mood.
我相信天氣可以對一個人的情緒產生顯著的影響。

I don't think there is direct connection between weather and mood.
我不認為天氣與情緒有直接的關聯。

### 參考範例

The weather can greatly affect my mood. On sunny days, the warmth and brightness of the sun can make me feel happy and positive. On the contrary, cloudy and rainy days often evoke sadness and depression. That's why I like to go to the south when it's gloomy in winter.

天氣會大大影響我的情緒。在晴朗的日子，太陽的溫暖與光亮能讓我感覺快樂而正面。相反地，多雲和下雨的日子常常引起悲傷和沮喪的感覺。那就是我在冬天天氣陰沉時喜歡去南部的原因。

### 詞彙

warmth 溫暖
brightness 明亮
on the contrary 相反地
evoke 喚起，引起
depression 沮喪

# Have you ever experienced a typhoon?

你經歷過颱風嗎？

Prologue

21 在地生活

22 天氣

23 我的個性

24 穿著風格

25 兒時回憶

Epilogue

......................................................................

......................................................................

......................................................................

......................................................................

### 你可以這樣回答

Yes, I've experienced typhoons many times.
是的，我經歷過許多次颱風。

I haven't really experienced the most intense aspects of typhoons.
我還沒有真正經歷過颱風最強烈的樣子。

### 參考範例

Yes, one of the most unforgettable experiences for me is Typhoon Morakot. During that time, the strong winds blew out the window glass, and we even experienced power outage. As a result, my family and I had to clean up our home, and we had quite a hard time then.

是的，我最難忘的經驗之一是莫拉克颱風。那時候，強風把窗戶玻璃吹破，而我們甚至遇到停電。結果，我和家人必須清掃家裡，那時候我們過得挺糟糕的。

### 詞彙

unforgettable 難忘的
power outage 停電
clean up 把…打掃乾淨
have a hard time 處境困難

169

Prologue

21 在地生活

22 天氣

23 我的個性

24 穿著風格

25 兒時回憶

Epilogue

# What will you do if it rains and you don't have an umbrella?

如果下雨而你沒有帶傘，你會怎麼做？

................................................................

................................................................

................................................................

................................................................

### 你可以這樣回答

I will use something like a jacket to cover myself until I can find a shelter.
我會用像是外套的東西來遮蔽自己，直到找到避雨處為止。

I will call a friend to pick me up with their car.
我會打電話給朋友，請朋友開車接我。

### 參考範例

I'll first look for nearby buildings to seek shelter and wait for the rain to lessen or stop. However, if it still rains a lot, I'll find a convenience store to buy an umbrella. If none of these ways are available, I'll consider borrowing an umbrella from others temporarily.

我會先找附近的建築物來避雨，並且等待雨變小或停止。不過，如果雨還是很大，我會找便利商店買傘。如果這些方法都不可行，我會考慮暫時跟別人借雨傘。

### 詞彙

shelter 躲避處
lessen 減輕，減少
temporarily 暫時

# How do you usually know the weather condition?

你通常怎樣知道天氣狀況？

.......................................................................

.......................................................................

.......................................................................

.......................................................................

Prologue

21 在地生活

22 天氣

23 我的個性

24 穿著風格

25 兒時回憶

Epilogue

### 你可以這樣回答

I watch the weather segment on the news.
我看電視新聞的天氣單元。

Sometimes I simply step outside to observe the weather.
有時我就只是走出門觀察天氣。

### 參考範例

I usually check weather conditions through weather sites or mobile applications dedicated to providing up-to-date weather reports. However, the weather conditions sometimes change rapidly, so I also check the social media to see if there are any immediate updates or real-time reports.

我通常透過氣象網站，或者專門提供最新氣象報告的手機應用程式來查看天氣狀況。不過，天氣狀況有時會快速轉變，所以我也查看社交媒體，看看是否有任何即時更新或即時報導。

### 詞彙

dedicated to 專注於…的
up-to-date 最新的
rapidly 迅速地
immediate
立即的，即時的
real-time 實時的，即時的

# Do you trust weather forecasts?

你相信天氣預報嗎？

Prologue

21 在地生活

22 天氣

23 我的個性

24 穿著風格

25 兒時回憶

Epilogue

**你可以這樣回答**

I trust weather forecasts to some extent.
我一定程度上相信天氣預報。

I am generally doubtful of weather forecasts.
我通常懷疑天氣預報。

**參考範例**

I usually don't rely on weather forecasts. Weather forecasts are not always accurate because the weather condition can easily change. I once trusted a forecast that predicted clear skies, only to end up caught in a downpour. That's when I stopped making decisions simply based on forecasts.

我通常不依賴天氣預報。天氣預報並不總是準確的，因為天氣狀況可能很容易改變。有一次我相信了預測天氣晴朗的預報，結果被困在傾盆大雨中。從那時候我就不再只根據天氣預報做決定了。

**詞彙**

rely on 依賴⋯
accurate 準確的
end up 結果變成⋯
downpour 傾盆大雨
based on 根據⋯

# Do you have a positive or negative attitude toward changes?

你對於改變的態度是積極還是消極？

Prologue

21 在地生活

22 天氣

23 我的個性

24 穿著風格

25 兒時回憶

Epilogue

........................

........................

........................

........................

### 你可以這樣回答

I generally have a positive/negative attitude towards changes.
我對改變的態度通常是積極／消極的。

I tend to respond positively/negatively to changes.
我對改變的反應通常是積極／消極的。

### 參考範例

I think changes can be seen as an opportunity for growth and improvement. By adopting this perspective, I have the energy and motivation to solve problems, rather than focus on obstacles. In the process of adapting to changes, I can also develop my resilience.

我認為改變可以被視為成長與改進的機會。藉由採取這個觀點，我有精力與動力去解決問題，而不是專注於阻礙上。在適應改變的過程中，我也可以發展自己的心理韌性。

### 詞彙

adopt 採取，採用
perspective 觀點
motivation 動機，動力
obstacle 障礙（物）
adapt 適應
resilience （心理）韌性

173

Prologue

21 在地生活

22 天氣

23 我的個性

24 穿著風格

25 兒時回憶

Epilogue

# What is your best personality trait?

你最好的人格特質是什麼？

........................................................................

........................................................................

........................................................................

........................................................................

### 你可以這樣回答

I consider my dedication to be my best personality trait.
我認為專心致力是我最好的人格特質。

Continuous learning is my best personality trait.
持續學習是我最好的人格特質。

### 參考範例

My best trait is my optimism. When I encounter challenges, I always seek out the silver lining. This perspective helps me maintain a positive outlook and believe that things will improve. This optimism also has a ripple effect, positively affecting those around me and leading to meaningful interactions.

我最好的特質是樂觀。當我遇到挑戰時，我總是會找出一線希望。這個觀點幫助我維持（對未來的）正面展望，並且相信情況會好轉。這樣的樂觀也有漣漪效果，正面影響我周遭的人，並且產生有意義的互動。

### 詞彙

optimism 樂觀

encounter 遇到

silver lining
困境中的一線希望

perspective 觀點

outlook 展望

ripple effect 漣漪效果

# Do you consider yourself a selfish or a generous person?

你認為你自己是自私還是慷慨的人？

Prologue

21 在地生活

22 天氣

23 我的個性

24 穿著風格

25 兒時回憶

Epilogue

**你可以這樣回答**

I demonstrate my generosity through my actions.
我透過行動展現我的慷慨。

I admit that there have been times when I've acted selfishly.
我承認自己有些時候行為自私。

**參考範例**

I consider myself a generous person, particularly when it comes to aiding those in need. An example of this is my active involvement in regular voluntary work to assist those struggling with poverty. I firmly believe in the saying that "it is more blessed to give than to receive."

我認為我自己是個慷慨的人，尤其說到幫助有需要的人這方面。一個例子是我積極參與定期的志工活動來協助處於貧窮困境的人。我堅定相信「施比受更有福」這句格言。

**詞彙**

aid 幫助
involvement 參與
voluntary 自願的
poverty 貧窮

Prologue
21 在地生活
22 天氣
23 我的個性
24 穿著風格
25 兒時回憶
Epilogue

# Do you think birth order can influence one's personality?

你認為出生順序可以影響一個人的個性嗎？

................................................................

................................................................

................................................................

................................................................

**你可以這樣回答**

Birth order might play a role, but it's not the only factor.
出生順序可能有其重要性，但那不是唯一的因素。

I'm skeptical about birth order's influence on personality.
我懷疑出生順序對於個性的影響。

**參考範例**

I believe that birth order can influence one's personality. As the eldest among my siblings, I've noticed myself more concerned about responsibility and organization. Conversely, my youngest sister displays a more outgoing and creative nature, along with a bit of mischief.

我相信出生順序可以影響一個人的個性。身為兄弟姊妹中最年長的，我注意到自己比較關心責任與組織。相反地，我最小的妹妹展現出比較外向而有創意的天性，還伴隨一點淘氣。

**詞彙**

responsibility 責任

organization 組織（性），條理

conversely 相反地

outgoing 外向的

mischief 淘氣

# Do you and your friends have different ideas about your personality?

對於你的個性，你自己和你朋友有不同的想法嗎？

Prologue

21 在地生活

22 天氣

23 我的個性

24 穿著風格

25 兒時回憶

Epilogue

........................................................................

........................................................................

........................................................................

........................................................................

### 你可以這樣回答

In some aspects, my friends and I share similar perceptions of my personality. 在某些方面，我朋友和我對於我的個性看法類似。

They see sides of me I might not notice.
他們會看到我可能沒注意的方面。

### 參考範例

My friends and I have different ideas about my personality. Some of them see me as an outgoing person who enjoys adventurous activities, but I consider myself an introvert and deep thinker. Actually, I often reflect on myself, and I can stay calm and composed in stressful situations.

對於我的個性，我朋友和我有不同的想法。他們有些人把我看成喜歡冒險活動的外向人，但我認為自己是內向者、深思熟慮的人。事實上，我常常反省自己，在壓力大的情況也能保持冷靜與沉著。

### 詞彙

adventurous 冒險的
introvert 內向的人
reflect on 反省…
composed
沉著的，冷靜的
stressful 壓力大的

177

Prologue

21 在地生活

22 天氣

23 我的個性

24 穿著風格

25 兒時回憶

Epilogue

# If you could change one thing about your personality, what would it be?

如果你可以改變自己個性中的一點，那會是什麼？

......

......

......

......

你可以這樣回答

I wish I could be more patient.
我希望我可以比較有耐心。

I'd like to cultivate more optimism.
我想要培養更多的樂觀心態。

參考範例

I would like to change my tendency to procrastinate. I often wait until the last minute to complete tasks and miss deadlines. To counter this, I'll begin with setting smaller and more specific goals. Additionally, I'll try practicing time management techniques and prioritizing tasks.

我想要改變自己拖延的傾向。我常等到最後一刻才要完成工作而錯過期限。為了對抗這個情況，我會先從設定比較小而具體的目標開始。另外，我會試著實踐時間管理技巧，並且排定工作的優先順序。

詞彙

tendency 傾向
procrastinate 拖延
deadline 截止期限
counter 反擊，對抗
prioritize
決定…的優先順序

# Do you think your personality has changed over time?

你認為自己的個性隨著時間而改變了嗎？

Prologue

21 在地生活

22 天氣

23 我的個性

24 穿著風格

25 兒時回憶

Epilogue

### 你可以這樣回答

I have observed some changes in my personality.
我觀察到自己個性的一些變化。

I think I am still the same person.　我認為我還是同樣的人。

### 參考範例

My personality has changed over time through various experiences. When I was younger, I was shy and introverted. However, when I became part of the photography club in high school, I developed better social skills and learned to enjoy spending time with people, making me now a more extroverted person.

透過各種經驗，我的個性隨著時間而改變了。當我年紀比較小的時候，我害羞而內向。不過，當我加入高中的攝影社，我發展出比較好的社交技巧，並且學習喜歡和別人共度時間，使得我現在成為比較外向的人。

### 詞彙

introverted 內向的

photography
（照相）攝影

social skill 社交技巧

extroverted 外向的

# Do you prefer classic, timeless clothing pieces or more trendy styles?

你偏好經典款、超越時代潮流的衣服，還是比較時髦的風格？

Prologue

21 在地生活

22 天氣

23 我的個性

24 穿著風格

25 兒時回憶

Epilogue

................................................................

................................................................

................................................................

................................................................

### 你可以這樣回答

I like classic/trendy styles better.
我比較喜歡經典／時髦的風格。

Classic/trendy styles are more to my taste.
經典／時髦的風格比較符合我的喜好。

### 參考範例

I have a personal preference for timeless clothing pieces. Choosing a classic style relieves me from the need to constantly chase trends and adapt to ever-changing fashions, which in turn helps me save on my clothing budget. Moreover, dressing in a classic manner means I never fall out of style.

我個人偏好超越時代潮流的衣服。選擇經典的風格，讓我不必持續追逐趨勢以及適應不斷改變的時尚，進而幫助我節省置裝預算。此外，穿著經典的風格也意味著我永遠不會過時。

### 詞彙

timeless 不受時間影響的，超越時代的

relieve 救援，解圍

constantly 持續地

ever- 始終，總是…

fall out of style
過時，退流行

# What kind of colors do you find yourself wearing the most?

你發現自己最常穿什麼樣的顏色？

Prologue

21 在地生活

22 天氣

23 我的個性

24 穿著風格

25 兒時回憶

Epilogue

........................................

........................................

........................................

........................................

**你可以這樣回答**

Dark/Bright/Warm/Cold colors dominate my closet.
我的衣櫃裡大多是暗色／亮色／暖色／冷色的衣服。

I wear… most of the time.
我大多時候穿…（顏色）。

**參考範例**

I often wear blue, not only because it suits me, but also because it is suitable for both formal and informal occasions. Additionally, due to my preference for monochromatic outfits, I've collected various blue clothes, shoes, and accessories to express my personal style.

我常穿藍色，不只是因為它適合我，也是因為它同樣適合正式與非正式的場合。另外，因為我偏好單色的服裝搭配，所以我收集了各種藍色衣服、鞋子以及配件來表現個人的風格。

**詞彙**

suitable 適合的
formal 正式的
informal 非正式的
monochromatic 單色的
outfit 全套服裝

# Do you buy second-hand clothes? Why or why not?

你買二手衣嗎？為什麼？

Prologue

21 在地生活

22 天氣

23 我的個性

24 穿著風格

25 兒時回憶

Epilogue

....................

....................

....................

....................

你可以這樣回答

Yes, I am a fan of second-hand clothes.
是的，我是二手衣熱愛者。

No, I prefer to buy new pieces that are in line with current trends and styles. 不，我比較喜歡買符合目前趨勢與風格的新衣服。

參考範例

I enjoy purchasing second-hand clothes since I can find unique items at more affordable prices. Although it might require visiting multiple vintage shops to discover what I love, the process itself is a delightful adventure. Additionally, this approach helps reduce waste and is thus more sustainable.

我喜歡買二手衣，因為我可以找到價格比較便宜的獨特品項。雖然可能需要去多間古著店才能發現我愛的東西，但這個過程本身就是令人愉快的冒險。另外，這個方式也幫助減少浪費，而比較具有永續性。

詞彙

**affordable**
可負擔的，買得起的

**vintage shop** 古著店

**delightful** 令人愉快的

**approach** 方式

**sustainable**
可持續發展的，永續性的

# Do you prioritize comfort or style when buying clothes?

買衣服的時候，你優先考慮舒適還是風格？

........................................................................

........................................................................

........................................................................

........................................................................

Prologue

21 在地生活

22 天氣

23 我的個性

24 穿著風格

25 兒時回憶

Epilogue

### 你可以這樣回答

Comfort/Style is my priority.
舒適／風格是我的優先。

I prefer comfortable/stylish clothes.
我比較喜歡舒適／時尚的衣服。

### 參考範例

Comfort is undoubtedly one of my top concerns when shopping for clothes. In my view, it is crucial to choose comfortable clothing as it directly touches my skin throughout the day. Moreover, prioritizing comfort doesn't mean sacrificing style. It's about the art of finding the right balance.

舒適毫無疑問是我選購衣服時的優先考量之一。在我看來，選擇舒適的衣物非常重要，因為它一整天都直接接觸我的皮膚。而且，優先考慮舒適並不意味著犧牲風格。這關係到尋找正確平衡的藝術。

### 詞彙

undoubtedly 無疑地
concern 關心的事
crucial 至關重要的
prioritize 優先考慮
sacrifice 犧牲

# Do you prefer to shop for clothes online or in stores? Why?

你比較喜歡在網路還是店面選購衣服？為什麼？

Prologue

21 在地生活

22 天氣

23 我的個性

24 穿著風格

25 兒時回憶

Epilogue

### 你可以這樣回答

I prefer to shop for clothes online/in stores.
我比較喜歡在網路／店面選購衣服。

I favor online/in-store shopping.
我偏好網路／店內購物。

### 參考範例

I prefer to shop for clothes in stores because I can try on clothes and ensure they fit my size and my style. Also, online shopping involves more packaging and shipping, which cause extra carbon footprint and result in more impact on the environment.

我比較喜歡在店面選購衣服，因為我可以試穿衣服，並且確保它們適合我的尺寸與風格。而且，網路購物需要比較多的包裝與運送，它們會造成額外的碳足跡，而對環境產生比較多影響。

### 詞彙

ensure 確保

packaging 包裝

shipping 運送

carbon footprint 碳足跡

impact 衝擊，影響

# Do you follow fashion influencers on social media to get inspired?

你會在社交媒體上追蹤時尚網紅來獲得靈感嗎？

Prologue

21 在地生活

22 天氣

23 我的個性

24 穿著風格

25 兒時回憶

Epilogue

**你可以這樣回答**

I follow a few style icons online, such as…
我在網路上追蹤一些時尚偶像，例如…

I create my own style rather than follow someone.
我創造自己的風格，而不是追蹤別人。

**參考範例**

I do follow plus-size fashion influencers on social media for style inspiration. In our society, the conventional beauty standards often exclude plus-size individuals, leading to limited representation in fashion media. Social media helps me find references and create my unique style.

我在社交媒體上追蹤大尺碼時尚網紅來獲得風格的靈感。在我們的社會中，慣常的美麗標準常常排除大尺碼的人，導致在時尚媒體中（對於大尺碼）的呈現有限。社交媒體幫助我找到參考，並且創造我獨特的風格。

**詞彙**

plus-size 大尺碼的
influencer 有影響力的人物（常指網紅）
inspiration 靈感
conventional 慣常的
reference 參考

Prologue

21 在地生活

22 天氣

23 我的個性

24 穿著風格

25 兒時回憶

Epilogue

# Do you like to wear accessories? Why or why not?

你喜歡穿戴配件嗎？為什麼？

........................................................

........................................................

........................................................

........................................................

### 你可以這樣回答

I love/enjoy wearing accessories.
我喜愛穿戴配件。

I don't particularly care for accessories.
我並不特別關心配件。

### 參考範例

I adore accessories as they enable self-expression beyond clothing. They are integral to my outfit, elevating my style and providing the finishing touch. Whether it's a bold necklace or a well-chosen scarf, an accessory allows me to play with different looks and add flair to even basic outfits.

我熱愛配件，因為它們能夠呈現衣服以外的自我表達。它們是我服裝中必需的一部分，提升我的風格並且做最後的潤色。不管是一條粗項鍊或者精挑細選的圍巾，配件都讓我能嘗試不同的風貌，就連基本的服裝都能增添風采。

### 詞彙

adore 熱愛

integral 整體之中必需的

elevate 提升

finishing touch
最後的修飾、潤色

flair 才華；風采

186

# What is the earliest childhood memory that still remains in your mind?

留在你心中最早的童年記憶是什麼？

Prologue

21 在地生活

22 天氣

23 我的個性

24 穿著風格

25 兒時回憶

Epilogue

......

......

......

......

### 你可以這樣回答

One of my earliest memories is baking cookies with my grandmother.
我最早的記憶之一是和祖母一起烤餅乾。

The earliest memory that I can still recall is my first day of kindergarten.
我還記得最早的記憶是第一天上幼稚園。

### 參考範例

When I was about three years old, I visited a beach with my grandparents. I remember dipping my finger into the seawater and tasting it. When my grandpa asked me how it tasted, I exclaimed, "So salty!" It is one of my earliest and most vivid discoveries about the world.

我大約三歲的時候，和祖父母造訪一座海灘。我記得我把手指泡在海水裡並且嚐味道。當我的祖父問我嚐起來怎麼樣的時候，我大叫「好鹹！」這是我對這個世界最早也最鮮明的發現之一。

### 詞彙

dip 浸一下
exclaim 呼喊
vivid 鮮明的
discovery 發現

# Are there any funny moments from your childhood that still make you smile?

有什麼有趣的兒時片刻仍然會讓你微笑嗎？

Prologue

21 在地生活

22 天氣

23 我的個性

24 穿著風格

25 兒時回憶

Epilogue

........................................................................................

........................................................................................

........................................................................................

........................................................................................

### 你可以這樣回答

I have a funny memory involving my pet dog.
我有個和寵物狗的有趣回憶。

One funny memory I have is from when I was around seven years old.
一個有趣的回憶是我七歲左右的時候。

### 參考範例

On my first day of kindergarten, I was confused about why we sat in the classroom. When I saw the playground through the window, I couldn't help but happily shouted, "I want to go outside!" Hilariously, the entire class followed me until the teacher managed to calm us down.

在我上幼稚園的第一天，我很困惑為什麼我們坐在教室。當我透過窗戶看到遊戲場的時候，我忍不住快樂地大叫「我想去外面！」好笑的是，整個班都跟著我，直到老師好不容易讓我們冷靜下來為止。

### 詞彙

confused 感到困惑的

playground 遊戲場

shout 大聲叫

hilariously
滑稽地，好笑地

manage to V 勉強做到⋯

# What would you tell your childhood self if you could go back in time?

如果你能回到過去，你會對小時候的自己說什麼？

......................................................................................................

......................................................................................................

......................................................................................................

......................................................................................................

### 你可以這樣回答

I would tell my younger self to value friendships more.
我會告訴小時候的自己要更重視友誼。

I'd advise my childhood self to believe in his/her abilities.
我會建議小時候的自己相信他／她的能力。

### 參考範例

If I could go back in time, I would tell my childhood self to be brave. As a timid child, I often struggled to express my feelings. I wish I could tell her that she has the right to speak for herself instead of always holding back.

如果我能回到過去，我會告訴小時候的自己要勇敢。身為膽小的小孩，我常常很難表達我的心情。我希望我能告訴她，她有為自己發聲的權利，而不是總是退縮。

### 詞彙

brave 勇敢的
timid 膽小的
struggle to V 艱難地做…
hold back 退縮

Prologue
21 在地生活
22 天氣
23 我的個性
24 穿著風格
25 兒時回憶
Epilogue

Prologue

21 在地生活

22 天氣

23 我的個性

24 穿著風格

25 兒時回憶

Epilogue

# Were there any life-changing experiences in your childhood?

你童年時有什麼改變你人生的經歷嗎？

........................................................................................

........................................................................................

........................................................................................

........................................................................................

### 你可以這樣回答

The loss of a family member during my childhood was life-changing to me. 在小時候失去一位家人，對我而言是改變人生的經歷。

Joining a school play was a life-changing moment for me.
加入學校戲劇表演，對我而言是改變人生的時刻。

### 參考範例

One of the most transformative times in my childhood was when I fell in love with reading. It began with a captivating story that introduced me to a whole new world. I started visiting the library regularly, reading around ten books a week. This experience nurtured my passion for literature.

我小時候造成最大改變的時刻之一，是我愛上閱讀的時候。那是從一個帶領我進入全新世界的迷人故事開始的。我開始定期上圖書館，每週讀大約十本書。這個經驗培養了我對文學的熱愛。

### 詞彙

transformative
造成大改變的，顛覆性的

captivating 迷人的

introduce 介紹，引見

nurture 培育

literature 文學

# Which childhood friend do you think means a lot to you?

你認為哪一位小時候的朋友對你而言意義重大？

....................................................................................

....................................................................................

....................................................................................

....................................................................................

### 你可以這樣回答

Sandy holds a significant place in my life.
Sandy 在我的人生中有很重要的地位。

Among my childhood friends, Henry is truly special.
在我小時候的朋友中，Henry 真的很特別。

### 參考範例

I think Wendy is the most special childhood friend to me. We shared many first-time experiences together, such as watching a horror movie, exploring beyond our town, and fangirling over idols. We hung out almost every weekend, and the sisterhood we built was very precious to me.

我認為 Wendy 是我小時候最特別的朋友。我們共同經歷許多第一次，例如看恐怖電影、探索我們城市以外的地方，以及當偶像的迷妹。我們幾乎每個週末都一起打發時間，而我們建立的姊妹情對我而言非常珍貴。

### 詞彙

horror movie 恐怖電影
fangirl
（偶像的）迷妹；（行為）當迷妹 [ ⟷ fanboy]
hang out 消磨時間
sisterhood 姊妹情誼
precious 珍貴的

Prologue

21 在地生活

22 天氣

23 我的個性

24 穿著風格

25 兒時回憶

Epilogue

# What was your favorite activity or hobby as a child?

你小時候最愛的活動或嗜好是什麼？

Prologue

21 在地生活

22 天氣

23 我的個性

24 穿著風格

25 兒時回憶

Epilogue

......................................................................................

......................................................................................

......................................................................................

......................................................................................

### 你可以這樣回答

I loved riding my bike around my neighborhood.
我愛在我家附近騎腳踏車。

I spent a lot of time reading stories.
我花很多時間讀故事。

### 參考範例

As a kid, my favorite activity was playing in my grandparents' orchard with my brother. We would go there every day after school. I loved chasing after ducks and petting our dog. The orchard provided us freedom to explore nature and gave us countless precious memories.

小時候，我最愛的活動是和哥哥在爺爺奶奶的果園玩。我們每天放學後都會去那裡。我很愛追鴨子、摸我們的狗。那座果園提供我們探索自然的自由，也帶給我們無數的珍貴回憶。

### 詞彙

orchard 果樹園

chase after 追趕…

pet 撫摸

countless 無數的

# How did your childhood experiences shape your personality?

你的兒時經歷如何形塑你的個性？

........................................................................

........................................................................

........................................................................

........................................................................

Prologue

21 在地生活

22 天氣

23 我的個性

24 穿著風格

25 兒時回憶

Epilogue

### 你可以這樣回答

Growing up in a large family, I learned the importance of cooperation.
因為在大家庭長大，所以我學到合作的重要性。

Being the eldest child in my family, I learned leadership at a young age.
因為我是家裡最年長的小孩，所以我在小時候就學會領導。

### 參考範例

I remember when I struggled with learning to play the violin, my parents encouraged me to stick with it, and they emphasized the value of perseverance. In the end, not only did I become proficient, but I also learned to apply that same determination in my adulthood.

我記得當我為學拉小提琴所苦的時候，我爸媽鼓勵我堅持下去，而且他們強調堅持不懈的價值。結果，我不但變得熟練，也學到在成年時發揮同樣的決心。

### 詞彙

struggle with
因為…而辛苦

stick with it 堅持下去

emphasize 強調

perseverance 堅持不懈

proficient 精通的，熟練的

determination 決心

# Topics

# Do you prefer to travel abroad or domestically?

你比較喜歡到海外還是國內旅遊？

Prologue

26
旅遊

27
交通方式

28
手機通訊

29
網路媒體

30
我的外貌

Epilogue

.................................................................................................

.................................................................................................

.................................................................................................

.................................................................................................

**你可以這樣回答**

I prefer international/domestic travel.
我偏好國際／國內旅遊。

I enjoy both. Domestic travel is budget-friendly, while international travel provides more adventures.
我都喜歡。國內旅遊對預算友善（低廉），而國際旅遊提供更多冒險。

**參考範例**

I prefer traveling abroad to explore diverse cultures. It offers me the chance to broaden my horizons and gain fresh perspectives on different ways of life. In foreign countries, I can also meet people from various backgrounds and build international friendships.

我偏好到海外旅遊，去探索各種文化。這給我機會去拓展視野，並且對於不同的生活方式獲得新鮮的觀點。在外國，我也能遇見來自各種背景的人，並且建立跨國友誼。

**詞彙**

diverse 多種多樣的
broaden 拓寬
horizon 眼界，視野
perspective 觀點
various
各種的，形形色色的

Prologue

26 旅遊

27 交通方式

28 手機通訊

29 網路媒體

30 我的外貌

Epilogue

# Are you interested in traveling on a cruise? Why?

你對於在遊輪上旅行有興趣嗎？為什麼？

............................................................

............................................................

............................................................

............................................................

## 你可以這樣回答

I'm interested in cruising because it offers a luxurious experience.
我對遊輪旅行有興趣，因為它提供豪華的體驗。

No, I'm not interested in being on a ship for an extended period.
不，我對於長時間待在船上沒有興趣。

## 參考範例

I'm interested in cruise travel. I would like to know how it feels like to dine in the exquisite restaurants aboard. I've also heard that there are live music and dance performances for passengers to enjoy and stay entertained. In addition, I also want to witness the breathtaking ocean views.

我對遊輪旅行有興趣。我想知道在船上高雅的餐廳用餐感覺怎麼樣。我也聽說那裡有現場音樂和舞蹈表演讓乘客享受並且保持愉快。除此之外，我也想要親眼看到壯觀的海景。

## 詞彙

exquisite 精美的，高雅的
aboard 在船上
entertain 娛樂，使快樂
witness 見證，親眼看到
breathtaking 令人屏息的，壯觀的

# Do you like to travel with your family?

你喜歡和家人一起旅行嗎？

Prologue

26 旅遊

27 交通方式

28 手機通訊

29 網路媒體

30 我的外貌

Epilogue

........................................................

........................................................

........................................................

........................................................

## 你可以這樣回答

I love to travel and create memories with my family.
我喜愛和家人一起旅行並且創造回憶。

No, I prefer to travel alone.
不，我比較喜歡一個人旅行。

## 參考範例

I love to travel with my family. While there may be less freedom compared to traveling solo, what really matters is the experiences we can share. I remember when we drove to Taitung, we laughed, sang, and exclaimed with excitement when seeing spectacular views, making the trip truly unforgettable.

我愛和家人一起旅行。雖然和獨自旅行比起來可能比較不自由，但真正重要的是我們能夠共享的經驗。我記得當我們開車去台東的時候，我們大笑、唱歌，也在看到壯觀的景觀時興奮大叫，使得那次旅行真的很難忘。

## 詞彙

solo 獨自
exclaim 呼喊，驚叫
excitement 興奮
spectacular 壯觀的

# What country do you want to visit the most?

你最想拜訪哪個國家？

Prologue

26 旅遊

27 交通方式

28 手機通訊

29 網路媒體

30 我的外貌

Epilogue

........................................................................

........................................................................

........................................................................

........................................................................

**你可以這樣回答**

I've always dreamed of visiting Iceland/Italy/Nepal.
我一直夢想拜訪冰島／義大利／尼泊爾。

I want to visit Greece/Thailand/Morocco more than other places.
我想拜訪希臘／泰國／摩洛哥勝過其他地方。

**參考範例**

Australia is my dream destination, primarily because of its unparalleled natural beauty. With stunning coral reefs and picturesque beaches, it seems to be the perfect place for those who enjoy activities along the shore. I'm particularly eager to go snorkeling and bask in the sunshine there.

澳洲是我夢想的目的地，主要是因為它無與倫比的自然美景。那裡有非常迷人的珊瑚礁和風景如畫的海灘，對於喜歡海岸活動的人似乎是完美的地方。我特別想去那裡浮潛和做日光浴。

**詞彙**

unparalleled 無與倫比的
stunning 非常迷人的
picturesque 風景如畫的
be eager to V 很想做…
snorkeling 浮潛

Prologue

26 旅遊

27 交通方式

28 手機通訊

29 網路媒體

30 我的外貌

Epilogue

## Q.187

# Do you like package tours?

你喜歡套裝旅行嗎？

...................................................................

...................................................................

...................................................................

...................................................................

### 你可以這樣回答

I think package tours provide a convenient way to explore new destinations.
我認為套裝旅行提供探索新目的地的便利方式。

I prefer independent travel over package tours.
我偏好獨自旅遊勝過套裝旅行。

### 參考範例

No, I don't like following a predetermined travel plan. I prefer to have more freedom and flexibility when I travel. More specifically, package tours tend to focus only on popular tourist spots, while I prefer to explore and be surprised by hidden gems.

不，我不喜歡遵循預先決定的旅行計畫。我比較喜歡在旅行時有較多的自由和彈性。更具體地說，套裝旅行傾向於只聚焦在熱門的觀光景點，但我比較喜歡探索，並且因為隱藏的寶石而感到驚奇。

### 詞彙

**predetermined**
預先決定好的

**flexibility** 靈活性，彈性

**specifically** 具體地

**tourist spot** 觀光景點

**hidden gem**
隱藏的寶石（比喻很棒但少人知道的地點或事物）

Prologue

26 旅遊

27 交通方式

28 手機通訊

29 網路媒體

30 我的外貌

Epilogue

# Would you rather stay in a hotel or a bed & breakfast?

你比較想住在飯店還是民宿？

### 你可以這樣回答

I prefer hotels because their quality of service is generally higher.
我偏好飯店，因為它們的服務品質通常比較高。

I prefer bed & breakfasts because they have an intimate atmosphere.
我偏好民宿，因為它們有親密的氣氛。

### 參考範例

I prefer to stay in a hotel. Hotels provide a variety of amenities and services that make my stay more comfortable. The cleanliness and professional staff also bring me a sense of reliability. What's more, it feels more private than staying in a bed & breakfast.

我比較喜歡住在飯店。飯店提供多樣的便利設施和服務，讓我的住宿更加舒適。飯店的清潔與專業人員也帶給我可靠的感覺。而且，住在飯店比在民宿感覺更有隱私。

### 詞彙

amenities 便利設施
cleanliness 清潔
reliability 可靠
private
私人的，不受打擾的

# Do you like traveling alone or in a group?
你喜歡獨自還是團體旅行？

Prologue

26 旅遊

27 交通方式

28 手機通訊

29 網路媒體

30 我的外貌

Epilogue

......................................................

......................................................

......................................................

......................................................

**你可以這樣回答**

I enjoy traveling alone because it allows me to have complete freedom.
我喜歡獨自旅行，因為它讓我有徹底的自由。

It depends on the destination and the kind of experience I'm seeking.
取決於目的地和我尋求的體驗。

**參考範例**

I prefer to travel in a group because it is generally more affordable than traveling alone. Most attractions and activities offer discounts for groups. In addition, exploring the world with like-minded individuals makes the trip more enjoyable. It also provides an opportunity to make new friends.

我比較喜歡團體旅行，因為通常比獨自旅行便宜。大部分的景點和活動提供團體折扣。此外，和志趣相投的人一起探索世界，會讓旅行更加愉快。這也提供交新朋友的機會。

**詞彙**

generally 一般，通常

affordable
（價格等）負擔得起的

attraction 景點

like-minded 志趣相投的

enjoyable 令人愉快的

Prologue

26
旅遊

27
交通方式

28
手機通訊

29
網路媒體

30
我的外貌

Epilogue

## Q.190

# What form of transportation do you prefer?

你比較喜歡哪一種交通方式？

........................................................................................

........................................................................................

........................................................................................

........................................................................................

**你可以這樣回答**

I prefer walking / biking / flying / traveling by train.
我比較喜歡走路／騎單車／坐飛機／搭火車旅行。

I prefer to take public transportation.
我比較喜歡搭乘大眾運輸。

**參考範例**

I prefer to drive because it allows me to go wherever I want. The sense of independence that comes with driving is unmatched. Whether it's a road trip or a quick escape to unwind after a long day at work, I can drive at my own pace without hurry.

我比較喜歡開車，因為能讓我去任何想去的地方。伴隨駕駛而來的獨立感是無與倫比的。不管是公路旅行，還是在一天漫長工作後去放鬆的短暫逃避，我都可以不慌不忙地用自己的步調駕駛。

**詞彙**

independence 獨立

unmatched 無與倫比的

road trip 公路旅行

unwind 放鬆

at one's own pace
用自己的步調

# Do you enjoy walking in your commuting process?

你享受在通勤過程中走路嗎？

....................................................................................

....................................................................................

....................................................................................

....................................................................................

Prologue

26 旅遊

27 交通方式

28 手機通訊

29 網路媒體

30 我的外貌

Epilogue

### 你可以這樣回答

I find walking during my commute quite enjoyable.
我覺得在通勤時走路挺愉快的。

I find it tiring and time-consuming to walk during my commute.
我覺得在通勤時走路又累又花時間。

### 參考範例

While walking offers some health benefits, I don't like to walk for a long distance. I don't mind walking as a part of the commuting process, but my daily schedule is tight, so I prefer a mode of transportation that minimizes the need for walking.

雖然走路提供一些健康上的好處，但我不喜歡走很長的距離。我不介意走路作為通勤過程的一部分，但我每天的行程很緊湊，所以我偏好將走路的需求降到最低的交通方式。

### 詞彙

tight （時間上）緊湊的

mode of transportation
交通方式

minimize 最小化

Prologue

26 旅遊

27 交通方式

28 手機通訊

29 網路媒體

30 我的外貌

Epilogue

# Do you like to take public transportation?

你喜歡搭乘大眾運輸嗎？

........................

........................

........................

........................

### 你可以這樣回答

I like public transportation because it allows me to relax during my commute. 我喜歡大眾運輸，因為它讓我在通勤時可以放鬆。

No. Public transportation tends to be crowded and less comfortable during rush hours.
不喜歡。大眾運輸在尖峰時段通常是擁擠而比較不舒服的。

### 參考範例

I like taking public transportation because it's an eco-friendly choice that reduces carbon emissions and traffic congestion. It is also more cost-effective compared to taxis and carpools. Plus, it allows me to use my commute time more productively, such as reading or answering emails.

我喜歡搭乘大眾運輸，因為它是減少碳排放與交通堵塞的環保選擇。和計程車、共乘汽車比起來，它也比較有成本效益（划算）。而且，它讓我能更有生產力地運用通勤時間，例如閱讀或者回電子郵件。

### 詞彙

eco-friendly 環保的

carbon emissions 碳排放

traffic congestion
交通堵塞，塞車

carpool 汽車共乘

productively 有生產力地

# In your experience, do you think it is comfortable to take a train?

在你的經驗中，你認為搭火車舒適嗎？

................................................................

................................................................

................................................................

................................................................

Prologue

26 旅遊

27 交通方式

28 手機通訊

29 網路媒體

30 我的外貌

Epilogue

**你可以這樣回答**

I've had mostly positive experiences with train travel.
我搭火車旅行的經驗大多是正面的。

The announcements and noise from other passengers make train travel less comfortable.
公告和來自其他乘客的噪音，使得火車旅行不那麼舒適。

**參考範例**

Based on my experience, taking a train is uncomfortable. Even when I've reserved a seat, the trains are often overcrowded with passengers who can't secure their own seats, making it difficult to relax and enjoy the journey. I don't even have enough space to stretch in that situation.

根據我的經驗，搭火車並不舒適。即使我預約了座位，火車還是常常擠滿無法取得座位的乘客，造成很難放鬆並享受旅程。在這種情況下，我甚至沒有足夠的空間伸展。

**詞彙**

reserve 預約
overcrowded 過度擁擠的
secure 取得，獲得
journey 旅程
stretch 伸展

Prologue

26 旅遊

27 交通方式

28 手機通訊

29 網路媒體

30 我的外貌

Epilogue

# How do you usually get to work or school?

你通常怎麼上班或上學？

........................................................

........................................................

........................................................

........................................................

### 你可以這樣回答

I drive my motorcycle / take the bus / take the metro to get to work/ school. 我騎摩托車／搭公車／搭捷運上班／上學。

I usually drive/cycle/walk to work/school.
我通常開車／騎單車／走路上班／上學。

### 參考範例

I usually get to work by car because of its convenience and flexibility. I can leave home and arrive at my company at my desired time without being constrained by the timetable of public transportation. In addition, I can carry my personal belongings or documents without the limitations of space.

因為便利性和彈性，我通常開車上班。我可以在我想要的時間離開家、抵達公司，而不用受到大眾運輸的時間表限制。除此之外，我還可以攜帶自己的個人物品或文件，而不受到空間上的限制。

### 詞彙

flexibility 彈性
constrain 限制，約束
timetable 時間表
limitation 限制

# Have you ever used an app to call a taxi?
你曾經用 app 叫計程車嗎？

........................................

........................................

........................................

........................................

Prologue
26 旅遊
27 交通方式
28 手機通訊
29 網路媒體
30 我的外貌
Epilogue

### 你可以這樣回答

I frequently/sometimes call taxis through an app.
我經常／有時透過 app 叫計程車。

No, I hail taxis on the street / I call taxi companies to request taxis.
不，我在路上叫車／我打電話給計程車公司叫車。

### 參考範例

Yes, I am using a taxi-hailing app, which helps me find the nearest available taxis based on my location. Once I confirm the pickup location, the taxi will often arrive within a few minutes. Besides, I can track the taxi's current location, which is convenient.

是的，我正在使用一款叫車 app，它幫我依照自己的位置找到距離最近的可利用計程車。我確認上車地點後，計程車通常會在幾分鐘內抵達。而且，我也可以追蹤計程車目前的位置，這一點很方便。

### 詞彙

hail 招呼（計程車）
location 地點，位置
pickup （車輛）接人
track 追蹤

Prologue

26 旅遊

27 交通方式

28 手機通訊

29 網路媒體

30 我的外貌

Epilogue

# What do you think is the best way to travel on a trip?

你認為旅行中最好的移動方式是什麼？

........................................................

........................................................

........................................................

........................................................

## 你可以這樣回答

For me, road trips are the ideal way to travel.
對我而言，公路旅行是理想的移動方式。

I'm a fan of cycling, so I believe riding a bicycle is the best way.
我是熱愛單車運動的人，所以我相信騎腳踏車是最好的方式。

## 參考範例

Taking a train is a good way to travel on a trip. You can relax in spacious seats and enjoy the scenery passing by. In luxury trains, you can even visit the dining car for a delightful meal. In a train, you can slow down and appreciate the journey itself.

搭火車是旅行時很好的移動方式。你可以在寬敞的座位上放鬆，並且享受經過（眼前）的風景。在豪華列車上，你甚至可以去餐車享用令人愉快的餐點。在火車上，你可以慢下來，並且欣賞旅途本身。

## 詞彙

spacious 寬敞的

luxury 奢華

dining car
（列車上的）餐車

delightful 令人愉快的

appreciate 欣賞

Prologue

26 旅遊

27 交通方式

28 手機通訊

29 網路媒體

30 我的外貌

Epilogue

## Q.197

# How often do you use your smartphone? What do you use it to do?

你多常使用智慧型手機？你用它做什麼？

.................................................

.................................................

.................................................

.................................................

### 你可以這樣回答

I check my phone almost all the time. 我幾乎隨時都在查看我的手機。

I hardly ever touch my phone. 我幾乎不碰我的手機。

### 參考範例

I reach for my smartphone about every two hours, mostly for browsing social media, such as Instagram and Facebook. I also use it to stay in touch through phone calls and messages on Line or WhatsApp. Additionally, I use it to check emails, read news on websites, and take photos.

我大約每兩個小時伸手拿一次智慧型手機，大多是為了瀏覽社交媒體，例如 Instagram 和 Facebook。我也用它透過打電話和 Line 或 WhatsApp 的訊息來保持連繫。另外，我用它來查看電子郵件、看網站上的新聞，還有拍照。

### 詞彙

reach for 伸手拿…

social media 社交媒體

stay in touch
（和人）保持連繫

Prologue

26 旅遊

27 交通方式

28 手機通訊

29 網路媒體

30 我的外貌

Epilogue

## Q.198

# Do you prefer to talk on the phone or send messages?

你比較喜歡講電話還是傳訊息？

.................................................................................................................

.................................................................................................................

.................................................................................................................

.................................................................................................................

### 你可以這樣回答

I prefer Ving to Ving.
我偏好…勝過…

I don't have a preference. It depends on the situation.
我沒有偏好。那取決於情況。

### 參考範例

I prefer sending messages to talking on the phone. One reason is that it's a more private form of communication. If I make a phone call in public, people around might overhear. Moreover, it's also easier to multitask while messaging.

我偏好傳訊息勝過講電話。一個理由是那是比較私密的溝通形式。如果我在公共場所打電話，周遭的人可能會聽到。而且，在傳訊息時也比較容易同時做多件事。

### 詞彙

prefer A to B
偏好 A 勝過 B

in public 在公共場所

overhear 無意中聽到

multitask 同時做多件事

message 傳訊息

# Do you think you are addicted to using smartphones?

你認為自己對於使用智慧型手機上癮了嗎？

Prologue

26 旅遊

27 交通方式

28 手機通訊

29 網路媒體

30 我的外貌

Epilogue

### 你可以這樣回答

Yes, I believe I have a smartphone addiction.
是的，我相信我有智慧型手機成癮症。

No, I'm not really into using my phone.
不，我對於用手機沒什麼興趣。

### 參考範例

I think I may be addicted to my smartphone, as I find myself starting and ending each day by compulsively checking notifications and scrolling through social media. Furthermore, I get extremely anxious when I realize I've left my phone at home. It feels like I can't live without it.

我認為我可能對自己的智慧型手機上癮了，因為我發現自己在一天開始和結束時難以抑制地查看通知、瀏覽社媒體。而且，我發現自己把手機留在家裡時，會變得非常焦慮。感覺就好像沒有它我活不下去一樣。

### 詞彙

**be addicted to** 對…上癮

**compulsively** （心理上）強迫性地，難以抑制地

**notification** 通知（訊息）

**scroll through** 捲動（螢幕、視窗中的頁面），「滑過」，瀏覽

**anxious** 焦慮的

211

# Without electronic devices, what do you think your life would be like?

如果沒有電子設備，你認為自己的生活會怎麼樣？

Prologue

26 旅遊

27 交通方式

28 手機通訊

29 網路媒體

30 我的外貌

Epilogue

.........................................................................................

.........................................................................................

.........................................................................................

.........................................................................................

### 你可以這樣回答

I might be more focused on outdoor activities and reading.
我可能會更專注於戶外活動和閱讀。

I think I would get more peace of mind without electronic devices.
我認為沒有電子設備，我會得到更多心靈平靜。

### 參考範例

Life without electronic devices would be hard and inconvenient for me as technology plays an important role in many aspects of daily life. For example, I would not be able to take online courses without electronic devices. Also, it would be difficult to stay connected with family and friends.

對我而言，沒有電子設備的生活會是困難而不便的，因為科技在日常生活的許多方面扮演重要的角色。舉例來說，沒有電子設備，我會沒辦法上線上課程。而且，和家人與朋友保持聯絡也會很困難。

### 詞彙

inconvenient 不便的
play a role 扮演角色
aspect 方面
stay connected with 和…保持聯絡

# What kinds of apps do you often use?
你常常用什麼樣的 app ？

Prologue

26 旅遊

27 交通方式

28 手機通訊

29 網路媒體

30 我的外貌

Epilogue

### 你可以這樣回答

I often use communication apps like WhatsApp and Line.
我常常使用像是 WhatsApp 和 Line 的溝通（傳訊）app。

I often use shopping/fitness/news apps, such as…
我常常使用購物／健康／新聞 app，像是…

### 參考範例

Besides social media apps, I also use Netflix and YouTube to stream movies, music, and videos. Netflix is my go-to platform for watching TV series and exploring movies. YouTube, on the other hand, is for the times when I want to watch some music videos or vlogs.

除了社交媒體的 app 以外，我也用 Netflix 和 YouTube 串流播放電影、音樂和影片。Netflix 是我看電視影集和探索電影（發現想看的電影）時一定會使用的平台。另一方面，YouTube 則是在我想要看一些 MV 或者 vlog（生活紀錄影片）時使用的。

### 詞彙

stream 以串流方式播放

go-to （做某件事情時）一定會去的，一定會使用的

platform 平台

vlog 生活紀錄影片

Prologue

26 旅遊

27 交通方式

28 手機通訊

29 網路媒體

30 我的外貌

Epilogue

# Do you find it hard to focus at work or school since you started using a smartphone? 自從開始使用智慧型手機之後，你覺得自己在上班或上學時很難專注嗎？

........................................................

........................................................

........................................................

........................................................

### 你可以這樣回答

I'm more easily distracted at work/school since I began using a smartphone.
自從開始使用智慧型手機之後，我在上班／上學時比較容易分心。

No, I don't think that's the case for me.
不，我不認為那是我的情況。

### 參考範例

I used to be able to concentrate on my work for hours. However, since I started using my smartphone regularly, I find it hard to focus. I'm easily distracted by the constant notifications' interruption, making me lose my train of thought and end up unproductive.

我以前可以專注在自己的工作長達幾小時。不過，自從我開始規律使用智慧型手機，就覺得很難專注。我很容易因為持續通知的打擾而分心，使我的思路中斷，結果就變得沒有生產力。

### 詞彙

concentrate on 專注於…

distract 使分心

interruption 打擾

lose one's train of thought 思路中斷

unproductive 沒有生產力的

# Are you aware of privacy issues when using your smartphone?

使用智慧型手機時，你會意識到隱私問題嗎？

Prologue

26 旅遊

27 交通方式

28 手機通訊

29 網路媒體

30 我的外貌

Epilogue

### 你可以這樣回答

Yes, I'm very conscious about privacy issues when using my smartphone.
是的，我在使用智慧型手機時非常意識到隱私問題。

I think it's impossible not to give up some privacy when using a smartphone.
我認為使用智慧型手機時不可能不放棄一些隱私。

### 參考範例

I'm aware of the issue. Every electronic device could constantly collect and transmit data as long as it is connected to the Internet. Therefore, before downloading any apps, I always check the permissions and privacy settings first to ensure security.

我有意識到這個問題。只要連上網路，每個電子設備都可能持續收集並傳送資料。所以，在下載任何 app 之前，我總是先查看（權限的）許可與隱私權設定以確保安全。

### 詞彙

constantly 持續地
transmit 傳送
permission 許可
ensure 確保
security 安全

# Have you ever made new friends using social media?

你曾經用社交媒體交到新朋友嗎？

Prologue

26 旅遊

27 交通方式

28 手機通訊

29 網路媒體

30 我的外貌

Epilogue

**你可以這樣回答**

Yes, I've made a few new friends through social media.
是的，我透過社交媒體交了一些新朋友。

No, I've never made new friends on the Internet.
不，我從來沒在網路上交過新朋友。

**參考範例**

Yes, I've made some new friends who share my passion for mountain climbing online. I initially messaged a guy who enjoys outdoor activities like hiking and climbing. After getting to know him, he introduced me to more fellow enthusiasts, and we frequently went on mountain expeditions together.

是的，我在網路上曾經交到一些和我一樣熱愛爬山的朋友。我一開始傳訊息給一個喜歡健行和爬山之類戶外活動的男人。逐漸認識他之後，他把我介紹給更多（戶外活動）愛好者同伴，我們就經常一起去登山探險。

**詞彙**

initially 一開始

get to know 逐漸認識

fellow 同伴的

enthusiast 熱衷者

expedition 探險，遠征

Prologue

26 旅遊

27 交通方式

28 手機通訊

29 網路媒體

30 我的外貌

Epilogue

# Q.205

## Are you following any celebrities on social media? Who are they?

你在社交媒體有追蹤任何名人嗎？他們是誰？

........................................................................

........................................................................

........................................................................

........................................................................

### 你可以這樣回答

I am one of the followers of... 我是…的追蹤者之一。

No, I use social platforms to stay connected with my friends rather than know about celebrities.

不，我用社交平台和朋友保持聯絡，而不是了解名人。

### 參考範例

I am following Kim Kardashian on Instagram, where she regularly shares her beauty routines and outfits. I can stay updated on her interests and activities, which often reflect current trends in fashion, beauty, and lifestyle. I also find inspiration in her posts for my own wardrobe.

我在 Instagram 追蹤 Kim Kardashian，她在那裡定期分享自己的美妝日常步驟和服裝。我可以持續得知關於她的興趣與活動的最新消息，其中經常反映目前的時尚、美妝與生活風格趨勢。我也在她的發文中得到自己的服裝靈感。

### 詞彙

beauty routine 日常習慣使用的全套美妝步驟

stay updated on 持續得知關於…的最新消息

lifestyle 生活方式

inspiration 靈感

wardrobe （某人的）全部衣服

217

# Have you ever thought about taking a break from social media?

你曾經想過休息一陣子不用社交媒體嗎？

Prologue

26 旅遊

27 交通方式

28 手機通訊

29 網路媒體

30 我的外貌

Epilogue

你可以這樣回答

I do have taken a short break in the past, and it was refreshing.
我以前的確休息過一陣子，那是讓人精神一振的經驗。

I can't imagine living a day without social media.
我不能想像度過沒有社交媒體的一天。

參考範例

Sometimes I want to take a break from social media. The constant stream of information has made me overwhelmed and stressed. I also find myself spending too much time scrolling through my newsfeed and comparing my life to others, which makes me unhappy.

有時候我想要休息一陣子不用社交媒體。持續的資訊流讓我感覺難以承受、有壓力。我也發現自己花太多時間捲動我的動態消息頁面，並且拿自己的生活和別人比較，而這讓我感到不快樂。

詞彙

stream 流，流動

overwhelmed 感到難以承受的

stressed 感到有壓力的

newsfeed （展示新消息和朋友動態的）動態消息頁面

# Do you prefer to share your life or simply browsing on social media?

在社交媒體上，你比較喜歡分享自己的生活，還是只是瀏覽？

Prologue

26 旅遊

27 交通方式

28 手機通訊

29 網路媒體

30 我的外貌

Epilogue

........................................................

........................................................

........................................................

........................................................

**你可以這樣回答**

I prefer to share aspects of my life on social media.
我比較喜歡在在社交媒體上分享生活的各方面。

I find they are both enjoyable to me.
我覺得它們對我而言都很令人愉快。

**參考範例**

I prefer simply browsing on social media. For me, social media is just a way to keep in touch with others and stay informed about the world. While sharing my life could make my friends understand me better, I prefer to keep my private life offline.

我偏好只是在社交媒體上瀏覽。對我而言，社交媒體只是和別人保持聯絡、持續得知世界上消息的方法。雖然分享我的生活可能會讓朋友們更了解我，但我比較希望把私生活保持在線下（不在網路上）。

**詞彙**

keep in touch with
和…保持聯絡

stay informed about
持續得知關於…的消息

private 私人的

offline 在線下，離線的，不在網路上

Prologue

26 旅遊

27 交通方式

28 手機通訊

29 網路媒體

30 我的外貌

Epilogue

## Q.208

# What kind of videos do you usually watch on YouTube or similar platforms?

你在 YouTube 或類似的平台通常看什麼樣的影片？

........................................................................................................

........................................................................................................

........................................................................................................

........................................................................................................

### 你可以這樣回答

I enjoy watching gaming walkthroughs / stand-up comedies / travel vlogs. 我喜歡看遊戲破關攻略／單口喜劇／旅遊紀錄影片。

I usually watch videos about makeup/fitness/politics.
我通常看關於化妝／身體健康／政治的影片。

### 參考範例

My favorite kind of videos are cooking tutorials. Whether it's classic comfort foods or exotic flavors, I always find something new to learn. Watching these videos makes it easier to follow the instructions. Even when I'm not in the mood for cooking, I still find such videos satisfying to watch.

我最愛的一種影片是烹飪教學。不管是經典的安慰食物還是異國風味，我總是能找到可以學的新東西。看這些影片讓跟隨指示變得比較容易。就算在我沒心情煮東西的時候，我還是覺得這種影片讓人看得很滿足。

### 詞彙

tutorial
教學（影片、手冊等等）

classic 經典的

comfort food
安慰食物（能提振心情，通常富含碳水或油脂的食物）

exotic 異國風情的

be in the mood for
有（做）…的心情

220

Prologue

26 旅遊

27 交通方式

28 手機通訊

29 網路媒體

30 我的外貌

Epilogue

## Q.209

# How do you feel when your posts do not get many likes?

當你的發文沒有得到很多讚的時候,你感覺如何?

..............................................................................................................

..............................................................................................................

..............................................................................................................

..............................................................................................................

### 你可以這樣回答

I feel down/upset/disheartened when my posts aren't getting as many likes as I hoped.
當我的發文沒得到我希望的那麼多讚,我覺得心情低落/煩悶/灰心。

I am not affected by the number of likes I get.
我不會受得到的讚數影響。

### 參考範例

I tend to feel disappointed when seeing my posts on social media not receiving many likes. It feels like my content is judged as worthless by others. While I know that the lack of likes does not mean insignificance in society, it does make me have lower self-esteem.

看到我在社交媒體上的貼文沒有得到很多讚,我通常會覺得失望。感覺就像我的內容被別人評斷為沒有價值。雖然我知道缺少讚並不意味著在社會上不重要,但那的確讓我的自尊變得比較低。

### 詞彙

judge 評判,判斷
worthless 沒有價值的
insignificance
不重要,無足輕重
self-esteem 自尊

Prologue

26 旅遊

27 交通方式

28 手機通訊

29 網路媒體

30 我的外貌

Epilogue

# Do you listen to podcasts? Why or why not?

你聽 podcast（播客）嗎？為什麼？

...................................................................

...................................................................

...................................................................

...................................................................

### 你可以這樣回答

I occasionally listen to podcasts when I have the time.
當我有時間的時候，我偶爾會聽 podcast。

I'm not particularly interested in podcasts.
我對 podcast 不是特別有興趣。

### 參考範例

I listen to podcasts daily, particularly when I'm commuting or doing chores. One of the benefits of podcasts is that I don't need to stare at a screen, which makes them perfect for multitasking. I especially love podcasts about true crimes, and such content is rare on traditional radio.

我每天聽 podcast，尤其在通勤或者做家事的時候。podcast 的一項優點是我不需要盯著螢幕，這使得 podcast 非常適合同時做多件事的時候。我特別喜歡關於真實犯罪事件的 podcast，這樣的內容在傳統廣播中很少聽到。

### 詞彙

podcast 「播客」（可供下載收聽的預錄節目）

commute 通勤

chore 日常雜事，家事

stare at 盯著…

multitasking
同時做多件事

# Are you happy with your overall appearance?
你對於自己整體的外貌（包括臉和身體）滿意嗎？

........................................................

........................................................

........................................................

........................................................

Prologue

26 旅遊

27 交通方式

28 手機通訊

29 網路媒體

30 我的外貌

Epilogue

### 你可以這樣回答

I am quite content with my overall appearance.
我對自己整體的外貌挺滿意的。

I am not confident about my appearance.
我對自己的外貌沒有自信。

### 參考範例

I feel OK with my appearance, but I'm not totally happy with it. There are still some aspects I wish were different. For instance, I would like to have an athletic physique. I also want smaller lips and a sharper nose.

我覺得自己的外貌還可以，但我並不完全滿意。仍然有一些方面是我但願有所不同的。舉例來說，我希望擁有運動員的體格。我也想要比較小的嘴唇和比較尖挺的鼻子。

### 詞彙

be happy with 對…滿意
athletic 運動員的
physique 體格

Prologue

26 旅遊

27 交通方式

28 手機通訊

29 網路媒體

30 我的外貌

Epilogue

# Do you feel that your appearance affects your confidence in social situations?

你覺得你的外貌會影響自己在社交場合的自信嗎？

......................................................................

......................................................................

......................................................................

......................................................................

### 你可以這樣回答

Appearance can impact how confident I feel.
外貌會影響我感覺有自信的程度。

I feel confident no matter how I look.
不管我看起來怎樣，我都感覺有自信。

### 參考範例

Yes, I believe that my appearance is closely tied to my self-confidence, particularly in social situations with many people around. If someone makes unkind comments or reacts negatively to my appearance, I may feel depressed and be less willing to socialize.

是的，我相信我的外貌和我的自信有密切的關係，尤其在周遭有許多人的社交場合。如果有人對我的外貌做出不友善的評論或負面的反應，我可能會覺得沮喪，而且比較不願意社交。

### 詞彙

be closely tied to
和…有密切的關係

unkind
不友善的，不客氣的

depressed 感到沮喪的

socialize 社交

224

# Which part of your face do you like best?

你最喜歡自己臉上的哪個部分？

Prologue

26 旅遊

27 交通方式

28 手機通訊

29 網路媒體

30 我的外貌

Epilogue

### 你可以這樣回答

I really like my freckles/jawline/smile.
我真的很喜歡自己的雀斑／下巴輪廓／笑容。

I'm quite happy with my cheekbones / nose / skin tone.
我對自己的顴骨／鼻子／膚色挺滿意的。

### 參考範例

I particularly love my eyebrows. They're naturally arched and round, following the contour of my eyes perfectly. I'm especially proud that they require very little maintenance. I rarely need to trim or tweeze them to keep their shape intact.

我特別愛自己的眉毛。它們天生又彎又圓滑，完美地跟隨我眼形的輪廓。我特別自豪的是它們幾乎不需要維護。我很少需要藉由修剪或拔毛來保持眉毛的形狀完好。

### 詞彙

arched 拱形的

contour 輪廓

maintenance 維護，保養

tweeze 用鑷子拔除

intact 完好無損的

Prologue

26 旅遊

27 交通方式

28 手機通訊

29 網路媒體

30 我的外貌

Epilogue

# Do you think you have a unique appearance that makes you stand out?

你認為你擁有讓自己顯得突出的獨特外貌嗎？

### 你可以這樣回答

I don't consider myself to have a unique appearance.
我不認為自己有獨特的外貌。

I guess I have a unique look because…
我猜我有獨特的外貌，因為…

### 參考範例

Even though I have a few unique features, I still think that I look ordinary overall. My distinctive aspects include a small birthmark on my cheek and slightly thicker lips. However, I don't think these features are enough to make me stand out.

儘管我有一些獨特的特徵，但我仍然認為自己整體而言看起來很普通。我獨特的方面包括臉頰上小小的胎記，還有稍微厚一點的嘴唇。不過，我不認為這些特徵足以讓我顯得突出。

### 詞彙

ordinary 普通的，平凡的

distinctive
獨特的，與眾不同的

birthmark 胎記

cheek 臉頰

stand out 突出

# Do you use beauty products to enhance your appearance?

你使用美妝產品（包括保養品和化妝品）來改善自己的容貌嗎？

........................................................................

........................................................................

........................................................................

........................................................................

Prologue

26 旅遊

27 交通方式

28 手機通訊

29 網路媒體

30 我的外貌

Epilogue

## 你可以這樣回答

I use cosmetics / skincare products to improve my appearance.
我用化妝品／保養品來改善自己的容貌。

No, I never apply any beauty products.
不，我從來不使用任何美妝產品。

## 參考範例

Wearing makeup is important for me to feel confident. Whenever I go out, I typically apply lipstick to enhance my appearance. Additionally, when I have important engagements, I use foundation and concealer to cover any blemishes or freckles on my skin.

帶著妝（處於有化妝的狀態）對於讓我感覺自信很重要。只要在我出門的時候，我通常都會塗口紅來改善我的容貌。此外，當我有重要的社交約會時，我會用粉底和遮瑕膏蓋掉皮膚上的任何瑕疵或雀斑。

## 詞彙

lipstick 口紅
engagement 社交約會
foundation 粉底
concealer 遮瑕膏
blemish 瑕疵，疤痕

Prologue

26 旅遊

27 交通方式

28 手機通訊

29 網路媒體

30 我的外貌

Epilogue

# Do you think it is a good idea to get plastic surgery?

你認為接受整型手術是個好主意嗎？

### 你可以這樣回答

I think it's a personal decision. The choice should be based on an individual's circumstances.
我認為這是個人決定。選擇應該基於個人的情況而定。

I think people should embrace their natural appearance rather than alter it. 我認為人們應該擁抱自己天生的外貌，而不是改變它。

### 參考範例

I think plastic surgery should be viewed positively. For some people, it may contribute to increased self-confidence and potentially have a positive impact on mental well-being. With an appearance they feel more comfortable with, they may be more willing to engage in social situations.

我認為整型手術應該得到正面的看待。對一些人而言，它可能使自信增加，也可能對心理健康產生正面的影響。因為有了感到比較自在的外貌，他們可能會更願意參與社交場合。

### 詞彙

contribute to 促成…

potentially 可能

mental well-being
心理健康

be comfortable with
對…感到自在

engage in 從事，參加…

# Do you spend a lot of time and/or money on your hair?

你花很多時間和／或金錢在頭髮上嗎？

Prologue

26 旅遊

27 交通方式

28 手機通訊

29 網路媒體

30 我的外貌

Epilogue

### 你可以這樣回答

Yes, I consider my hair a significant part of my overall appearance.
是的，我認為頭髮是我整體外貌很重要的部分。

I prefer low-maintenance hairstyles, so I don't spend much time or money on my hair.
我偏好維護工夫少的髮型，所以我並沒有花很多時間或錢在頭髮上。

### 參考範例

I spend a lot of time and money on my hair. I go to the salon once a month to dye my hair and do hair treatment, which often takes me at least two hours. Sometimes, I get a perm to have a different look.

我很多時間和金錢在頭髮上。我每個月去沙龍一次，染我的頭髮並且做護髮，這常常會花我至少兩小時。有時候，我會燙髮來獲得不同的造型。

### 詞彙

salon 美容／美髮沙龍

dye 染

hair treatment 護髮

perm 燙髮

# Topics

# What is your advantage in personality, and how do you use it well?

你個性的優點是什麼，你如何善用它？

Prologue

31 優點與缺點

32 日常作息

33 我的遺憾

34 人生清單

35 快樂與幸福

Epilogue

....................................................

....................................................

....................................................

....................................................

### 你可以這樣回答

My advantage lies in my strong empathy / sense of responsibility / sense of humor.
我的優點在於強烈的同理心／責任感／幽默感。

I have a highly adaptable/sociable/adventurous personality.
我有適應性很強的／很善於交際的／很有冒險精神的個性。

### 參考範例

One of my strengths is my excellent communication skills. I can express my thoughts with clarity and establish meaningful connections with people. I actively employ these skills to enhance team collaboration and create a positive atmosphere in my workplace.

我的優點之一是優秀的溝通技巧。我可以清楚地表達我的想法，並且和別人建立有意義的連結。我在職場積極運用這些技巧來提升團隊合作，並且創造正面的氣氛。

### 詞彙

strength 優點，長處
clarity 清楚
employ 使用
enhance 提升，改善
collaboration 合作

Prologue

31
優點與缺點

32
日常作息

33
我的遺憾

34
人生清單

35
快樂與幸福

Epilogue

# What weakness troubles you the most? How do you want to improve it?

什麼弱點最讓你困擾？你想要怎麼改善？

........................................................................................

........................................................................................

........................................................................................

........................................................................................

### 你可以這樣回答

Impatience/Forgetfulness/Procrastination is my biggest weakness.
沒耐性／健忘／拖延是我最大的弱點。

I have a hard time making decisions / staying focused / accepting criticism.
我很難下決定／保持專注／接受批評。

### 參考範例

Sometimes I find myself behaving excessively like a perfectionist, and this tendency often results in low efficiency and procrastination. To address this weakness, I think I should learn the lessons of embracing imperfections and accepting the mistakes I have made.

有時候我覺得自己的行為太像個完美主義者，而這樣的傾向常常會造成低效率和拖延。為了處理這個弱點，我想我應該學習擁抱不完美，以及接受我所犯的錯誤這些課題。

### 詞彙

excessively 過度地
perfectionist 完美主義者
tendency 傾向
procrastination 拖延
imperfection 不完美

# Are you good at analyzing things?

你擅長分析事物嗎？

Prologue

31 優點與缺點

32 日常作息

33 我的遺憾

34 人生清單

35 快樂與幸福

Epilogue

.................................................................................

.................................................................................

.................................................................................

.................................................................................

### 你可以這樣回答

I am quite proficient at analyzing things.
我很熟練於分析事物。

Analyzing things is not my strength.
分析事物不是我的強項。

### 參考範例

I have a knack for analyzing things. When faced with complex information or problems, I can quickly break them down and recognize their underlying patterns. Moreover, I find it easy to provide insights and point out core issues by reviewing relevant data.

我有分析事物的本事。面對複雜的資訊或問題時，我可以快速將它們拆解，並且認出潛在的模式。而且，我覺得藉由檢視相關數據來提供洞見並指出核心問題很簡單。

### 詞彙

have a knack for Ving
有…的本事

be faced with 面對…

underlying 潛在的

insight 洞察，洞見

relevant 相關的

233

Prologue

31 優點與缺點

32 日常作息

33 我的遺憾

34 人生清單

35 快樂與幸福

Epilogue

## Q.221

# Do you tend to procrastinate or stay ahead of schedule?

你通常會拖延還是保持超前進度？

你可以這樣回答

I do my best to stay ahead of schedule.
我盡力保持超前進度。

I have a tendency to procrastinate.
我有拖延的傾向。

參考範例

I usually prefer to stay ahead of schedule rather than procrastinate. I prioritize my tasks by considering their importance and urgency, and I rely on my calendar to monitor their progress. This approach not only helps me manage stress but also enhances the quality of my work.

我通常偏好保持超前進度而不是拖延。我考慮工作的重要性和緊急性來區分它們的優先順序，而我靠我的行事曆來監控工作的進度。這個方式不但幫助我管理壓力，也提升我的工作品質。

詞彙

prioritize 決定優先順序

urgency 緊急性

monitor 監控

progress 進度

# Do you feel confident when socializing with people?

與人社交時，你覺得有自信嗎？

........................................

........................................

........................................

........................................

**你可以這樣回答**

I feel at ease when interacting with people.
和人互動時我覺得自在。

I'm confident when socializing within my comfort zones.
我在舒適圈裡和人社交時有自信。

**參考範例**

I often feel uncomfortable and unconfident in social situations. This is partly due to my introverted nature, which makes me anxious about interacting with others. Additionally, at larger social events, I tend to compare myself to others, which often makes me feel inferior.

我在社交場合常常覺得不自在、不自信。這有一部分是因為我內向的天性，讓我對於和人互動感到焦慮。而且，在比較大的社交活動中，我通常會拿自己跟別人比較，而這常常讓我感覺低人一截。

**詞彙**

uncomfortable 不自在的
unconfident 不自信的
introverted 內向的
anxious 焦慮的
inferior
等級比較低的，比較差的

# Do you think you are a good leader?

你認為自己是好的領導者嗎？

Prologue

31
優點與缺點

32
日常作息

33
我的遺憾

34
人生清單

35
快樂與幸福

Epilogue

### 你可以這樣回答

I have some experience being a leader, but there's still room for improvement.
我有一些當領導者的經驗，但還是有改善的空間。

I would rather be a subordinate.
我寧願當個下屬。

### 參考範例

I consider myself a good leader. I am good at setting goals and distributing tasks to those who are suitable. Besides, I make an effort to communicate with and motivate them. That's why I am usually chosen to lead a new project.

我認為自己是好的領導者。我擅長設定目標，以及把工作分配給適合的人。另外，我努力和人們溝通並且激勵他們。這就是我經常被選中領導新企畫案的原因。

### 詞彙

distribute 分配

make an effort to V
努力做⋯

motivate 激勵

# What kind of task are you skilled at doing?

你擅長做什麼樣的工作任務？

Prologue

31
優點與缺點

32
日常作息

33
我的遺憾

34
人生清單

35
快樂與幸福

Epilogue

............................................................

............................................................

............................................................

............................................................

**你可以這樣回答**

I am proficient in graphic design / data analysis / writing and editing.
我對於平面設計／數據分析／寫作與編輯很熟練。

I have a talent for negotiation / project management / social media management.
我有談判／專案管理／社群媒體管理的天分。

**參考範例**

I am skilled at arranging events. It takes attention to details such as venue preparation and participant invitations, which are quite familiar and interesting to me. My detail-oriented nature ensures that every aspect of an event is executed perfectly.

我擅長安排活動。它需要對細節的注意，例如場地準備與參加者的邀請，這些對我而言很熟悉而且有趣。我注重細節的天性，能確保活動的每個細節都得到完美的執行。

**詞彙**

venue
（公開活動的）場地

participant 參加者

detail-oriented
注重細節的

ensure 確保

execute 執行

# Are you an early bird or a night owl?
你是早起的鳥兒還是夜貓子？

> 你可以這樣回答

I am more of an early bird / a night owl.
我比較算是早起的鳥兒／夜貓子。

I am neither of them.
我兩者都不是。

> 參考範例

A night owl describes me better. Unlike early birds, I prefer to stay up late when most people are asleep. I often feel drowsy during the daytime, while the tranquility of the night helps me think more clearly and boosts my creativity.

夜貓子比較能形容我。不像早起的鳥兒，我比較喜歡在大多數人睡覺的時候熬夜到很晚。我在白天的時候常常感覺昏昏欲睡，而夜晚的寧靜幫助我思考更清晰，也能提高我的創意。

> 詞彙

stay up late 熬夜到很晚
drowsy 昏昏欲睡的
tranquility 寧靜
boost 提高，增加
creativity 創造力，創意

# What makes you feel refreshed in the beginning of a day?

在一天開始的時候，什麼讓你感到精神一振？

Prologue

31 優點與缺點

32 日常作息

33 我的遺憾

34 人生清單

35 快樂與幸福

Epilogue

........................................................................................

........................................................................................

........................................................................................

........................................................................................

### 你可以這樣回答

A shower / A hearty breakfast makes me feel refreshed in the morning.
淋浴／豐盛的早餐讓我在早上感到精神一振。

I start my day with jogging/meditating.
我用慢跑／冥想開始我的一天。

### 參考範例

Having a cup of coffee in the morning definitely helps me feel refreshed. With my own coffee machine, I can enjoy homemade coffee tailored to my taste. It has become a cherished part of my daily routine, providing an energizing start to each day.

早上喝一杯咖啡肯定會幫助我感到精神一振。靠著我自己的咖啡機，我能享受依照自己的喜好量身訂做的自家沖泡咖啡。這已經成為我每天例行公事中很珍惜的一部分，為每天提供令人振奮的開始。

### 詞彙

homemade 自家製的

be tailored to
依照…量身訂做的

cherish 珍惜

daily routine 每天從事例行事項的習慣模式

energizing 令人振奮的

Prologue

31 優點與缺點

32 日常作息

33 我的遺憾

34 人生清單

35 快樂與幸福

Epilogue

## Q.227

# Is your morning routine different on weekends?

你的早晨習慣在週末有所不同嗎？

........................................................................................

........................................................................................

........................................................................................

........................................................................................

你可以這樣回答

I have a separate morning routine for weekends.
我在週末有分別的早晨習慣。

My weekday and weekend morning routines are quite similar.
我的平日和週末早晨習慣相當類似。

參考範例

Compared to weekdays, my morning routine is quite different on weekends. Instead of waking up early, I can enjoy a bit of a lie-in and then have a leisurely brunch. For the rest of the day, I either play sports with friends or simply relax and read at home.

和平日比起來，我的早晨習慣在週末相當不同。我不會早起，而可以稍微享受睡懶覺，然後吃悠閒的早午餐。至於一天當中的其他時間，我不是和朋友進行體育活動，就是在家裡單純放鬆和閱讀。

詞彙

lie-in
懶覺（比平常晚起床）

leisurely 悠閒的

brunch 早午餐

# What time of day do you usually exercise?

你通常在一天當中的什麼時候運動？

Prologue

31 優點與缺點

32 日常作息

33 我的遺憾

34 人生清單

35 快樂與幸福

Epilogue

### 你可以這樣回答

I typically exercise in the morning / late at night.
我通常早上／深夜運動。

I exercise at different times on different days, depending on my shifts.
我每天有不同的運動時間，取決於我的值班時間。

### 參考範例

I usually exercise in the afternoon or the early evening. Working out at this time helps me release stress and switch from work mode to personal time. After my exercise, I enjoy a healthy dinner to replenish my body.

我通常在下午或者傍晚運動。在這個時段運動，幫助我釋放壓力，並且從工作模式切換到個人時間。在運動過後，我會享受健康的晚餐來為身體補充營養。

### 詞彙

release stress 釋放壓力

switch 切換

replenish 為⋯補充

Prologue

31
優點與缺點

32
日常作息

33
我的遺憾

34
人生清單

35
快樂與幸福

Epilogue

# Do you think you have a healthy work-life/study-life balance? Why?

你認為自己有健康的工作／學業與生活平衡嗎？

......

......

......

......

你可以這樣回答

I think my work-life/study-life balance is generally healthy.
我認為自己的工作／學業與生活平衡大致上健康。

I am still trying to strike a balance between work/study and life.
我還在努力達成工作／學習與生活的平衡。

參考範例

I think my study-life balance is less than ideal because I stay up late studying. I also sacrifice leisure activities for school assignments and preparation for group presentations. While I dedicate a substantial amount of time to academic pursuits, I find that I often neglect my personal life.

我認為自己的學業與生活平衡不太理想，因為我熬夜讀書到很晚。我也為了學校作業與團體報告的準備而犧牲休閒活動。在我為課業奉獻許多時間的同時，我覺得自己經常忽略個人的生活。

詞彙

sacrifice A for B
為了 B 而犧牲 A

dedicate 奉獻

substantial
很多的，很大的

academic 學術的，學校的

pursuit 追求

# Do you meditate regularly? If not, do you want to try?

你規律地進行冥想（靜心）嗎？如果不是的話，你想試試看嗎？

Prologue

31 優點與缺點

32 日常作息

33 我的遺憾

34 人生清單

35 快樂與幸福

Epilogue

........................................................

........................................................

........................................................

........................................................

### 你可以這樣回答

Meditation is an essential part of my daily routine.
冥想是我每天例行事項中不可或缺的一部分。

I am not a regular meditator, but I've been curious about meditation.
我不是規律進行冥想的人，但我對冥想感到好奇。

### 參考範例

While I don't meditate regularly, I do practice it occasionally, especially when I feel stressed and anxious. Meditation helps me to clarify my thoughts, calm my nerves, and find inner peace. Since I have greatly benefited from meditation, I'd like to make it a habit.

雖然不是規律地做，但我偶爾會冥想，尤其在我感到有壓力而焦慮的時候。冥想幫助我把思緒變得清晰、讓焦躁鎮定下來，並且找到內在平靜。因為我從冥想中得到很大的好處，所以我想把它變成習慣。

### 詞彙

meditate 冥想（靜心）
occasionally 偶爾
clarify 使清晰
nerves 神經過敏，焦躁
benefit 受益；對…有益

Prologue

31
優點與缺點

32
日常作息

33
我的遺憾

34
人生清單

35
快樂與幸福

Epilogue

# Do you tend to stay consistent or frequently change your daily routine?

你的每天例行事務通常始終如一，還是經常改變？

....................

....................

....................

....................

你可以這樣回答

I stick to a regular daily routine.
我堅持規律的每天例行事務。

I'm naturally inclined to change things up frequently.
我天生傾向於經常做出大幅度的改變。

參考範例

I frequently adjust my daily routine.
I adapt it to factors such as weather
and my mental or physical condition.
This flexibility allows me to explore
new possibilities and adds a sense of
spontaneity to my life.

我經常調整每天的例行事務。我會讓它適合
天氣、我的心理或身體狀態之類的因素。這
樣的彈性讓我能探索新的可能性，並且為我
的生活增加自發性的感覺。

詞彙

adapt A to B 使 A 適應 B
mental 心理的，心智的
physical 身體的
flexibility 靈活性，彈性
spontaneity 自發性（自然
發生而不是預先計畫）

# Are there any relationships or friendships you regret ending? Why?

有什麼情感關係或友誼是你後悔結束的嗎？為什麼？

Prologue

31 優點與缺點

32 日常作息

33 我的遺憾

34 人生清單

35 快樂與幸福

Epilogue

........................................................

........................................................

........................................................

........................................................

### 你可以這樣回答

I regret breaking up with… / stopping being friends with…
我後悔和…分手／不再和…當朋友。

I have no regrets about growing apart from anyone.
我對於和人疏遠沒有任何遺憾。

### 參考範例

I regret losing touch with my college friends. When I began my career, I didn't make an effort to stay in touch with them. Now, five years have passed, and I've come to realize how difficult it is to form meaningful connections. Looking back, I should have cherished my friendships more.

我後悔和大學朋友失去聯繫。當我開始就職時，我沒有努力和他們保持聯絡。現在，五年過去了，我開始了解要建立有意義的關係（連結）有多難。回顧過去，我當時應該更珍惜我的友誼的。

### 詞彙

lose touch with
和…失去聯絡

stay in touch with
和…保持聯絡

come to V 開始變得…

connection
聯繫；人際關係

cherish 珍惜

Prologue

31
優點與缺點

32
日常作息

33
我的遺憾

34
人生清單

35
快樂與幸福

Epilogue

# Are there any regretful things that have profoundly impacted you?

有什麼後悔的事對你造成深遠的影響嗎？

................................................................................................

................................................................................................

................................................................................................

................................................................................................

**你可以這樣回答**

I regret (not) Ving…
我後悔做了…（沒做…）

I wish I had (never) p.p.…
我希望自己以前做了…（從來沒做…）

**參考範例**

I regret not making self-care a priority in college. Back then, I often burned the midnight oil for my assignments, presentations, and exams. If I had eaten better, slept more, and paid more attention to my well-being, I might not get sick so often now.

我後悔在大學的時候沒有把照顧自己當成優先的事。在那時候，我常常為了作業、報告和考試而熬夜到很晚。要是我當時吃得比較好、睡得比較多，並且多注意自己的身心健康，我現在或許就不會這麼常生病了。

**詞彙**

self-care 自我照顧

burn the midnight oil
工作到深夜

well-being 身心健康

# Do you have any unfulfilled dreams? Why haven't you realized them yet?

你有什麼沒實現的夢想嗎？為什麼你還沒有實現？

Prologue

31 優點與缺點

32 日常作息

33 我的遺憾

34 人生清單

35 快樂與幸福

Epilogue

### 你可以這樣回答

I have always dreamed about Ving... but never made it come true.
我一直夢想…但從來沒有讓它實現。

I haven't fulfilled my dream of Ving… yet.
我還沒有實現…的夢想。

### 參考範例

My dream of becoming a novelist remains unfulfilled because I am preoccupied with meeting others' expectations. I care too much about my friends and parents' thoughts about my career. Also, I am too afraid of the potential failures in the process of pursuing my dream.

我成為小說家的夢想仍然沒有實現，因為我心裡總想著要滿足別人的期望。我太在乎朋友和父母對於我職業生涯的想法。另外，我也太過害怕在追逐夢想的過程中可能遇到的失敗。

### 詞彙

novelist 小說家

be preoccupied with
心頭縈繞著…這件事

expectation 期望

potential 潛在的，可能的

# Have you ever missed a significant opportunity? Why?

你曾經錯過重要的機會嗎？為什麼？

.................................................................................

.................................................................................

.................................................................................

.................................................................................

Prologue

31 優點與缺點

32 日常作息

33 我的遺憾

34 人生清單

35 快樂與幸福

Epilogue

### 你可以這樣回答

I have missed a significant job opportunity because I wasn't prepared for the interview. 我因為沒有準備好面試而錯過了重要的工作機會。

I had a chance to get a scholarship, but I missed the application deadline. 我曾經有得到獎學金的機會，但我錯過了申請期限。

### 參考範例

I have missed a chance to exchange abroad due to the COVID-19 pandemic. Even though my application was successful, the exchange could not but be delayed. In the end, I decided to give up the opportunity so I could graduate on time and accumulate practical experience in a job.

我曾經因為 COVID-19 疫情而錯過到國外當交換學生的機會。儘管我的申請成功了，但交換計畫不得不被延期。結果。我決定放棄這個機會，讓我能準時畢業，並且在工作中累積實際的經驗。

### 詞彙

pandemic
傳染病的大流行，疫情

application 申請

accumulate 累積

practical 實用的，實際的

# Are there any decisions you'd like to change if you could travel back in time?

如果可以回到過去，有什麼決定是你想要改變的嗎？

Prologue

31 優點與缺點

32 日常作息

33 我的遺憾

34 人生清單

35 快樂與幸福

Epilogue

### 你可以這樣回答

I would change the decision of not taking a job opportunity abroad.
我會改變沒接受海外工作機會的決定。

I wish I had made up my mind to buy a house five years ago.
但願我五年前就下定決心買房子。

### 參考範例

I would change the decision of always hanging out with my friends instead of spending more time with my grandparents when they were alive. If I had visited them more often, I could have created more memories with them. I realized too late the importance of cherishing those moments.

我會改變總是和朋友一起玩，而不是在祖父母在世時和他們度過更多時間的決定。要是我更常拜訪他們，就能和他們創造更多回憶了。我太晚才了解到珍惜那些時刻的重要性。

### 詞彙

hang out with
和（人）混在一起

alive 活著的

cherish 珍惜

249

# Have you ever hurt someone's feelings and regretted it?

你曾經傷了誰的感情而後悔嗎？

.................................................................................

.................................................................................

.................................................................................

.................................................................................

Prologue

31 優點與缺點

32 日常作息

33 我的遺憾

34 人生清單

35 快樂與幸福

Epilogue

### 你可以這樣回答

I have hurt X's feelings by saying that…
我曾經因為說…而傷了 X 的感情。

I always try to be considerate, and hopefully no one has been hurt by my words. 我總是努力體貼別人，也希望沒有人曾經因為我說的話而受傷。

### 參考範例

I have hurt one of my close friends before. I was so inconsiderate that I made a thoughtless joke about his personality, so he didn't talk to me for a whole month. I deeply regretted it and apologized to him, and the experience made me learn a valuable lesson.

我以前曾經傷害過一位親近的朋友。我太欠考慮了，以致於針對他的個性開了一個不顧他想法的玩笑，所以他整整一個月不跟我講話。我非常後悔，也向他道歉，而這次經驗讓我上了寶貴的一課。

### 詞彙

**inconsiderate** 沒有慎重考慮的

**thoughtless** 不為他人著想的

**personality** 個性

**apologize** 道歉

# Have you ever lost your temper/patience with others and regretted it?

你曾經對別人發脾氣／失去耐性而後悔嗎？

### 你可以這樣回答

I have once lost my cool with…
我曾經對…控制不住而發脾氣。

I regret losing my temper with…
我後悔對…發脾氣。

### 參考範例

I have lost my patience and blew up at my parents one time. I deeply regret that I said something disrespectful to them. I believe it was extremely unwise and unthankful to repay their love in such a manner.

我有一次失去耐性，並且對我的爸媽發怒（爆發）。我非常後悔自己說了些不尊重他們的話。我相信用這種方式回報他們的愛是非常不明智而且不知感恩的。

### 詞彙

blow up at 對…發怒
disrespectful 不尊重的
extremely 極度地
unwise 不明智的
unthankful 不知感恩的

Prologue

31 優點與缺點

32 日常作息

33 我的遺憾

34 人生清單

35 快樂與幸福

Epilogue

# What is the most important thing on your bucket list?

在你的人生夢想清單中，最重要的事是什麼？

........................................................................................

........................................................................................

........................................................................................

........................................................................................

你可以這樣回答

My ultimate dream is to visit Machu Picchu / to travel around the world.
我終極的夢想是拜訪馬丘比丘／環遊世界。

Mastering Spanish / Writing a book is at the top of my bucket list.
精通西班牙語／寫書是我人生清單中最重要的事。

參考範例

One of the most important items on my bucket list is to witness the northern lights. I've heard this natural phenomenon is captivating, so it must be a magical experience to see it in solitude. However, the cost of traveling to the Arctic is still not affordable for me now.

我的人生清單中最重要的事情之一，是親眼看見北極光。我聽說這個自然現象很令人著迷，所以獨自看到這個現象一定會是很奇妙的經驗。不過，去北極圈旅行的費用我現在還沒辦法負擔。

詞彙

witness 親眼看見；目擊

natural phenomenon
自然現象

captivating 令人著迷的

solitude 獨處

affordable 可負擔的

Prologue

31 優點與缺點

32 日常作息

33 我的遺憾

34 人生清單

35 快樂與幸福

Epilogue

## Q.240

# Are there any adventurous activities or extreme sports you want to try?

有什麼冒險活動或者極限運動是你想要嘗試的嗎？

........................................................................

........................................................................

........................................................................

........................................................................

你可以這樣回答

I've always wanted to try bungee jumping / rock climbing.
我一直想要嘗試高空彈跳／攀岩。

I have to admit that I'm too scared to try extreme sports.
我必須承認自己太害怕了，沒辦法嘗試極限運動。

參考範例

I would like to try skydiving. The idea of jumping out of an airplane and free falling before deploying a parachute is always intriguing to me. It's not only about the joy of defying gravity but also about conquering my fear.

我想要嘗試高空跳傘。跳出飛機、在展開降落傘前自由落下的概念，總是讓我很有興趣。這不只是關於反抗地心引力的快樂，也是關於克服我的恐懼。

詞彙

skydiving 高空跳傘
deploy 使展開
parachute 降落傘
intriguing 令人感興趣的
defy 反抗
conquer 克服

Prologue

31 優點與缺點

32 日常作息

33 我的遺憾

34 人生清單

35 快樂與幸福

Epilogue

# Are there any places that you want to visit at least once in your life?

有什麼地方是你這輩子至少想去一次的嗎？

........................................

........................................

........................................

........................................

你可以這樣回答

I've always dreamed of visiting the Egyptian pyramids / the Amazon Rainforest. 我一直夢想拜訪埃及金字塔／亞馬遜雨林。

I'd love to explore the countryside of Italy.
我想要探索義大利的鄉間。

參考範例

I want to visit the Nordic countries. The region seems to be vastly different from Taiwan in its natural environment and climate, particularly since Taiwan is experiencing longer and hotter heat waves in recent years. It must be an eye-opening experience to witness the stark contrast.

我想要拜訪北歐國家。這個地區的自然環境和氣候似乎和台灣有很大的不同，特別是因為台灣近年正在經歷更長、更熱的熱浪。能見證這個鮮明的對比，一定會是讓人大開眼界的經驗。

詞彙

Nordic 北歐的

vastly 龐大地，極大地

heat wave 熱浪

eye-opening
令人大開眼界的

stark （對比）鮮明的

# Do you think it is possible to fulfill everything on your bucket list before retirement?

你覺得在你退休前有可能實現人生夢想清單上的每件事嗎?

....................

....................

....................

....................

Prologue

31 優點與缺點

32 日常作息

33 我的遺憾

34 人生清單

35 快樂與幸福

Epilogue

### 你可以這樣回答

It's challenging, but I'll strive to complete as much as I can.
這很有挑戰性,但我會努力儘量完成。

I don't think it's realistic to fulfill everything before retirement.
我不認為在退休前實現每件事是現實可行的。

### 參考範例

I think it is unlikely to do everything before retirement. Because I spend most of my effort doing my daily work, it is only after retirement that most items on my bucket list would be feasible. I might have less strength then, but there would definitely be more free time.

我認為在退休前不太可能做每一件事。因為我把大部分的努力用在做每天的工作上,所以只有在退休之後,人生清單上大部分的項目才有可能實行。我那時候可能比較沒有體力了,但一定會有比較多的空閒時間。

### 詞彙

unlikely 不太可能的
retirement 退休
feasible 可行的
strength 力量,體力

# Is there anything you would definitely like to do with your family in the future?

有什麼事情是未來你一定想和家人一起做的嗎？

Prologue

31 優點與缺點

32 日常作息

33 我的遺憾

34 人生清單

35 快樂與幸福

Epilogue

**你可以這樣回答**

I'd love to go on a family camping trip someday.
將來有一天我想進行家庭露營旅行。

I look forward to skiing with my family in Japan.
我期待和我的家人在日本滑雪。

**參考範例**

I want to take my parents on a trip abroad as a way to show my gratitude for their dedication to the family. More importantly, we meet less frequently after I started to work, so I want to create an opportunity for us to savor life together.

我想帶父母去海外旅行，作為對他們為家庭所做的奉獻表示謝意的方法。更重要的是，在我開始工作之後，我們就比較不常見面了，所以我想要創造讓我們一起品味人生的機會。

**詞彙**

gratitude 謝意
dedication 奉獻
frequently 頻繁地
savor 細細品味

## Q.244

# Have you ever tried bungee jumping? If not, would you like to try it?

你嘗試過高空彈跳嗎？如果沒有的話，你想試試看嗎？

......................................................................

......................................................................

......................................................................

......................................................................

**你可以這樣回答**

I've tried bungee jumping once, and it was an incredible experience.
我試過高空彈跳一次，那是很棒的經驗。

I haven't tried bungee jumping, and I'm not sure if I ever will.
我沒試過高空彈跳，也不確定會不會去。

**參考範例**

I want to try bungee jumping someday. It requires a lot of courage, while I tend to hesitate and feel scared when the situation seems risky. However, I believe that once I overcome my fear, I will be amazed by the breathtaking views and perhaps attain personal growth.

將來有一天我想嘗試高空彈跳。它需要許多勇氣，而我在情況看起來危險的時候通常會猶豫並感覺害怕。不過，我相信一旦我克服恐懼，就會因為令人屏息的景象而感到驚豔，或許也會達到個人的成長。

**詞彙**

courage 勇氣
hesitate 猶豫
risky 危險的
overcome 克服
breathtaking
令人屏息的，壯觀的

Prologue

31 優點與缺點

32 日常作息

33 我的遺憾

34 人生清單

35 快樂與幸福

Epilogue

Prologue

31
優點與缺點

32
日常作息

33
我的遺憾

34
人生清單

35
快樂與幸福

Epilogue

# Is there any musical instrument you would like to learn in the future?

有什麼樂器是你未來想學的嗎？

........................................................................................

........................................................................................

........................................................................................

........................................................................................

### 你可以這樣回答

I've been thinking about learning the piano/violin/flute.
我一直在考慮學鋼琴／小提琴／長笛。

I'm interested in learning the saxophone/cello/harp.
我對學薩克斯風／大提琴／豎琴有興趣。

### 參考範例

I want to learn the guitar because its sound is very pleasant. Moreover, many of my favorite musicians excel at songwriting with the guitar, inspiring me to learn this instrument and sing while playing it, just like they do.

我想學吉他，因為它的聲音非常悅耳。而且，許多我最愛的音樂人擅長用吉他創作歌曲，激勵我學這種樂器並且自彈自唱，就像他們一樣。

### 詞彙

pleasant 令人愉快的

excel at 擅長…

songwriting 創作歌曲

inspire 激勵

# What makes you feel happy in your daily life?
在日常生活中，什麼讓你感到快樂？

Prologue

31 優點與缺點

32 日常作息

33 我的遺憾

34 人生清單

35 快樂與幸福

Epilogue

．．．．．．．．．．．．．．．．．．．．

．．．．．．．．．．．．．．．．．．．．

．．．．．．．．．．．．．．．．．．．．

．．．．．．．．．．．．．．．．．．．．

### 你可以這樣回答

Simply having a cup of coffee can make me happy.
只是喝一杯咖啡就能讓我快樂。

Listening to music I like brings me joy.
聆聽我喜歡的音樂，會為我帶來快樂。

### 參考範例

My dog, Relty, is my daily source of happiness. Going on a walk with him is a true pleasure. It provides me with the energy to start a brand-new day and helps me refresh after a busy day at work.

我的狗 Relty 是我每天快樂的來源。和他去散步真的是件愉快的事。這件事給我開始全新一天的能量，也幫助我在忙碌工作的一天之後恢復活力。

### 詞彙

source 來源
pleasure 愉快（的事）
brand-new 全新的
refresh 恢復活力

# What kind of activity do you feel happiest doing?

你做什麼樣的活動時感覺最快樂？

Prologue

31 優點與缺點

32 日常作息

33 我的遺憾

34 人生清單

35 快樂與幸福

Epilogue

### 你可以這樣回答

Painting / Volunteering / Practicing yoga brings me a deep sense of happiness.
繪畫／做志願服務／做瑜伽帶給我深深的快樂。

Hiking/Dancing/Reading novels allows me to experience pure happiness.
健行／跳舞／讀小說讓我能體驗到純粹的快樂。

### 參考範例

I am the happiest person when I'm cooking. It allows me to be creative with flavors and ingredients, while the aroma filling the kitchen creates a pleasant atmosphere. Moreover, preparing delicious meals for my loved ones makes me feel fulfilled and valuable.

我在烹飪時是最快樂的人。烹飪讓我能用味道和食材發揮創意，而充滿廚房的香氣創造出令人愉快的氣氛。而且，為我所愛的人準備美味的餐點，讓我感到滿足而且有價值。

### 詞彙

creative 有創意的
flavor 味道
ingredient 原料，食材
aroma 香氣
fulfilled 滿足的

# Do you think buying things can lead to happiness?

你認為買東西可以帶來快樂嗎？

Prologue

31 優點與缺點

32 日常作息

33 我的遺憾

34 人生清單

35 快樂與幸福

Epilogue

### 你可以這樣回答

Buying things can be a source of happiness, but we should avoid excessive consumption.
買東西可以是快樂的來源，但我們應該避免過度消費。

I don't believe buying things can lead to lasting happiness.
我不認為買東西可以帶來持久的快樂。

### 參考範例

I do think that buying things leads to happiness, as long as the purchase truly resonates with your desires and needs. In that case, it will feel like a well-deserved reward rather than a pursuit of superficial gratification. Also, it is important to spend within your means.

我認為買東西會帶來快樂，只要購買的東西真正符合你的渴望和需求。在這種情況下，它就會感覺像是應得的獎勵，而不是對膚淺滿足的追求。另外，在收入範圍內花錢也是很重要的。

### 詞彙

resonate with 和⋯共鳴
well-deserved 應得的
superficial 表面的，膚淺的
gratification 滿足
within one's means 量入為出，在收入範圍內（花費、生活）

261

Prologue

31
優點與缺點

32
日常作息

33
我的遺憾

34
人生清單

35
快樂與幸福

Epilogue

## Q.249

# What do you usually do to make someone happy?

你通常做什麼來讓人快樂？

.......................................................................................

.......................................................................................

.......................................................................................

.......................................................................................

### 你可以這樣回答

I enjoy preparing their favorite food to make my loved ones happy.
我喜歡準備他們最喜歡的食物，讓我所愛的人們開心。

I make someone happy by sending thoughtful messages.
我藉由傳體貼的訊息來讓人開心。

### 參考範例

I usually play the guitar to amuse my loved ones. It allows me to bring smiles to their faces without saying a word. Unlike verbal communication, it's a special way to connect with them on a deeper level. Music simply conveys emotions more effectively than words do.

我通常彈吉他來娛樂我所愛的人。這讓我不用說話就能帶來他們臉上的笑容。不像言語溝通，這是在比較深的層次和他們連結的特別方式。音樂就是比話語更能有效傳達情緒。

### 詞彙

amuse 娛樂，逗樂

verbal 言語的

convey 傳達

emotion 情緒

effectively 有效地

# Would you be happier single or in a relationship?

你覺得自己單身還是在關係中會比較快樂？

**你可以這樣回答**

I currently find happiness in being single.
我目前單身覺得很快樂。

I believe that a right relationship could enhance my happiness.
我相信對的關係可以提升我的幸福感。

**參考範例**

I find myself happier being single. Being single allows me to prioritize my personal growth and make decisions independently, without the need to compromise for a shared future. It also gives me the freedom to concentrate on self-discovery.

我覺得自己單身比較快樂。單身讓我能優先考慮個人成長，並且獨立做決定，而不需要為了（兩人）共同的未來妥協。單身也給我專注於自我發現的自由。

**詞彙**

prioritize 優先考慮
personal growth 個人成長
independently 獨立地
compromise 妥協
self-discovery 自我發現

Prologue | 31 優點與缺點 | 32 日常作息 | 33 我的遺憾 | 34 人生清單 | 35 快樂與幸福 | Epilogue

Prologue

31
優點與缺點

32
日常作息

33
我的遺憾

34
人生清單

35
快樂與幸福

Epilogue

# What is the happiest period of time in your life?

你人生中最快樂的時期是什麼時候？

................................................................................

................................................................................

................................................................................

................................................................................

**你可以這樣回答**

One of the happiest periods in my life was during my high school years.
我人生中最快樂的時期之一是高中的時候。

The time when I was volunteering remains the happiest period in my life. 我以前做志願服務的時候，仍然是我人生中最快樂的時期。

**參考範例**

The happiest period in my life was when I joined the guitar club during my sophomore year. It was my first time learning to play an instrument, and I quickly fell in love with playing it. Moreover, I met many awesome people there, including my first love.

我人生中最快樂的時期，是在大學二年級加入吉他社的時候。那是我第一次學習演奏樂器，我也很快愛上彈吉他的感覺。而且，我在那裡遇到了許多很厲害的人，也包括我的初戀。

**詞彙**

sophomore
（大學）二年級的

instrument 樂器

fall in love with 愛上…

awesome
（口語）很好的，了不起的

# Do you think happiness is the ultimate goal of life?

你認為幸福／快樂是人生的終極目標嗎？

Prologue

31 優點與缺點

32 日常作息

33 我的遺憾

34 人生清單

35 快樂與幸福

Epilogue

........................................................................

........................................................................

........................................................................

........................................................................

### 你可以這樣回答

Absolutely. Happiness is the driving force behind life.
當然。幸福是人生的驅動力。

I don't think happiness is the only goal of life.
我不認為幸福是人生唯一的目標。

### 參考範例

I agree that happiness is the ultimate goal of life. Many of us pursue things like wealth or power, but ultimately, we all hope our pursuits will contribute to our happiness. Only when we can find true happiness in these pursuits will our lives be meaningful.

我同意幸福是人生的終極目標。我們許多人追求財富或權力之類的事物，但最終我們都希望自己的追求將會帶來幸福。只有當我們能在這些追求中找到真正的幸福時，我們的人生才會有意義。

### 詞彙

pursue 追求（動詞）
ultimately 最終；終極地
pursuit 追求（名詞）
contribute to 促成…
meaningful 有意義的

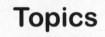

# Topics

# Have you ever experienced or witnessed a car accident? How did you feel?

你曾經經歷或者目擊車禍嗎？你有什麼感受？

Prologue

36 意外事件

37 資訊交流

38 八卦話題

39 祕密

40 社會議題

Epilogue

### 你可以這樣回答

My car was once hit when I was driving.
我曾經在開車時被撞上。

I haven't had such experience, but I guess it must be very shocking.
我沒有這種經驗，但我猜一定很嚇人。

### 參考範例

I once witnessed a collision between two cars, and although it wasn't severe, it left a lasting impression on me. The incident happened so suddenly that I was shocked and standing still for a while. It was only when other passersby called for an ambulance that the situation began to be resolved.

我曾經目擊兩輛車相撞，雖然並不嚴重，卻讓我留下長久的印象。這起事件發生得很突然，讓我受到驚嚇，並且有一陣子站著不動。直到其他路過的人打電話叫救護車，狀況才開始獲得解決。

### 詞彙

collision 撞擊
severe 嚴重的
lasting 持久的
incident 事件
passer(s)by 路過的人
ambulance 救護車
resolve 解決

# Do you become afraid of flying when there is a plane crash in the news?

新聞出現墜機事故時，你會害怕搭飛機嗎？

Prologue

36 意外事件

37 資訊交流

38 八卦話題

39 祕密

40 社會議題

Epilogue

........................................................

........................................................

........................................................

........................................................

### 你可以這樣回答

Yes, news of plane crashes does increase my fear of flying.
會，墜機的消息會增加我對搭飛機的恐懼。

No, I believe it is much rarer than car accidents.
不會，我相信那遠比車禍少發生。

### 參考範例

Seeing news about plane crashes always makes me fearful about flying. I can imagine the helplessness that the crew and passengers feel. It must be scary as there is no one to turn to for immediate assistance. That is why I find myself anxious before boarding a flight.

看到墜機的消息，總是會讓我害怕搭飛機。我可以想像機組人員和乘客感受到的無助。那一定很可怕，因為沒有可以尋求立即協助的對象。那就是我登機前感到焦慮的原因。

### 詞彙

fearful 感到害怕的
crew 全體機組人員
helplessness 無助
turn to 向⋯尋求幫助
assistance 協助

# Have you ever experienced flooding or seen it in the news?

你曾經經歷過洪水，或者在電視上看到過嗎？

Prologue

36 意外事件

37 資訊交流

38 八卦話題

39 祕密

40 社會議題

Epilogue

### 你可以這樣回答

I haven't experienced it before, and I hope I never will.
我從來沒經歷過，希望未來也不會。

I have seen footage of floods in the news.
我曾經在新聞中看過洪水的影片。

### 參考範例

I haven't experienced it myself, but I have seen the news about floods. The footage of houses being washed away in an instant was truly horrifying. I couldn't bear to continue watching, but the immense pain endured by the affected families weighed heavily on my mind.

我不曾親身經歷過，但我曾經看過關於洪水的消息。房屋在一瞬間被沖走的影片真的很嚇人。我不忍繼續看下去，但受影響的家庭所忍受的極大痛苦，讓我的心感到很沉重。

### 詞彙

**footage**
影片片段（不可數名詞）

**horrifying**
嚇人的，令人震驚的

**cannot bear to V**
無法忍受做…

**immense** 巨大的

**endure** 忍受

# Do you think an accident is more of a destiny or a coincidence?

你認為意外事故比較像是命中注定還是巧合？

Prologue

36 意外事件

37 資訊交流

38 八卦話題

39 祕密

40 社會議題

Epilogue

你可以這樣回答

I think that accidents are often a result of coincidences rather than destiny. 我認為意外事故通常是一些巧合而非命運的結果。

For me, accidents sometimes appear as a part of a larger destiny. 對我而言，意外事故有時像是更大的命運的一部分。

參考範例

I feel it's more like a coincidence rather than destiny. No matter how unreasonable an accident may seem, we can always identify the factors that contribute to its occurrence. Rather than resign ourselves to fate, we should analyze these factors and take measures to prevent similar incidents in the future.

我認為那比較像是巧合而不是命中注定。不管一件意外事故看起來多不合理，我們總是可以找出造成它發生的因素。與其聽天由命，我們應該分析這些因素，並且採取措施來預防未來的類似事件。

詞彙

unreasonable 不合理的
identify 認出，發現
contribute to 促成…
occurrence 發生
resign oneself to 順從、屈服於…
incident 事件

## Q.257

# Are you more afraid of natural disasters or man-made tragedies? Why?

你比較怕天災還是人為的悲劇？為什麼？

..................................................................................

..................................................................................

..................................................................................

..................................................................................

36 意外事件

37 資訊交流

38 八卦話題

39 祕密

40 社會議題

Epilogue

### 你可以這樣回答

I am more scared of… because…
我比較怕…因為…

I find myself more concerned about…
我覺得自己比較擔心…

### 參考範例

For me, man-made tragedies are more horrifying, as they result from preventable errors. We tend to believe that people do their best to make things right, but the reality is that negligence and poor judgment are prevalent and can unexpectedly lead to serious consequences.

對我而言，人為的悲劇比較可怕，因為它們是可預防的錯誤造成的結果。我們通常相信人們會盡全力把事情打理好，但真實情況是疏忽與糟糕的判斷很普遍，而有可能意外導致嚴重的後果。

### 詞彙

horrifying
令人恐懼的，可怕的

preventable 可預防的

negligence 疏忽

judgment 判斷

prevalent 普遍的

consequence 後果

# Do you have a feeling that natural disasters are more frequent than before?

你覺得天然災害比以前頻繁嗎？

Prologue

36 意外事件

37 資訊交流

38 八卦話題

39 祕密

40 社會議題

Epilogue

你可以這樣回答

I do sense that natural disasters are more frequent compared to the past.
我確實感覺到天然災害比以前頻繁。

I think it is just that we are more informed and connected now.
我認為那只是因為我們現在比較容易獲知消息、和世界更有連結。

參考範例

Yes, I feel that natural disasters are occurring more frequently now, especially instances of extreme weather. The rise seems closely related to human activities. For instance, the increase in greenhouse gas emissions has been linked to a higher frequency and greater intensity of heatwaves and storms.

是的，我感覺現在天然災害發生得比較頻繁，尤其是極端天氣事件。天災的增加似乎和人類活動有密切關係。舉例來說，溫室氣體排放增加被認為和熱浪、風暴較高的發生頻率與強度有關。

詞彙

**extreme weather**
極端天氣

**greenhouse gas**
溫室氣體

**emission** 排放

**intensity** 強度

**heatwave** 熱浪

# Are you sensitive to earthquakes? What do you do when an earthquake occurs?

你對地震敏感嗎?地震發生時你會做什麼?

Prologue

36 意外事件

37 資訊交流

38 八卦話題

39 祕密

40 社會議題

Epilogue

........................................................................

........................................................................

........................................................................

........................................................................

### 你可以這樣回答

I tend to feel even smaller earthquakes.
我就連比較小的地震都往往會感覺到。

I'm not particularly sensitive to earthquakes.
我對地震不是特別敏感。

### 參考範例

I am very sensitive to earthquakes, and when one occurs, I will jump from my seat and scream. After a moment, however, I will calm down and rush to open doors and windows so that they don't get stuck due to distorted frames.

我對地震很敏感,而當地震發生時,我會從座位上彈起來尖叫。不過,一會兒之後,我會冷靜下來並且衝去打開門窗,好讓它們不會因為變形的外框而卡住。

### 詞彙

sensitive 敏感的
rush 衝
get stuck 卡住
distort 使扭曲
frame 外框

Prologue

36
意外事件

37
資訊交流

38
八卦話題

39
祕密

40
社會議題

Epilogue

# Which social platform do you use the most to vent your feelings?

你最常用什麼社群平台來發洩你的心情？

..................
..................
..................
..................

## 你可以這樣回答

I primarily use Tiktok to express my emotions.
我主要用抖音來表達我的情緒。

When I need to let out my feelings, I usually post an Instagram story.
當我需要發洩我的心情時，我通常會發表 Instagram 的限時動態。

## 參考範例

When I feel distressed, I use Facebook and Instagram to vent my feelings. Since many of my friends are on these social platforms, when I post my stories and share my challenges, they can understand how I'm doing and offer me suggestions immediately.

當我感到痛苦的時候，我會用 Facebook 和 Instagram 來發洩我的心情。因為我有許多朋友在這些社群平台上，所以當我發表我的故事並分享我面臨的挑戰時，他們可以了解我的近況並且立即提供建議給我。

## 詞彙

distressed
（心理上）痛苦的
vent 發洩（負面情緒）
social platform 社群平台
suggestion 建議
immediately 立即

# Do you think being anonymous is necessary when expressing opinions online?

你認為在網路上發表意見時，匿名是必要的嗎？

Prologue

36 意外事件

37 資訊交流

38 八卦話題

39 祕密

40 社會議題

Epilogue

### 你可以這樣回答

Anonymity can be beneficial for expressing opinions online.
匿名性對於在網路上發表意見可能是有益的。

Being anonymous isn't essential when expressing opinions online.
在網路上發表意見時，匿名不是必要的。

### 參考範例

I believe that being anonymous can be important when expressing opinions online. This anonymity provides a sense of security, and it can shield us from potential repercussions that might arise due to expressing divergent viewpoints. That is, we can freely share our thoughts without the fear of harassment.

我相信在網路上發表意見時，匿名可能是重要的。這樣的匿名性提供一種安全感，而且能保護我們避免因為表達不同的觀點而遭受可能發生的後果。也就是說，我們可以自由分享想法，而不用害怕遭到騷擾。

### 詞彙

anonymity 匿名性

shield 保護

repercussions
（不良的）後果

divergent 分歧的，不同的

harassment 騷擾

275

Prologue

36 意外事件

37 資訊交流

38 八卦話題

39 祕密

40 社會議題

Epilogue

# Q. 262

# Do you still watch the news? Why?

你現在還看電視新聞嗎？為什麼？

........................................................................................

........................................................................................

........................................................................................

........................................................................................

**你可以這樣回答**

Yes, I do watch the news regularly.
是的，我經常看電視新聞。

Instead of watching the news, I prefer Ving...
比起看電視新聞，我比較喜歡…

**參考範例**

Instead of watching the news on TV, I prefer absorbing new information from Youtube, podcasts, and other kinds of new media. Compared to traditional news reporting, the new media platforms offer a more diverse range of perspectives and the flexibility to choose content that cater to my interests.

比起看電視新聞，我比較喜歡從 Youtube、podcast（播客）和其他類型的新媒體吸收新資訊。和傳統的新聞播報比起來，新媒體平台提供比較多樣的觀點，以及選擇符合我興趣的內容的彈性。

**詞彙**

absorb 吸收
diverse 多樣的
perspective 觀點
flexibility 彈性
cater to 迎合…

# Do you often express your thoughts about social issues? Why?

你經常表達對於社會議題的想法嗎？為什麼？

Prologue

36 意外事件

37 資訊交流

38 八卦話題

39 祕密

40 社會議題

Epilogue

**你可以這樣回答**

I am quite vocal about social issues.
我對於社會議題直言不諱。

I usually keep my opinions on social issues to myself.
我通常會隱藏對社會議題的意見而不說出來。

**參考範例**

Yes, I frequently express my thoughts about social issues. I believe that individual perspectives should be valued, and I want my voice to be heard. By sharing my views, I hope to inspire others to question the mainstream opinion and think of ways that can truly contribute to progress in society.

是的，我常常表達對於社會議題的想法。我相信個人的觀點應該受到重視，而我希望自己的聲音被聽見。藉由分享我的看法，我希望激勵別人去質疑主流意見，並且想出能真正促成社會進步的方法。

**詞彙**

value 重視

inspire 激勵

question 質疑

mainstream opinion 主流意見

contribute to 促成…

Prologue

36 意外事件

37 資訊交流

38 八卦話題

39 祕密

40 社會議題

Epilogue

# Do you think the Internet promotes or hinders rational discussion?

你認為網路是促進還是妨礙理性討論？

......................................................................................................

......................................................................................................

......................................................................................................

......................................................................................................

**你可以這樣回答**

I think the Internet generally promotes/hinders rational discussion.
我認為網路整體而言促進／妨礙理性討論。

I believe the Internet has both positive and negative impacts on rational discussion. 我認為網路對理性討論有正面和負面的影響。

**參考範例**

In my opinion, the Internet hinders rational discussion because of its lack of in-person interaction. Without facing or knowing who they talk to online, people tend to feel no responsibility for their comments and leave rude or mean words toward others. Consequently, it's harder to make constructive discussions online.

在我看來，網路因為缺少面對面的互動而妨礙理性討論。因為在網路上不會面對談話的對象，也不知道那是誰，所以人們往往對自己發表的意見沒有責任感，而會對別人留下無禮或刻薄的話語。結果，在網路上要做有建設性的討論就比較難。

**詞彙**

hinder 妨礙

rational 理性的

in-person
當面的（面對面的）

consequently 結果

constructive 建設性的

# Do you try to meet new people and talk with them to broaden your horizons?

你會努力認識新朋友，並且和他們交談來擴展視野（增廣見聞）嗎？

## 你可以這樣回答

I believe meeting new people is essential for personal growth.
我相信認識新朋友對於個人成長而言是必要的。

I am not into meeting new people just for the sake of it.
我不喜歡為交而交新朋友。

## 參考範例

I love meeting and befriending new people because it's the best way to enrich my knowledge. I enjoy talking with people of different backgrounds and listening to their unique stories. Their insights not only expand my understanding of the world, but also encourage me to continuously learn and grow.

我很愛遇見新的人並且和他們交朋友，因為這是豐富我知識最好的方法。我很喜歡和不同背景的人談話，並且聽他們獨特的故事。他們的洞見不但拓展我對這個世界的了解，也鼓勵我持續學習並且成長。

## 詞彙

befriend 和…交朋友

enrich 使豐富

background
（經歷方面的）背景

insight 洞察力，洞見

continuously 持續地

279

# Do you prefer to talk in person or communicate online?

你比較喜歡當面交談還是在網路上溝通？

Prologue

36 意外事件

37 資訊交流

38 八卦話題

39 祕密

40 社會議題

Epilogue

### 你可以這樣回答

I find in-person/online communication more comfortable.
我覺得當面／網路上的溝通讓我比較自在。

In-person/online communication suits me better.
當面／網路上的溝通比較適合我。

### 參考範例

I prefer to communicate online because I can have more time to react and conserve energy. Face-to-face conversations demand immediate responses and sometimes discourage us from giving candid feedback. On the other hand, online exchanges allow us the space to structure our thoughts and talk honestly.

我比較喜歡在網路上溝通，因為我可以有比較多時間反應，也能節省精力。面對面的溝通需要立即的反應，而且有時候會讓我們不想給出率直的回饋意見。另一方面，線上交流讓我們有組織想法與誠實交談的空間。

### 詞彙

conserve 節省

discourage someone from Ving
使某人打消…的念頭

candid 率直的

feedback 回饋意見

exchange 交流

## What do you think is the reason that people like to talk about rumors?

你認為人們喜歡談論傳聞的原因是什麼？

.................................................

.................................................

.................................................

.................................................

Prologue

36 意外事件

37 資訊交流

38 八卦話題

39 祕密

40 社會議題

Epilogue

**你可以這樣回答**

In my opinion, talking about rumors might stem from our curiosity.
在我看來，談論傳聞可能源自我們的好奇心。

People love discussing rumors because it provides a sense of excitement.
人們很愛討論傳聞，因為那會帶來一種興奮感。

**參考範例**

It seems to me that sharing rumors is a way of fitting into a community and enhancing social ties. Being in the know gives us a sense of belonging because it means we are included in the exchange of information and provided with the chance to share our opinions.

在我看來，分享傳聞似乎是一種融入社群並增強社會連結的方法。知道內幕消息會給我們歸屬感，因為那意味著我們被包括在資訊的交流中，並且得到了分享意見的機會。

**詞彙**

fit into 融入…

social ties 社會連結

be in the know
熟悉內幕，知道詳情

sense of belonging
歸屬感

include 包括

Prologue

36 意外事件

37 資訊交流

38 八卦話題

39 祕密

40 社會議題

Epilogue

# When a rumor appears in the media, do you tend to believe or doubt it?

當傳聞出現在媒體時，你傾向於相信還是懷疑？

......

......

......

......

你可以這樣回答

I'm more likely to believe/doubt rumors in the media.
我比較會相信／懷疑媒體報導的傳聞。

When a rumor emerges in the media, I tend to believe it is true to some extent. 當傳聞出現在媒體時，我傾向於相信某個程度上是真的。

參考範例

I tend to doubt the credibility of rumors in the media. The reason is that many rumors are reported because of their ability to grab people's attention, while their authenticity is not guaranteed. Therefore, I always approach rumors with suspicion, even if they are reported by reputable sources.

我傾向於懷疑媒體傳聞的可信度。原因是，許多傳聞是因為它們能吸引人們的注意而獲得報導，而它們的真實性則沒有保證。所以，我總是抱著懷疑來對待傳聞，就算是有信譽的來源所報導的也一樣。

詞彙

credibility 可信度
authenticity 真實性
approach 接近，處理
suspicion 懷疑
reputable 聲譽好的

# Would you accept someone who likes to gossip as a friend?

你會接受愛八卦的人當朋友嗎？

Prologue

36 意外事件

37 資訊交流

38 八卦話題

39 祕密

40 社會議題

Epilogue

................................................................

................................................................

................................................................

................................................................

### 你可以這樣回答

I would hesitate to befriend someone who enjoys gossiping.
我會猶豫和愛八卦的人交朋友。

I wouldn't mind having a friend who enjoys gossiping.
我不介意有個愛八卦的朋友。

### 參考範例

I have no interest in making friends with someone who enjoys gossiping. I question their choice to invest time in discussing others rather than self-improvement. Additionally, I'd worry about becoming a target of their gossip in the future. I prefer to surround myself with more positive influences.

我沒興趣跟愛八卦的人交朋友。我質疑他們選擇投資時間（花時間）來討論其他人而不是提升自己。另外，我也會擔心自己未來成為他們八卦的目標。我偏好讓比較正面的影響圍繞在我身邊。

### 詞彙

self-improvement
自我改善（自我成長）

additionally 另外

target 目標

surround 包圍，圍繞

influence 影響

Prologue

36 意外事件

37 資訊交流

38 八卦話題

39 祕密

40 社會議題

Epilogue

# What would you do if you find that someone is speaking ill of you?

如果你發現有人說你壞話，你會怎麼做？

你可以這樣回答

If I discover that someone is speaking ill of me, I would assess my relationship with them.
如果我發現有人說我壞話，我會評估自己和他們的關係。

I would communicate openly to resolve any misunderstandings.
我會公開溝通來消除誤會。

參考範例

I'd initially feel disheartened. However, I would recognize that their words may stem from misunderstandings, and my primary concern would be maintaining my mental and emotional well-being despite the negativity around me. I would also talk about the matter with my friends so I can see it more objectively.

我一開始會覺得沮喪。不過，我會認識到他們所說的可能是源自誤解，而我主要關心的會是維持自己的心理與情緒健康，就算我身邊圍繞著負面的事。我也會和朋友談這件事，讓我能更客觀地看待它。

詞彙

disheartened 沮喪的
recognize 承認，認識到
stem from 源於…
negativity 消極，負面
objectively 客觀地

Prologue

36 意外事件

37 資訊交流

38 八卦話題

39 祕密

40 社會議題

Epilogue

## Q.271

# Do you think celebrity relationships deserve more privacy?

你認為名人的感情關係應該得到更多隱私嗎？

........................................................................................

........................................................................................

........................................................................................

........................................................................................

### 你可以這樣回答

Celebrity relationships should be respected just like anyone else's.
名人的感情關係應該像其他任何人一樣受到尊重。

I don't think so. Their fame relies on public interest, so some degree of attention is inevitable.
我不認為。他們的名氣要靠大眾感興趣，所以一定程度的關注是無可避免的。

### 參考範例

I think celebrity relationships deserve more privacy, as it is a fundamental right. While it is undeniable that being a celebrity comes with public attention, it is important to recognize that they are ordinary people outside of work. No one should have their private life constantly examined by the public.

我認為名人的感情關係應該得到更多隱私，因為這是（人）基本的權利。雖然無法否認當名人就會伴隨著大眾的關注，但認知到他們在工作之餘是一般人，是很重要的。沒有人的私生活應該持續受到大眾檢視。

### 詞彙

fundamental 基本的
undeniable 無可否認的
ordinary 普通的
constantly 持續地
examine 檢視

285

# What do you do to spot false information?

你如何辨識假消息？

Prologue

36 意外事件

37 資訊交流

38 八卦話題

39 祕密

40 社會議題

Epilogue

**你可以這樣回答**

I check if there are credible sources cited to back it up.
我檢查它是否有引用可靠的來源作為支持。

I seek out experts in the field to validate its accuracy.
我尋找該領域的專家來證實它的正確性。

**參考範例**

I always check the credibility of the source and compare the information with reliable sources. Fact-checking websites are useful, too. I also consider the tone of an article to be an important clue. When the language is sensational or overly emotional, it can be a red flag for misinformation.

我總是確認來源的可信度，並且將資訊和可靠的來源比較。事實查核網站也很有用。我也認為文章的語氣是重要的線索。當語言風格很聳動或者過度情緒化時，可能就是假消息的警訊。

**詞彙**

credibility 可信度

tone 音調；語氣

sensational
（新聞）聳動的

red flag 警訊

misinformation 假消息

# Do you agree that "Rumors are spices of our daily life"?

你同意「傳聞是我們日常生活中的趣味」嗎？

Prologue

36 意外事件

37 資訊交流

38 八卦話題

39 祕密

40 社會議題

Epilogue

........................................................................................

........................................................................................

........................................................................................

........................................................................................

### 你可以這樣回答

I believe rumors can make our daily life more interesting.
我認為傳聞能使我們的日常生活比較有趣。

While rumors can be entertaining, they can also be harmful.
雖然傳聞可以是有趣的，但也有可能造成傷害。

### 參考範例

I agree with the saying because rumors offer a form of entertainment. More precisely, they often feature stories that are novel and captivating. Even if the content goes against social norms or remains anecdotal, it at least offers some excitement to the audience.

我同意這句俗語，因為傳聞提供一種娛樂的形式。更精確地說，它們常常有新奇而令人著迷的故事。就算內容違反社會常規，或者只是趣聞軼事，至少也為聽眾帶來一些興奮感。

### 詞彙

precisely 精確地
novel 新奇的
captivating 令人著迷的
norm 常態，規範
anecdotal 趣聞軼事的
excitement 刺激，興奮

Prologue

36 意外事件

37 資訊交流

38 八卦話題

39 祕密

40 社會議題

Epilogue

# What kind of thing do you want to keep secret?
你想要把什麼事保持祕密？

........................................................................

........................................................................

........................................................................

........................................................................

你可以這樣回答

I prefer to keep my personal struggles private.
我比較希望把個人的困難保持隱私。

I keep family issues to myself.
我不會把家庭問題說出來。

參考範例

I want to keep details about my relationships secret. By keeping certain details confidential, I can protect the intimacy and trust between me and my partner. If I talk too much about my love life, other people's judgments may negatively affect the way I interact with my partner.

我想要把感情關係的細節保持祕密。藉著把某些細節保持機密，我可以保護我和伴侶之間的親密與信任。如果我對於自己的感情生活說得太多，別人的評判可能會負面影響我和伴侶的互動方式。

詞彙

relationship 感情關係
confidential 機密的
intimacy 親密
judgment
判斷，評判，意見
negatively 負面地

# Do you think it is kind or cruel to tell a white lie?

你認為說善意的謊言是好心還是殘忍？

..................................................................................

..................................................................................

..................................................................................

..................................................................................

Prologue

36 意外事件

37 資訊交流

38 八卦話題

39 祕密

40 社會議題

Epilogue

### 你可以這樣回答

Telling a white lie can be a kind gesture in certain situations.
在某些情況下，說善意的謊言可能是好意的表示。

White lies can lead to distrust if the truth is discovered.
如果真相被發現，善意的謊言可能導致不信任。

### 參考範例

In my view, it is rather kind tell a white lie, especially when it is about one's opinion of the listener. Instead of causing unnecessary hurt with blunt comments, I think choosing words that spare their feelings is more socially acceptable. Honesty works only when one is willing to hear.

在我看來，說善意的謊言可以算是好心，尤其是它和對於聽者的意見有關的時候。比起用直言不諱的評論造成不必要的傷害，我認為選擇不傷他們感情的措詞是在社交上比較可以接受的。誠實只有在一個人願意聽的時候才有用。

### 詞彙

unnecessary 不必要的

blunt 直言不諱的

spare one's feelings
避免傷害某人的感情

acceptable 可接受的

honesty 誠實

Prologue

36 意外事件

37 資訊交流

38 八卦話題

39 祕密

40 社會議題

Epilogue

# Whom do you tell a secret to the most?

你最常對誰說你的祕密？

........................................................................

........................................................................

........................................................................

........................................................................

**你可以這樣回答**

In most cases, I share my secrets with…
在大部分情況下，我和…分享祕密。

I find comfort in telling my secrets to…
對…說祕密讓我覺得安慰。

**參考範例**

I tell my secrets to my parents the most.
Secrets are often too embarrassing to tell,
so I need to find a listener who will take
them seriously. When I reveal a secret to
my parents, I am confident that they are
respectful and will not disclose anything
to others.

我最常對我的父母說祕密。祕密通常太讓人
尷尬而難以啟齒，所以我需要找到會認真看
待的人。當我對父母揭露祕密的時候，我有
信心他們是尊重的，而且不會對別人透露任
何事。

**詞彙**

embarrassing 令人尷尬的
reveal 揭露
confident 有信心的
respectful 尊重的
disclose 透露

290

# What kind of thing do you think is better exposed than kept secret?

你認為什麼樣的事最好曝光而不是保密？

Prologue

36 意外事件

37 資訊交流

38 八卦話題

39 祕密

40 社會議題

Epilogue

### 你可以這樣回答

I believe an act of sexual misconduct should be exposed.
我相信性方面的不當行為應該要曝光。

Opening up about emotional struggles is often beneficial.
對於情緒方面的困難開誠布公，通常是有益的。

### 參考範例

I would say that an act of generosity is worth sharing rather than keeping as a secret. Regardless of its scale, a good deed can trigger a ripple effect and inspire others to follow suit. Therefore, I think spreading the word about such acts can make the world a better place.

我會說慷慨的行為值得分享而不是保密。不管程度大小如何，善行可以引起漣漪效應，並且激勵其他人照樣做。所以，我認為散布這種行為的消息可以讓世界變得更好。

### 詞彙

generosity 慷慨

scale 規模，大小

ripple effect 漣漪效應
（事物的影響力漸漸擴散）

inspire 激勵

follow suit 照樣做

spread the word 散布消息

Prologue

36
意外事件

37
資訊交流

38
八卦話題

39
祕密

40
社會議題

Epilogue

# Do you think it is possible to live without holding secrets?

你認為人活著有可能沒有祕密嗎？

........................................................................

........................................................................

........................................................................

........................................................................

**你可以這樣回答**

Achieving a life without secrets is virtually impossible.
達到沒有祕密的人生幾乎是不可能的。

With conscious effort, one can lead a life without secrets.
靠著有意識的努力，人可以過著沒有祕密的生活。

**參考範例**

I think it is difficult to live without holding secrets. Most of us will feel vulnerable if we expose everything about our traumatic experiences and intimate relationships, and that is why we have to keep some things to ourselves. There is nothing wrong in safeguarding our privacy when necessary.

我認為活著是很難沒有祕密的。如果曝露關於我們創傷經驗和親密關係的一切，我們大部分的人會覺得很容易受傷，這就是我們必須隱藏而不說出一些事情的原因。在必要時保護我們的隱私並沒有錯。

**詞彙**

vulnerable
容易受傷的，脆弱的

traumatic experience
創傷經驗

intimate 親密的

keep something to oneself 不說出某事，不讓人知道某事

safeguard 保護，防衛

privacy 隱私

# Do you think it is acceptable to keep some things to yourself in a relationship?

你認為在感情關係中不讓對方知道某些事是可以接受的嗎？

Prologue

36 意外事件

37 資訊交流

38 八卦話題

39 祕密

40 社會議題

Epilogue

....................................................................

....................................................................

....................................................................

....................................................................

**你可以這樣回答**

I think it's acceptable to have personal boundaries in a relationship.
我認為在感情關係中擁有個人界線是可以接受的。

I think that hiding things in a relationship is a betrayal of trust.
我認為在感情關係中隱藏事情是對信任的背叛。

**參考範例**

Some people think there should be no secret in a relationship, but it is actually important to keep a certain extent of privacy, especially when it is about personal traumas. Without this personal space, one may feel their autonomy is threatened, potentially leading to tension in a relationship.

有些人認為感情關係中不應該有祕密，但保持一定程度的隱私其實很重要，尤其是和個人的創傷有關的時候。沒有這個個人空間，人就可能覺得自主權受到威脅，而可能導致關係中的緊張。

**詞彙**

extent 程度
autonomy 自主
threaten 威脅
potentially 潛在地，可能
tension 緊張

# Would you reveal your private life to a stranger? Why?

你會對陌生人透露自己的私生活嗎？為什麼？

........................................................................................

........................................................................................

........................................................................................

........................................................................................

### 你可以這樣回答

I believe that sharing my private life with a stranger can be refreshing.
我相信和陌生人分享我的私生活可以是很新鮮的。

I am too embarrassed to share my private life with a stranger.
我會太尷尬而無法和陌生人分享我的私生活。

### 參考範例

Telling a stranger about my private life is actually a liberating experience for me. Having no prior knowledge of my life, a stranger can listen and offer insights with less bias. Besides, I can freely express myself without worrying that the information could be circulated within my social circle.

告訴陌生人我的私生活，對我而言其實是讓我得到解放的經驗。因為陌生人先前對我的生活一無所知，所以能帶著比較少的偏見聆聽並提供洞見。而且，我可以自由地表達自己的想法，而不用擔心資訊可能在我的社交圈中流傳。

### 詞彙

liberate 解放
prior 先前的
bias 偏見
circulate 流通，傳播
social circle 社交圈

# Do you think women are at a disadvantage in finding jobs?

你認為女性求職時處於不利地位嗎？

........................................................................

........................................................................

........................................................................

........................................................................

Prologue

36 意外事件

37 資訊交流

38 八卦話題

39 祕密

40 社會議題

Epilogue

## 你可以這樣回答

Yes, I think women still face challenges in various industries.
是的，我認為女性在各種業界仍然面臨著挑戰。

I think men and women are treated rather equally nowadays.
我認為男女現在算是得到相當平等的對待了。

## 參考範例

I think women often experience gender bias when seeking jobs, especially in male-dominated fields. Deep-rooted stereotypes may lead to women being overlooked or their abilities being underestimated. We still need to raise people's awareness to improve such a situation.

我認為女性在找工作時常常遭受到性別的偏見，尤其在男性支配的領域。根深柢固的刻板印象，可能導致女性受到忽略，或者使她們的能力被低估。我們還需要提升人們（對此議題）的意識，來改善這樣的情況。

## 詞彙

dominate 支配
deep-rooted 根深柢固的
stereotype 刻板印象
overlook 忽略
underestimate 低估
awareness 意識

Prologue

36 意外事件

37 資訊交流

38 八卦話題

39 祕密

40 社會議題

Epilogue

# What are your thoughts on yielding priority seats to older individuals?

你對於將博愛座讓給老人的想法是什麼？

........................................................................................

........................................................................................

........................................................................................

........................................................................................

### 你可以這樣回答

I think it's a meaningful way to show our kindness.
我認為這是表現好意的一種有意義的方式。

While I support such an act, I don't think people should be forced to do it. 雖然我支持這樣的行為，但我不認為人們應該被強迫做這件事。

### 參考範例

I believe in the importance of offering priority seats to older individuals. This practice not only ensures a more comfortable and secure journey for the elderly but also reflects the value of caring for those in need. Furthermore, this simple act can foster a sense of compassion among people.

我相信把博愛座讓給老人的重要性。這樣做不但能確保老人有更舒適而安全的旅程，也能反映出照顧有需要者的價值觀。而且，這個簡單的舉動還可以促進人們的同情心。

### 詞彙

priority seat
博愛座（優先的座位）

secure 安全的

the elderly 老年人（總稱）

foster 培養，促進

compassion 同情

# Do you think the death penalty should be abolished?

你認為死刑應該被廢除嗎？

Prologue

36 意外事件

37 資訊交流

38 八卦話題

39 祕密

40 社會議題

Epilogue

........................................................................

........................................................................

........................................................................

........................................................................

### 你可以這樣回答

I am in favor of / I object to the abolition of the death penalty.
我贊成／反對死刑的廢除。

I (don't) believe the death penalty can act as a deterrent against crimes.
我（不）相信死刑可以嚇阻犯罪。

### 參考範例

Yes, I think the death penalty should be abolished. In my opinion, it is a violation of human rights, as no individual or entity should be entitled to end another person's life. More importantly, the death penalty does not necessarily prevent serious crimes from happening.

是的，我認為死刑應該被廢除。在我看來，死刑違反人權，因為沒有一個人或者實體有資格結束另一個人的生命。更重要的是，死刑不一定能預防嚴重的犯罪發生。

### 詞彙

abolish 廢除
violation 違反
human rights 人權
entitle 使…有資格
necessarily 必然，必定

# Do you think it is necessary for a couple to get married?

你認為情侶必須結婚嗎？

Prologue

36 意外事件

37 資訊交流

38 八卦話題

39 祕密

40 社會議題

Epilogue

### 你可以這樣回答

I (don't) think marriage is essential for a successful relationship.
我（不）認為婚姻對於成功的關係是必要的。

Yes, I think marriage is a symbol of commitment.
是的，我認為婚姻是（對感情）承諾的象徵。

### 參考範例

I don't think a couple needs to get married. I believe a robust relationship is not reliant on marriage, but based on love, trust, and mutual respect. We don't need a marriage certificate or a ceremony to prove our love with someone.

我不認為情侶需要結婚。我相信穩健的關係並不是依靠婚姻，而是建立在愛、信任與互相尊重之上。我們不需要結婚證書或者婚禮來證明和一個人的愛。

### 詞彙

robust 強健的，堅實的
reliant 依賴的，依靠的
mutual 互相的
certificate 證書
ceremony 儀式，典禮

# How can we help end homelessness?
我們可以如何幫助終結遊民問題？

Prologue

36 意外事件

37 資訊交流

38 八卦話題

39 祕密

40 社會議題

Epilogue

### 你可以這樣回答

We can support the homeless by offering employment opportunities.
們可以藉由提供受雇機會來支援遊民。

We should first raise awareness of this issue.
我們應該先提升（大眾）對這個議題的認知度。

### 參考範例

To help end homelessness, we can begin by encouraging government actions aimed at providing affordable housing for the homeless. We can also donate our time or money to non-profit organizations that support homeless people by providing shelter and job training.

要幫助終結遊民問題，我們可以從鼓勵政府採取行動、為遊民提供可負擔的住宅開始。我們也可以貢獻時間（當義工）或錢給藉由提供住處與職業訓練來幫助遊民的非營利組織。

### 詞彙

**homelessness**
無家可歸，遊民問題
**aimed at** 以…為目標的
**affordable** 可負擔的
**housing** 住房
**shelter** 庇護所，收容處

# How can families and schools help prevent drug abuse?

家庭與學校可以如何幫助預防藥物濫用？

Prologue

36 意外事件

37 資訊交流

38 八卦話題

39 祕密

40 社會議題

Epilogue

你可以這樣回答

Families can build strong relationships based on trust and support.
家庭可以在信賴與支持的基礎上建立堅定的情感關係。

Schools can promote positive peer interactions that discourage drug use.
學校可以促進能打消用藥（吸毒）念頭的正向同儕互動。

參考範例

Both families and schools can encourage students to participate in extracurricular activities, which can help them focus on personal growth rather than escapism through drugs. Schools can also organize workshops that help parents and students develop communication strategies to address this issue.

家庭和學校都可以鼓勵學生參與課外活動，它們可以幫助學生聚焦在個人成長，而不是用藥物逃避現實。學校也可以舉辦工作坊，幫助父母與學生發展出溝通策略來處理這個問題。

詞彙

extracurricular 課外的

personal growth 個人成長

escapism 逃避現實

organize 組織，籌辦

workshop 工作坊（專題討論會）

# Do you think the unemployment rate is high in your country?

你認為你國家的失業率高嗎？

Prologue

36 意外事件

37 資訊交流

38 八卦話題

39 祕密

40 社會議題

Epilogue

......................................................................................................

......................................................................................................

......................................................................................................

......................................................................................................

### 你可以這樣回答

Yes, I've seen more job seekers making do with part-time jobs.
是的，我看到有比較多找工作的人靠兼職工作勉強過日子。

No, I've seen numerous job openings advertised across various sectors.
不，我看到各種行業刊登了許多職缺。

### 參考範例

I can tell that the unemployment rate is high because some of my friends online have been looking for jobs for quite a while. I've also seen news reports about large-scale layoffs and a decrease in job vacancies due to the recent economic recession.

我能感覺到失業率很高，因為我有些網路上的朋友已經找工作好一陣子了。我也看過一些關於最近的經濟衰退造成大規模裁員與職缺減少的新聞報導。

### 詞彙

unemployment 失業
large-scale 大規模的
layoff 臨時解雇，裁員
vacancy 空缺
recession 衰退

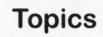

# Topics

# What do you do in your daily life to save energy?

你在日常生活中做什麼來節能？

## 你可以這樣回答

I limit my screen time and use energy-saving settings on my electronic devices.
我限制看螢幕的時間，並且在我的電子設備上使用節能（省電）模式。

I set the temperature of the air conditioner between 26 and 28 degrees Celsius.
我把冷氣的溫度設定在攝氏 26 和 28 度之間。

## 參考範例

I turn off lights and unplug appliances when they are not in use. Besides, I use energy-efficient lighting like LED bulbs instead of traditional light bulbs. Also, I won't turn on the air conditioner unless I can't tolerate the temperature.

用不到的時候，我會把燈關掉，並且把家電的插頭拔掉。此外，我使用 LED 燈泡之類的節能照明，而不是傳統的燈泡。還有，除非我受不了溫度，不然我不會打開冷氣。

## 詞彙

unplug 把…的插頭拔掉
appliance 器具，家電
energy-efficient
能源效率好的
light bulb 燈泡
tolerate 忍受

# Do you actively use eco-friendly products or services?

你積極使用環保的產品或服務嗎？

........................................................................................

........................................................................................

........................................................................................

........................................................................................

你可以這樣回答

I choose eco-friendly products whenever possible.
只要可能的話，我就會選擇環保的產品。

I seldom notice if a product or service is eco-friendly.
我很少注意產品或服務是否環保。

參考範例

As an environmentally conscious person, I make a conscious effort to incorporate eco-friendly products into my daily life. To achieve this, I check if a product is certified as eco-friendly or organic before buying it. In this way, I can contribute to sustainability through my purchase.

身為有環境意識的人，我有意識地努力將環保產品包含在日常生活中。為了達成這個目標，我在購買產品之前會查看它是否被認證為環保或者有機。這樣一來，我可以透過我的購買對永續性做出貢獻。

詞彙

conscious 有意識的
incorporate 包含，整合
certify 證明，認證
organic 有機的
sustainability 永續性

# Do you try to buy less to be more sustainable?

你試圖藉由買比較少的東西,讓自己更支持永續性嗎?

Prologue

41 環保

42 教育

43 工作

44 我的情緒

45 我的弱點

Epilogue

........................................................................

........................................................................

........................................................................

........................................................................

### 你可以這樣回答

Yes, I try to buy less to promote sustainability.
是的,我試著買比較少的東西來支持永續性。

No, I just can't help but buy a lot of stuff.
不,我就是忍不住買很多東西。

### 參考範例

I believe in promoting sustainability by reducing consumption. Before making any purchase, I always pause to consider if it's necessary. When it comes to clothing, I try to buy second-hand items instead of new ones. This not only extends the lifespan of clothing but also helps me save money.

我相信可以藉由減少消費對永續性作出貢獻。在購買任何東西之前,我總是會暫停一下,考慮它是否必要。至於衣服,我試著買二手衣物而不是新的。這樣不僅延長衣服的壽命,也會幫我省錢。

### 詞彙

promote 促進
consumption 消費
extend 延長
lifespan 壽命,使用期限

# What can we do to raise people's awareness of environmental issues?

我們可以做什麼來提升人們對環境議題的意識？

.................................................................................

.................................................................................

.................................................................................

.................................................................................

### 你可以這樣回答

We can develop environmental education programs in schools.
我們可以開發學校裡的環境教育課程。

We can reach a broad audience using the power of social media.
我們可以用社交媒體的力量來觸及廣泛的受眾。

### 參考範例

We can do so through a variety of media. Documentaries, for instance, have the ability to evoke emotions within the audience and inspire them to take action in support of our planet. Community events like tree planting also helps foster a sense of environmental responsibility.

我們可以藉由各種媒體做到這件事。例如紀錄片，就有能力激起觀眾的情緒，並且鼓勵他們採取行動來支持我們的星球。種樹之類的社區活動也對於培養環境責任感有幫助。

### 詞彙

a variety of 各種各樣的⋯
documentary 紀錄片
evoke 喚起，激起
inspire 激勵
foster 培養，促進

# In your opinion, why should we recycle?

在你看來，為什麼我們需要做資源回收？

......

......

......

......

### 你可以這樣回答

Recycling helps reduce the volume of waste.
資源回收有助於減少垃圾量。

Recycling reduces habitat destruction caused by resource extraction.
資源回收能減少資源開採造成的（生物）棲地破壞。

### 參考範例

To prevent the depletion of natural resources, we should do our best to recycle and reuse them. Recycling not only conserves resources but also reduces pollution and lowers greenhouse gas emissions. Additionally, recycling also creates jobs, such as collection, sorting, and processing.

為了預防天然資源的耗竭，我們應該盡全力將它們回收再利用。資源回收不只是節省資源，也能減少污染並降低溫室氣體排放。此外，資源回收也會創造工作，例如收集、分類與處理。

### 詞彙

depletion 耗盡
reuse 再利用
conserve 保存；節省
greenhouse gas
溫室氣體
emission 排放

# Do you think it is a lot of trouble to recycle?

你認為資源回收很麻煩嗎？

........................

........................

........................

........................

## 你可以這樣回答

Considering the environmental benefits, I think it's a small but worthwhile effort.

考慮到環境方面的好處，我認為它是很小但值得的努力。

Recycling feels like an additional chore in my daily routine.

資源回收感覺像是我例行事項裡額外的家事。

## 參考範例

Recycling has become effortless now that I've made it a habit. Since it is part of my routine, it no longer feels like trouble. By using different containers, I can sort my waste before disposing of it, so there isn't any hassle.

因為我已經把資源回收變成習慣，所以它已經變得毫不費力。因為它是我日常程序的一部分，所以感覺不再是件麻煩事了。藉由使用不同的容器，我可以在丟掉垃圾之前分類，所以並沒有任何麻煩。

## 詞彙

**effortless** 不費力的

**routine** 例行事項，日常程序

**container** 容器

**dispose of** 處理掉，捨棄…

**hassle** 麻煩

# What kind of clean energy do you think can replace fossil fuels?

你認為哪種乾淨能源可以取代化石燃料？

Prologue

41 環保

42 教育

43 工作

44 我的情緒

45 我的弱點

Epilogue

........................................................................

........................................................................

........................................................................

........................................................................

### 你可以這樣回答

Solar energy is now accessible and cost-effective.
太陽能現在容易利用，而且成本效益高。

Wind farms are being developed in various regions.
風電場現在正在各種地區開發中。

### 參考範例

Solar energy and wind power are two common types of clean energy that can replace fossil fuels. They have gained popularity due to their low operating cost. If they become more stable and affordable, they will definitely be adopted in more places.

太陽能與風力是可以取代化石燃料的兩種常見乾淨能源。由於很低的營運成本，它們已經變得普及。如果它們更穩定而且便宜，就一定會在更多地方獲得採用。

### 詞彙

solar energy 太陽能

gain popularity 變得普及

operating cost
營業成本，營運成本

stable 穩定的

affordable
（價格等方面）可負擔的

# Do you think students need to attend cram schools?

你認為學生需要上補習班嗎？

41 環保

42 教育

43 工作

44 我的情緒

45 我的弱點

Prologue

Epilogue

## 你可以這樣回答

I believe students can benefit from attending cram schools.
我認為學生可以因為上補習班而獲益。

Cram schools can be helpful, but they are not always necessary.
補習班可能有幫助，但並非總是必要的。

## 參考範例

I don't think cram schools are necessary for students. They focus on exam preparation rather than critical thinking or application of knowledge in real life. While they can be helpful in achieving short-term academic goals, they don't help students prepare themselves for the ever-changing environment.

我不認為補習班對於學生是必要的。它們專注於考試準備，而不是批判性思考或者將知識運用在實際生活中。雖然它們可能對於達成短期學業目標有幫助，但它們不能幫學生為不斷改變的環境做好準備。

## 詞彙

preparation 準備

critical thinking
批判性思考

application 應用

short-term 短期的

academic 學業的，學術的

# Do you have any experience of learning something by yourself?

你有過自學什麼事物的經驗嗎?

Prologue

41 環保

42 教育

43 工作

44 我的情緒

45 我的弱點

Epilogue

## 你可以這樣回答

I have learned programming independently.
我曾經自主學習程式設計。

No, I am too lazy to learn by myself.
沒有,我太懶了,沒辦法自己學習。

## 參考範例

When I was eight, I developed an interest in playing ukulele. I started to watch tutorial videos on YouTube and practiced every day. Over time, I not only made significant progress but also built the confidence to pursue other interests.

當我 8 歲的時候,我對於演奏烏克麗麗產生了興趣。我開始看 YouTube 上的教學影片,並且每天練習。隨著時間過去,我不但有了顯著的進步,還建立了追求其他興趣的信心。

## 詞彙

ukulele 烏克麗麗
tutorial 指導的,教學的
over time 隨著時間
make progress 取得進步
significant 顯著的

# Do you learn best by listening, reading, or by some other method?

你用聽的、讀的，還是用其他方法學習效果最好？

........................................................................................

........................................................................................

........................................................................................

........................................................................................

## 你可以這樣回答

Reading is my preferred learning method.
閱讀是我偏好的學習方法。

I've found that online courses and multimedia resources suit me best.
我發現線上課程和多媒體資源最適合我。

## 參考範例

I think I learn best by listening. For instance, during lectures or speeches, I find myself attentive to what the speakers say. Listening to audio recordings or engaging in group discussions also helps me absorb new knowledge and concepts quickly.

我認為我用聽的學習效果最好。舉例來說，在上課或者演講的時候，我發現自己會很專心聽講者說什麼。聽錄音或者參加團體討論，也會幫助我快速吸收新知識與概念。

## 詞彙

lecture 授課
attentive 專心的，注意的
audio 聲音的
engage in 參加，從事…
absorb 吸收

# Would you consider studying abroad?

你會考慮海外留學嗎？

Prologue

41 環保

42 教育

43 工作

44 我的情緒

45 我的弱點

Epilogue

### 你可以這樣回答

I'm very interested in studying abroad.
我對於海外留學非常有興趣。

I'm concerned about the cost of studying abroad.
我擔心海外留學的費用。

### 參考範例

I would consider studying abroad if I have the opportunity. Besides more advanced educational resources, it also provides a chance to immerse myself in diverse cultures, connect with people from all walks of life, and expand my global network.

如果有機會的話，我會考慮海外留學。除了有更先進的教育資源以外，海外留學也讓我有機會沉浸在多元文化中、和來自各行各業的人交際，並且拓展我的全球人脈。

### 詞彙

advanced 先進的
immerse 使沉浸
diverse 多種多樣的
all walks of life 各行各業
expand 拓展

## Q.299

# What would you do if the subject you want to learn is not offered at school?

如果你想要學的主題（科目）在學校裡沒有，你會怎麼做？

..................................................................................................

..................................................................................................

..................................................................................................

..................................................................................................

### 你可以這樣回答

I would check out relevant publications to gain some understanding.
我會查看相關的刊物來獲得一些了解。

I could find YouTube videos on the subject.
我可以找關於這個主題的 YouTube 影片。

### 參考範例

If the subject I want to learn is not available at school, I will try to find other resources. For instance, my school didn't offer courses about artificial intelligence, so I started by taking online courses. I also attended workshops on that topic to improve my understanding.

如果我想學的主題在學校裡沒有，我會試圖找到其他資源。舉例來說，（之前）我的學校不提供關於人工智慧的課程，所以我藉由上線上課來開始（學習）。我也參加關於這個主題的工作坊來增進我的了解。

### 詞彙

resource 資源

artificial intelligence
人工智慧

attend 出席，參加

workshop
工作坊（專題討論會）

# Has any teacher affected your attitude toward a subject?

有哪位老師改變了你對一個科目的態度嗎？

Prologue

41 環保

42 教育

43 工作

44 我的情緒

45 我的弱點

Epilogue

### 你可以這樣回答

My history teacher completely transformed my perspective on history.
我的歷史老師完全轉變了我對歷史的觀點。

My physics teacher made me frustrated about the subject.
我的物理老師讓我對這個科目感到挫敗。

### 參考範例

My English teacher in junior high school had a profound impact on my attitude toward learning English. She said that English comes to life only when we use it, and that test scores are not the most important. That's why I train my listening comprehension by watching English-language movies.

我國中時的英語老師，對於我學習英語的態度有很深的影響。她說英語只有在我們使用它的時候才是活的，而測驗分數並不是最重要的。那就是我之所以靠著看英語電影來訓練聽力理解的原因。

### 詞彙

profound 深深的
impact 影響；衝擊
come to life 活起來
comprehension 理解

Prologue

41
環保

42
教育

43
工作

44
我的情緒

45
我的弱點

Epilogue

## Which do you think plays a bigger role in achieving good grades, hard work or talent?

你認為哪一項對於得到好成績比較重要，是努力還是天分？

........................................................................

........................................................................

........................................................................

........................................................................

你可以這樣回答

Talent can provide a strong foundation for achieving good grades.
天分可以為得到好成績提供堅實的基礎。

Talent can provide a natural advantage, but it won't bloom without hard work. 天分可以提供天生的優勢，但沒有努力它就不會開花。

參考範例

I believe that hard work plays a bigger role in achieving good grades. Regardless of talent, students need to review and practice to master the knowledge they have learned. Talented students might perform better initially, but those who consistently put in effort will be more successful in the long term.

我相信努力對於得到好成績比較重要。不管天分如何，學生都需要複習與練習，才能精通他們學到的知識。有天分的學生一開始可能表現比較好，但長期來看，持續努力的人會比較成功。

詞彙

regardless of 不管…
master 精通，掌握
talented 有天分的
consistently
一貫地，始終如一地
in the long term 長期來看

# If you could have your own business, what would it be?

如果你能擁有自己的事業，那會是什麼？

Prologue

41 環保

42 教育

43 工作

44 我的情緒

45 我的弱點

Epilogue

### 你可以這樣回答

I would consider opening a restaurant/boutique/bakery.
我會考慮開一家餐廳／精品店／烘焙坊。

I would establish my own software company / online learning platform.
我會建立自己的軟體公司／線上學習平台。

### 參考範例

I would like to run a coffee shop because I have a deep affection for coffee. I would roast beans by myself and hire a professional team of baristas to ensure the best quality. It would be even better if we could offer freshly baked pastries to complement our coffee.

我想要經營一家咖啡店，因為我非常喜愛咖啡。我會自己烘咖啡豆，並且雇用一群專業的咖啡師，確保最好的品質。如果我們能供應新鮮出爐的糕點來搭配我們的咖啡，那就更好了。

### 詞彙

affection 喜愛；感情

roast 烤

barista 咖啡師

pastry （通常指酥皮的）糕點

complement 補充，搭配

# Do you prefer a workplace that offers challenges or one that provides stability?

你偏好提供挑戰還是穩定性的職場？

Prologue

41 環保

42 教育

43 工作

44 我的情緒

45 我的弱點

Epilogue

......................................................................

......................................................................

......................................................................

......................................................................

### 你可以這樣回答

Challenges keep me motivated.
挑戰讓我保持有動力。

I used to seek challenges, but now I prefer a more stable environment.
我以前總是追求挑戰，但現在我偏好比較穩定的環境。

### 參考範例

I prefer a workplace that provides stability and allows me to focus on my professional development. The sense of security and predictability enables me to fully dedicate myself to my work. Such a workplace also allows me to make long-term plans for my future.

我偏好提供穩定性，並且讓我能專注於職業發展的職場。安全感與可預測性讓我能完全投身於工作中。這樣的職場也讓我能對未來做長期計畫。

### 詞彙

workplace 職場
stability 穩定
sense of security 安全感
predictability 可預測性
dedicate oneself to
獻身於，致力於…

# Would you like to become a supervisor?

你想要當主管嗎？

Prologue

41 環保

42 教育

43 工作

44 我的情緒

45 我的弱點

Epilogue

......

......

......

......

**你可以這樣回答**

I aspire to be a supervisor.
我渴望成為主管。

I'm not interested in becoming a supervisor.
我對於當主管沒有興趣。

**參考範例**

I would like to be a supervisor if I get the chance. I would try my best to create a better workplace and positive work culture. It would also be satisfying to see how my subordinates work together and achieve organizational success under my leadership.

如果我有機會的話，我想要當主管。我會盡全力創造更好的職場與正面的工作文化。看到下屬如何在我的領導下合作並達成組織的成功，也會是一件令我滿足的事。

**詞彙**

work culture 工作文化
subordinate 下屬
work together 合作
organizational 組織的
leadership
領導，領導才能

Prologue

41 環保

42 教育

43 工作

44 我的情緒

45 我的弱點

Epilogue

## Q.305

# What would you do if your opinion is different from your superior's?

如果你的意見和上級不同，你會怎麼做？

........................................................................

........................................................................

........................................................................

........................................................................

### 你可以這樣回答

I will still voice my viewpoint even if they don't listen.
就算他們不聽，我還是會說出我的觀點。

I tend to trust their judgment and say nothing.
我傾向於相信他們的判斷並且不說什麼。

### 參考範例

I will still express my opinion while listening to my superior's perspective carefully. And then, I will try to find common ground and reach a consensus. I think the key is being open-minded and respecting each other.

我還是會表達我的意見，同時仔細聆聽上級的觀點。然後，我會試圖找到（想法上的）共同點，並且達成共識。我認為關鍵是心態開放，以及尊重彼此。

### 詞彙

perspective 觀點

carefully 仔細地，小心地

common ground
（想法上的）共同點

consensus
一致的意見，共識

open-minded 心態開放的

# What can you do to try to get a promotion?
你可以做什麼以試圖獲得升職？

Prologue

41 環保

42 教育

43 工作

44 我的情緒

45 我的弱點

Epilogue

### 你可以這樣回答

I may need to seek additional responsibilities beyond my current job.
我可能需要尋求目前工作以外的額外職責。

Actually, I am content with my current role and not seeking a promotion.
事實上，我對自己目前的角色滿足，也不尋求升職。

### 參考範例

Getting a promotion requires dedication and hard work, so I think I need to deliver high-quality work and finish every project on time. Additionally, I should develop some impressive skills and strive to get along with my colleagues and supervisor.

獲得升職需要奉獻精神與努力工作，所以我認為我需要實現高品質的工作，並且準時完成每項專案。此外，我也應該發展一些令人印象深刻的技能，並且努力和同事與主管相處融洽。

### 詞彙

dedication 奉獻精神

deliver 給出；實現

impressive
令人印象深刻的

strive to V 努力去做…

get along with
和…相處融洽

321

Prologue

41
環保

42
教育

43
工作

44
我的情緒

45
我的弱點

Epilogue

# Do you like to work overtime? Why or why not?

你喜歡加班工作嗎？為什麼？

..................................................

..................................................

..................................................

..................................................

### 你可以這樣回答

I prefer not to work overtime unless…
我比較希望不要加班，除非…

I like working overtime, especially because it comes with financial incentives.
我喜歡加班，尤其是因為加班有金錢上的獎勵。

### 參考範例

I try not to work overtime because I want to maintain a healthy work-life balance and avoid the risk of burnout. Additionally, I've found that my productivity and efficiency tend to decline during overtime, so I do my best to finish my work during regular hours.

我努力做到不加班，因為我想要維持健康的工作與生活平衡，並且避免工作倦怠的風險。另外，我發現我的生產力與效率在加班時通常會下降，所以我儘量在正常工作時段完成工作。

### 詞彙

work overtime 加班工作

(job) burnout （過度勞累造成的）（工作）倦怠

productivity 生產力

efficiency 效率

decline 下降

# At what age would you like to retire? Why?

你想在幾歲退休？為什麼？

Prologue

41 環保

42 教育

43 工作

44 我的情緒

45 我的弱點

Epilogue

........................................

........................................

........................................

........................................

### 你可以這樣回答

My ideal retirement age is…
我的理想退休年齡是…

I won't retire unless I feel financially secure enough.
除非我覺得財務夠安全，不然我不會退休。

### 參考範例

I plan to retire at the age of 60 because I believe that by that time, I may not have the strength and energy required for a 9-to-5 job. My goal is to have saved enough money by then to pursue my hobbies in the later stages of my life.

我打算 60 歲退休，因為我相信到那時候，我可能沒有朝九晚五工作所需的體力和活力。我的目標是在那之前存足夠的錢，好讓我在人生之後的階段從事我愛好的活動。

### 詞彙

retire 退休

strength 體力

9-to-5 job 朝九晚五的工作

stage 階段

# Do you find that your emotions fluctuate frequently?

你覺得自己的情緒經常波動嗎？

你可以這樣回答

I often find myself on an emotional rollercoaster.
我常常感覺自己的情緒在坐雲霄飛車。

My emotions usually remain stable.
我的情緒通常保持穩定。

參考範例

I think that's the case for me. I can suddenly go from feeling great to being moody and unpredictable. I'd like to change this situation because my friends and loved ones tend to keep their distance when I become difficult to be around.

我認為那符合我的情況。我可能突然從感覺很好變成心情不穩而難以預測。我想要改變這個情況，因為在我變得很難相處的時候，我的朋友和我所愛的人通常會和我保持距離。

詞彙

moody
心情不穩的；喜怒無常的

unpredictable 不可預測的

keep one's distance
保持距離

# What do you do when you are under pressure?

你感受到壓力的時候會做什麼？

Prologue

41 環保

42 教育

43 工作

44 我的情緒

45 我的弱點

Epilogue

........................................................................................

........................................................................................

........................................................................................

........................................................................................

### 你可以這樣回答

I talk to my friends to relieve pressure.
我跟朋友聊來緩解壓力。

I do exercise to change my mood.
我做運動來改變心情。

### 參考範例

When I'm under pressure, I might take a few deep breaths, go for a short walk, or practice meditation to calm my mind. This allows me to regain my composure and face the situation with a more relaxed and positive mindset.

當我有壓力時，我可能會做幾個深呼吸、進行短程的散步，或者練習冥想（靜心）好讓心平靜下來。這樣會讓我能夠重拾沉著的感覺，而且能用比較放鬆而積極的心態來面對情況。

### 詞彙

**take a deep breath**
深呼吸

**meditation** 冥想（靜心）

**regain** 找回，恢復

**composure**
沉著（的感覺）

**mindset** 心態

# What do you think is a good way to deal with negative thoughts?

你認為什麼是處理負面想法的好方法？

Prologue

41 環保

42 教育

43 工作

44 我的情緒

45 我的弱點

Epilogue

......................................................................

......................................................................

......................................................................

......................................................................

**你可以這樣回答**

When I have negative thoughts, I immerse myself in my hobbies.
當我有負面想法時，我會沉浸在嗜好活動裡。

Mindfulness allows me to observe my thoughts without judgment.
正念讓我能不帶批判地觀察我的想法。

**參考範例**

I think writing down what I feel right now is a good way to deal with negative thoughts. For one thing, writing itself makes me feel peaceful, no matter what I write. For another, I can identify my problems by writing them down and tackle them rationally.

我認為寫下我現在的感覺，是處理負面想法的好方法。首先，書寫本身就讓我感覺平靜，不管我寫什麼。再者，我可以藉由寫下來而認出我的問題，並且理性地處理它們。

**詞彙**

negative 負面的
peaceful 平靜的；和平的
identify 辨認，認出
tackle 著手處理，應對
rationally 理性地

# Have you ever experienced a long period of feeling down?

你曾經有過長期心情低落的經驗嗎？

Prologue

41 環保

42 教育

43 工作

44 我的情緒

45 我的弱點

Epilogue

**你可以這樣回答**

There was a time when I felt consistently down due to work.
我曾經有一段時間因為工作而持續心情低落。

Fortunately, I've always been quite resilient.
幸好，我一直挺有心理韌性的。

**參考範例**

I suffered from depression when I was in high school. It was caused by the suffocating schoolwork, which made me feel extremely stressed. However, with the company of my family and the guidance from my counselor, I overcame it and became much better.

我高中時得了憂鬱症。那是令人喘不過氣的課業造成的，它讓我覺得壓力非常大。不過，因為有家人的陪伴和諮商師的引導，我克服憂鬱症而且好多了。

**詞彙**

depression 憂鬱症
suffocating 令人窒息的，令人喘不過氣的
schoolwork 課業
company 陪伴
counselor 諮商師

Prologue

41
環保

42
教育

43
工作

44
我的情緒

45
我的弱點

Epilogue

# When do you feel energetic?
什麼時候你覺得精力充沛？

.........................................................................................

.........................................................................................

.........................................................................................

.........................................................................................

### 你可以這樣回答

I am full of energy in the morning after a good night's sleep.
我在一夜好眠後的早晨充滿活力。

Listening to upbeat music makes me feel alive.
聽歡快的音樂讓我感覺有活力。

### 參考範例

I feel energetic when doing outdoor activities. In nature, I can truly escape from tedious life and routines. I especially enjoy breathing in the fresh air, which has a refreshing effect on my body and mind.

我在做戶外活動時感覺有活力。在自然中，我可以真正逃離單調乏味的生活與例行公事。我尤其享受呼吸新鮮空氣，這對於我的身心有提振精神的效果。

### 詞彙

energetic 精力充沛的

tedious 單調乏味的

routine 例行公事

refreshing 提振精神的；令人耳目一新的

# What makes you feel nervous?
什麼讓你感覺緊張？

Prologue

41 環保

42 教育

43 工作

44 我的情緒

45 我的弱點

Epilogue

### 你可以這樣回答

My heart starts racing when I have to make a public speech.
當我必須公開演說的時候，我的心跳就開始加速。

Unexpected changes tend to make me feel nervous.
預料之外的改變通常會讓我感覺緊張。

### 參考範例

Talking to a superior can be nerve-wracking for me. In front of someone in a higher position of authority, I get anxious about not meeting their expectations. I also feel the pressure to maintain a professional demeanor and a respectful attitude at the same time.

對上司說話會讓我很傷腦筋。在權力地位比我高的人面前，我會擔心不符合對方的期待。我也會感受到同時要維持專業舉止和尊重態度的壓力。

### 詞彙

superior 上司
nerve-wracking 傷腦筋的
authority 權力
expectation 期待
demeanor 神態舉止
respectful 尊重的

# What would you feel when standing on a stage?

你站在舞台上會有什麼感覺?

Prologue

41 環保

42 教育

43 工作

44 我的情緒

45 我的弱點

Epilogue

### 你可以這樣回答

I would feel excited and nervous at the same time.
我會同時覺得興奮又緊張。

I experience a rush of adrenaline in the spotlight.
在聚光燈照射下,我會感覺腎上腺素爆發。

### 參考範例

I would be nervous because I am too afraid of making mistakes or making a fool of myself in front of an audience. My heart rate would increase, and my palms would get sweaty. Sometimes, I could even feel the shaking in my hands and legs.

我會很緊張,因為我太害怕在觀眾面前犯錯或者出醜。我的心跳會加速,手掌會出汗。有時候我甚至能感覺到手和腿的顫抖。

### 詞彙

make a fool of oneself
出醜,出糗

audience 觀眾,聽眾

heart rate 心率

palm 手掌

sweaty 出汗而濕透的

# What is the greatest weakness in your personality?

你性格最大的弱點是什麼？

Prologue

41 環保

42 教育

43 工作

44 我的情緒

45 我的弱點

Epilogue

**你可以這樣回答**

My greatest weakness is that I am too introverted/impatient/impulsive.
我最大的弱點是我太內向／沒耐性／衝動。

I would say my most prominent weakness is my procrastination/sensitivity/self-doubt.
我會說我最明顯的弱點是拖延／敏感／自我懷疑。

**參考範例**

My most significant personality weakness is my perfectionism. I have a tendency to pursue perfection in every task, usually overworking myself. To address this tendency, I seek guidance from books that provide insights on letting go and reducing excessive attachment to outcomes.

我最顯著的性格弱點是完美主義，我傾向於在每項工作中追求完美，這通常會讓我過勞。為了處理這個傾向，我從對於放下以及減少過度執著於結果等方面提供洞見的書中尋求引導。

**詞彙**

perfectionism 完美主義

tendency 傾向

overwork oneself
讓自己過度勞累

guidance 引導

insight 洞察，洞見

attachment
依附的情感，執著

# Do you talk about your weaknesses with your family or friends? Why or why not?

你會跟家人或朋友談論自己的弱點嗎？為什麼？

.........................................................................................................

.........................................................................................................

.........................................................................................................

.........................................................................................................

### 你可以這樣回答

I share my weaknesses with my close friends.
我會跟親近的朋友分享我的弱點。

I'm hesitant to discuss my weaknesses with my family.
我對於跟家人討論我的弱點感到猶豫。

### 參考範例

No, I rarely talk about my weaknesses with my family or friends. Instead, I tend to keep them to myself. I'm reluctant to reveal my vulnerabilities and struggles to them because I don't want to seem incapable in their eyes.

不，我很少跟我的家人或朋友談論我的弱點。我反而傾向於不讓別人知道。我很不願意對他們揭露自己的弱點和掙扎，因為我不想在他們的眼中看起來沒有能力。

### 詞彙

keep... to oneself 不讓別人知道（祕密的事物）

reluctant 不情願的

vulnerability 脆弱，弱點

struggle 掙扎

incapable 沒有能力的

# What have you done to tackle your weaknesses? Provide an example.

你做了什麼來處理你的弱點？提供一個例子。

......................................................................

......................................................................

......................................................................

......................................................................

Prologue

41 環保

42 教育

43 工作

44 我的情緒

45 我的弱點

Epilogue

## 你可以這樣回答

I struggled with / One of my weaknesses was…
我曾經苦於／我的弱點之一是…

To address/tackle/overcome it, I…
為了處理／對付／克服它，我…

## 參考範例

I was not efficient in managing my time, and I often missed deadlines. To tackle this, I started using time management apps and creating schedules for my tasks. These changes helped me become more organized and meet deadlines.

我在管理時間方面沒有效率，而且我常常趕不上期限。為了處理這個情況，我開始使用時間管理 app，並且為我的工作建立時間表。這些改變幫助我變得比較有條理，並且趕上期限。

## 詞彙

efficient 有效率的

manage 管理

miss a deadline 錯過期限
（ ⟷ meet a deadline 趕上期限）

organized 有條理的

# Do you have a fear of something?

你有什麼感到恐懼的事物嗎?

Prologue

41 環保

42 教育

43 工作

44 我的情緒

45 我的弱點

Epilogue

## 你可以這樣回答

I have a fear of flying / cockroaches / the dark.
我怕搭飛機╱蟑螂╱黑暗。

I'm scared/afraid of talking on the phone / riding roller coasters.
我怕講電話╱坐雲霄飛車。

## 參考範例

I have a fear of heights. I remember when I visited Tokyo with some of my friends, we went to a skyscraper where people can overlook the city at its observation deck. While my friends were enjoying the breathtaking view, I was too terrified to even look down.

我怕高。我記得當我和一些朋友拜訪東京的時候,我們去了一棟可以在觀景台俯瞰城市的摩天大樓。當我的朋友在享受壯觀的視野時,我則是太害怕了,根本沒辦法往下看。

## 詞彙

skyscraper 摩天大樓

overlook 俯瞰

observation deck 觀景台

breathtaking
令人屏息的,壯觀的

terrified 非常害怕的

# Is there anything in your daily life that you are not good at doing?

在日常生活中，有什麼事情是你不擅長做的嗎？

Prologue

41 環保

42 教育

43 工作

44 我的情緒

45 我的弱點

Epilogue

## 你可以這樣回答

I have a hard time remembering names / waking up early in the morning.
我很難記住名字／在早上很早起床。

I'm not skilled at small talk / DIY home repairs.
我不擅長閒聊／DIY 家庭修繕。

## 參考範例

I'm not good at cooking. I can't really cook anything beyond instant noodles. Even when I try to follow a recipe, I usually end up ruining the ingredients. That's why I prefer eating out or ordering takeout. It's just more convenient and guarantees a better meal.

我不擅長烹飪。我煮不了速食麵以外的任何東西。就算我試圖照著食譜做，也通常會把食材毀掉。那就是我偏好外食或者點外帶的原因。這樣就是比較方便，而且能保證比較好的一餐。

## 詞彙

recipe 食譜

ruin 毀壞

ingredient
（烹調的）原料

order takeout 點外帶

guarantee 保證

Prologue

41 環保

42 教育

43 工作

44 我的情緒

45 我的弱點

Epilogue

# Do you have any aspects that negatively affect your self-confidence?

你有什麼面向對自信造成負面影響嗎？

. . . . . . . . . . . . . . . . . . . . . . . . . . . . . . . . . . . . . . . . . . . . . . . . . . . . . . . . . . . . . . . . . . . . . . . . . . . . . . . . . . . . . . . . .

. . . . . . . . . . . . . . . . . . . . . . . . . . . . . . . . . . . . . . . . . . . . . . . . . . . . . . . . . . . . . . . . . . . . . . . . . . . . . . . . . . . . . . . . .

. . . . . . . . . . . . . . . . . . . . . . . . . . . . . . . . . . . . . . . . . . . . . . . . . . . . . . . . . . . . . . . . . . . . . . . . . . . . . . . . . . . . . . . . .

. . . . . . . . . . . . . . . . . . . . . . . . . . . . . . . . . . . . . . . . . . . . . . . . . . . . . . . . . . . . . . . . . . . . . . . . . . . . . . . . . . . . . . . . .

## 你可以這樣回答

I have a hard time socializing, and that's detrimental to my self-confidence.
我很不會和人社交，而那傷害了我的自信。

My sensitivity has a negative impact on my self-confidence.
我的敏感對我的自信有負面影響。

## 參考範例

I find myself quite critical of my appearance. I usually pay attention to my imperfections in my body shape and facial features, so I'm never confident of how I look. I really should accept myself as I am and focus on what makes me unique.

我覺得我對自己的外貌很挑剔。我通常注意自己體型和臉部特徵不完美的地方，所以我對於自己的外貌從來都沒有信心。我真的應該接受自己原本的樣子，並且專注於讓我獨特的地方。

## 詞彙

critical 批判的，挑剔的
imperfection 不完美
body shape 體型
facial feature
臉部特徵（包括五官）
confident 有信心的

# How can an ineloquent person improve their communication skills?

口才不好的人可以如何改善溝通技能？

Prologue

41 環保

42 教育

43 工作

44 我的情緒

45 我的弱點

Epilogue

### 你可以這樣回答

They can enroll in communication courses or workshops.
他們可以報名溝通課程或工作坊。

They can use body language such as eye contact and gestures to improve their communication.
他們可以用目光接觸和手勢之類的身體語言來改善溝通。

### 參考範例

I believe in the principle that practice leads to perfection. Whether it's casual conversation or formal communication, the key is to engage in regular dialogue to enhance fluency. Seeking professional guidance and advice through communication classes can also be helpful.

我相信熟能生巧（多練習就能達到完美）的法則。不管是非正式的對話或者正式的溝通，關鍵在於經常進行對話來提升流暢度。透過溝通課尋求專業指導與建議，可能也有幫助。

### 詞彙

principle 原則
perfection 完美
engage in 從事，參與…
fluency 流暢
guidance 指導

# Topics

# How would you cheer yourself up if you were in a bad mood?

如果你心情不好,你會怎樣讓自己振作起來?

........................................................

........................................................

........................................................

........................................................

**你可以這樣回答**

I'd meet up with a close friend / take a warm bath to cheer myself up.
我會和親密的朋友見面/泡熱水澡來讓自己振作起來。

Reading a good book / walking in nature helps me feel better.
讀一本好書/在自然中散步會幫助我感覺比較好。

**參考範例**

I would go jogging. Exercising helps me focus more on myself, giving me a sense of relief. I'd take advantage of my exercise time to reflect on my strengths and concentrate on positive thoughts to raise my spirits.

我會去慢跑。運動幫助我更專注在自己身上,帶給我解脫的感覺。我會利用運動的時間來思考我的優點,並且專注於正面的想法,以提振我的心情。

**詞彙**

relief 解脫,緩和

take advantage of 利用…

reflect on
仔細考慮,深思…

strength 長處,優點

raise one's spirits
提振心情

Q.324

# What would you do to ease your anxiety when facing challenges?

面對挑戰的時候，你會做什麼來緩和焦慮？

........................................................................................................

........................................................................................................

........................................................................................................

........................................................................................................

### 你可以這樣回答

I would practice meditation / take a short break to help myself calm down.
我會冥想（靜心）／短暫休息來幫助自己冷靜。

I find that deep breathing / doing yoga helps me calm my nerves.
我覺得深呼吸／做瑜伽會幫助我鎮定情緒。

### 參考範例

I would consult my friends when I'm anxious or facing challenges. Talking with them helps me relieve my pressure. Being surrounded by friends gives me a sense of connection, reminding me that I'm not alone and that I could weather the storm with their support.

當我焦慮或者面臨挑戰的時候，我會請教我的朋友。和他們交談會幫助我緩解我的壓力。身邊圍繞著朋友，帶給我與人連結的感覺，也提醒我並不是一個人，並且可以靠著他們的支持度過難關。

### 詞彙

consult 諮詢
anxious 焦慮的
relieve 緩和，減輕
connection 連結
weather the storm
度過難關

# Do you think exercising is a good way to keep yourself energized?

你認為運動是讓你保持活力的好方法嗎？

.................................................................

.................................................................

.................................................................

.................................................................

Prologue

46 自我激勵

47 偶像與榜樣

48 夢

49 信念

50 佳節團聚

Epilogue

## 你可以這樣回答

Exercising is a fantastic way to boost my energy.
運動是我增強活力很好的方法。

Exercising is not my thing, and I prefer more enjoyable activities.
我不喜歡運動，我偏好比較令我愉快的活動。

## 參考範例

Yes, exercising does have improved my strength and vitality. Moreover, regular exercise has also been a powerful stress and anxiety reliever for me. I would forget about my bad experiences and become a happier person after exercising.

是的，運動的確改善了我的體力和活力。而且，規律運動對我而言也是強大的壓力與焦慮紓緩工具。運動後我會忘掉不好的經驗，並且變成比較快樂的人。

## 詞彙

strength 力量，體力

vitality 活力

powerful 強大的

reliever
紓緩（痛苦之類）的事物

# Do you feel more motivated being alone or with people around you?

在獨自一個人還是周圍有人的情況下，你會感覺比較有動力？

.............................................................................................

.............................................................................................

.............................................................................................

.............................................................................................

### 你可以這樣回答

I'm an independent worker, so I feel motivated when I'm alone.
我是獨立的工作者，所以我一個人的時候感覺有動力。

I'm a social person, and I feel more motivated when I'm with others.
我是愛社交的人，我和別人在一起時感覺比較有動力。

### 參考範例

I find myself more motivated when I'm surrounded by people. Engaging in conversations with them allows me to enjoy moments of laughter and feel their support. Their comforting words and encouragement always inspire me to keep going.

我覺得自己在周圍有人的情況下比較有動力。和他們對話讓我能享受歡笑的時刻，並且感覺到他們的支持。他們安慰的話語和鼓勵，總是會激勵我繼續走下去。

### 詞彙

motivated
有動機的，有動力的
surround 圍繞
laughter 笑，笑聲
comforting 令人安慰的
encouragement 鼓勵
inspire 激勵

# Do you think meticulous planning can make you more confident in achieving a goal?

你認為縝密的計畫可以讓你對於達成目標比較有信心嗎？

## 你可以這樣回答

Meticulous planning gives me confidence by providing a clear roadmap.
縝密的計畫提供清楚的路線圖，而帶給我信心。

I find too much planning stifles my creativity and makes me less confident. 我覺得過度計畫會使我的創意窒息，而且讓我比較沒有信心。

## 參考範例

I believe that meticulous planning plays a crucial role in boosting my confidence to achieve a goal. Comprehensive planning helps me gain a clear understanding of my objectives and potential obstacles. In this way, I can be better-prepared and more confident in my ability to succeed.

我相信縝密的計畫對於提升我達成目標的信心，扮演很重要的角色。全面的計畫幫助我對目標和可能的阻礙有清楚的了解。這樣一來，我就能有比較妥善的準備，也會對自己成功的能力比較有信心。

## 詞彙

meticulous
非常仔細的，一絲不苟的

crucial 至關重要的

boost 提升，增加

comprehensive 全面的

objective 目標

obstacle 阻礙

343

# Would the possibility of winning an award encourage you to put in extra effort?

得獎的可能性會鼓勵你更加努力嗎？

Prologue

46 自我激勵

47 偶像與榜樣

48 夢

49 信念

50 佳節團聚

Epilogue

........................................................................

........................................................................

........................................................................

........................................................................

### 你可以這樣回答

I find that the possibility of winning an award boosts my motivation.
我覺得得獎的可能性會增加我的動力。

Awards are nice, but I don't feel the urge to be recognized with them.
獎項是不錯，但我並沒有想藉由獎項得到肯定的衝動。

### 參考範例

The possibility of winning an award serves as a strong incentive for me to work harder. Firstly, gaining an award provides a deep sense of satisfaction because it's a proof of accomplishment. Furthermore, awards are far more tangible than mere words of praise.

得獎的可能性是刺激我更努力的強大誘因。首先，得獎會帶來很深的滿足感，因為它是成就的證明。而且，和只是用言語稱讚比起來，獎項實在多了。

### 詞彙

incentive 刺激，激勵
satisfaction 滿足
accomplishment 成就
tangible
可觸摸到的；實實在在的
mere 僅僅的，只不過的

# Do you need to be praised to feel motivated?

你需要得到稱讚才會感覺有動力嗎？

Prologue

46 自我激勵

47 偶像與榜樣

48 夢

49 信念

50 佳節團聚

Epilogue

----

----

----

----

### 你可以這樣回答

I need constant praise to stay motivated.
我需要持續的稱讚來保持動力。

Praise feels good, but it's not my primary source of motivation.
稱讚感覺不錯，但那不是我主要的動力來源。

### 參考範例

I do find that praise is a strong motivator for me. I see praise as a meaningful form of recognition, and it encourages me to put in extra effort and maintain my enthusiasm for a task. If no one praises me when I'm doing well, I'll be frustrated.

我的確覺得稱讚對我而言是很強大的激勵因素。我將稱讚視為有意義的肯定形式，它也鼓勵我更加努力，並且保持對工作的熱情。如果在我表現好的時候沒有人稱讚我，我會覺得洩氣。

### 詞彙

motivator 激勵因素
meaningful 有意義的
recognition 認可
enthusiasm 熱情
frustrated 感到洩氣的

# Who is your primary role model, and why?

誰是你主要的榜樣，為什麼？

Prologue

46
自我激勵

47
偶像與榜樣

48
夢

49
信念

50
佳節團聚

Epilogue

........................................................

........................................................

........................................................

........................................................

### 你可以這樣回答

My primary role model is…
我主要的榜樣是…

His/Her/Their determination/innovation/selflessness inspires me to V…
他／她／他們的決心／創新／無私激勵我…

### 參考範例

My primary role model is my father because he is the most persistent person I've ever seen. When I was a child, he started his own business, which was not doing well at first. Nevertheless, he worked tirelessly and successfully turned things around, showing me the meaning of perseverance.

我主要的榜樣是我的爸爸，因為他是我看過最堅持不懈的人。在我小的時候，他創立了自己的事業，它一開始並不順利。儘管如此，他還是孜孜不倦地工作，並且成功扭轉局勢，向我展現了堅持不懈的意義。

### 詞彙

persistent 堅持不懈的

tirelessly 不知疲倦地

turn things around
扭轉局勢

perseverance 堅持不懈

# Do you think it is important to have a role model? Why?

你認為有一個榜樣很重要嗎？為什麼？

........................................................................

........................................................................

........................................................................

........................................................................

Prologue

46 自我激勵

47 偶像與榜樣

48 夢

49 信念

50 佳節團聚

Epilogue

### 你可以這樣回答

Role models offer a clear path to personal and professional growth.
榜樣提供（展現出）個人與職業成長的清晰途徑。

I believe that self-motivation can be more influential than having a role model.
我認為自我激勵可能比有一個榜樣更有影響力。

### 參考範例

I think it is important to have a role model. First and foremost, we often learn by imitation. Secondly, the process of choosing a role model allows us to gain a deeper understanding of ourselves. It helps us find the personality traits we aspire to develop.

我認為有一個榜樣是很重要的。首先，我們常常藉由模仿來學習。第二，選擇榜樣的過程讓我們能對自己有更深的了解。它幫助我們找到渴望發展的人格特質。

### 詞彙

imitation 模仿
personality trait 人格特質
aspire to do 渴望做…

# What kind of personality trait earns your respect?

什麼樣的人格特質會贏得你的尊敬？

Prologue

46 自我激勵

47 偶像與榜樣

48 夢

49 信念

50 佳節團聚

Epilogue

你可以這樣回答

Honesty/Integrity/Humility is a personality trait that earns my respect.
誠實／正直／謙卑是贏得我尊敬的一項人格特質。

I admire those who exhibit leadership/courage/resilience.
我欣賞展現出領導力／勇氣／心理韌性的人。

參考範例

I respect those who consistently demonstrate kindness. As we grow up, we may become indifferent to others, making it challenging to maintain our kindness in interpersonal relationships. It is those who manage to do so that earn my greatest respect.

我尊敬一貫表現出親切的人。隨著我們長大，我們可能變得對別人漠不關心，使得在人際關係中維持親切變得困難。那些設法做到這件事的人，會贏得我最大的尊敬。

詞彙

consistently 一貫地

kindness
仁慈，好意，體貼

indifferent 漠不關心的

interpersonal
relationship 人際關係

manage to V 設法做到⋯

# How might one benefit from having an idol?
一個人可能因為有偶像而得到什麼好處？

Prologue

46 自我激勵

47 偶像與榜樣

48 夢

49 信念

50 佳節團聚

Epilogue

........................................................

........................................................

........................................................

........................................................

### 你可以這樣回答

Idols often exemplify positive qualities that fans can learn to develop.
偶像常常示範粉絲可以學習發展的正面特質。

Having an idol can provide a sense of direction and purpose.
擁有偶像可以帶來方向感與目的感。

### 參考範例

One may get inspired by having an idol. Ideally speaking, idols set good examples for their fans, who in turn can learn from their experience of achieving their goals. This connection between idols and their fans can be a powerful force for personal growth.

一個人可能因為有偶像而獲得激勵。理想上來說，偶像為粉絲樹立好的榜樣，而粉絲進而可以從他們達成目標的經驗中學習。偶像與粉絲之間的這層連結，可以是個人成長的強大力量。

### 詞彙

inspire 激勵

ideally 理想上

set a good example
樹立榜樣

in turn 進而

personal growth
個人成長

# How might being a zealous fan negatively impact one's life?

當個狂熱粉絲可能會對生活造成什麼負面影響？

Prologue

46 自我激勵

47 偶像與榜樣

48 夢

49 信念

50 佳節團聚

Epilogue

### 你可以這樣回答

Being a zealous fan can lead to excessive spending on merchandise, concerts, or events.

當狂熱粉絲可能導致在商品、演唱會或活動上的過度花費。

Zealous fans may have unrealistic expectations about their idols and end up disappointed.

狂熱粉絲可能對偶像有不切實際的期待，而在最終感到失望。

### 參考範例

Being a zealous fan can divert the time we could have invested in personal life. While enthusiastically following our idols, we might unintentionally sacrifice the time that could have been spent on studying and exercising, or our precious moments with family and friends.

當個狂熱粉絲可能會轉移我們原本可以投資〔個〕人生活的時間。在熱情追隨偶像的時〔候，我〕們可能無意間犧牲可以用在學習與運〔動的時〕間，或者與家人和朋友共度的珍貴片〔刻〕。

### 詞彙

zealous 熱情的，狂熱的
divert 使轉向，轉移
unintentionally 非故意地
sacrifice 犧牲
precious 珍貴的

Prologue

46 自我激勵

47 偶像與榜樣

48 夢

49 信念

50 佳節團聚

Epilogue

# Do you think being an idol is an occupation worth pursuing?

你認為當偶像是值得追求的職業嗎？

........................................

........................................

........................................

........................................

## 你可以這樣回答

Being an idol can be rewarding for those who have a passion for performance.
當偶像對於有表演熱忱的人可能是很值得的。

I think being an idol comes with too much pressure on mental health.
我認為當偶像會對心理健康帶來太多壓力。

## 參考範例

I don't think so. Idol's careers are full of uncertainty and instability because the preference of the audience is always changing. It also takes a long period of training before debut, yet success is not guaranteed regardless of how much effort one has spent.

我不認為。偶像的職業生涯充滿不確定與不穩定，因為觀眾的偏好一直在改變。在出道前也需要很長的訓練期間，然而不管付出了多少努力，也不能保證成功。

## 詞彙

uncertainty 不確定

instability 不穩定

preference 偏好

debut （藝人）出道

guarantee 保證

# Would you stop being a fan if one of your idols did something wrong?

如果你有偶像犯了錯，你會停止當他的粉絲嗎？

..................................................

..................................................

..................................................

..................................................

### 你可以這樣回答

I have a zero-tolerance attitude toward certain wrongdoings.
我對於某些惡行有零容忍的態度。

I will still be a fan if they show their willingness to make amends.
如果他們展現出改過自新的意願，我還是會繼續當粉絲。

### 參考範例

It depends on the nature of the mistake they have made. If they have committed a crime, I will not be a fan anymore because it will be morally problematic to support a criminal. However, for less severe errors, I'd be interested in seeing how they make a fresh start.

取決於他們所犯的錯的性質。如果他們犯了罪，我就不會再當粉絲，因為支持罪犯在道德上是有問題的。不過，對於比較不嚴重的，我會想看他們如何重新出發。

### 詞彙

commit a crime 犯罪

morally 道德上

problematic 有問題的

criminal 罪犯

make a fresh start
重新開始

# Do you usually have good dreams, bad dreams, or no dreams at all?

你通常做好夢、惡夢,還是完全不會做夢?

Prologue

46 自我激勵

47 偶像與榜樣

48 夢

49 信念

50 佳節團聚

Epilogue

.........................................................................................

.........................................................................................

.........................................................................................

.........................................................................................

### 你可以這樣回答

I have quite a few bad dreams / nightmares.
我做很多惡夢。

I can't remember my dreams most of the time.
我大多不會記得自己的夢。

### 參考範例

I often have interesting dreams with magical or medieval elements. For instance, I once dreamed of being a princess leading the fight against mystical creatures. Additionally, I sometimes find myself in dreams where I possess magical abilities that allow me to control the elements.

我常做有魔法或中世紀元素的有趣的夢。舉例來說,我有一次夢到自己是帶頭對抗神祕生物的公主。另外,我有時候會發現自己在夢中擁有魔力,讓我能控制元素。

### 詞彙

magical 魔法的

medieval 中世紀的

mystical 神祕的

creature 生物

element 要素;元素
(在此指土、水、火、風之類的古典元素)

# Do you prefer to sleep with or without dreams?

你比較希望睡覺時做夢還是不做夢？

Prologue

46 自我激勵

47 偶像與榜樣

48 夢

49 信念

50 佳節團聚

Epilogue

### 你可以這樣回答

I enjoy having dreams, especially when they are pleasant or exciting.
我喜歡做夢，尤其當夢很愉快或刺激的時候。

I prefer dreamless sleep.
我比較喜歡不做夢的睡眠。

### 參考範例

I prefer to dream while I sleep. Dreams turn my sleeping time into an exciting adventure, and they are a potential source of inspiration for my artistic creations. Despite the fatigue after waking up from an intense dream, dreaming continues to fuel my creativity.

我比較希望睡覺時做夢。夢會把我的睡眠時間變成刺激的冒險，它們也是我藝術創作的潛在靈感來源。儘管從強烈的夢境醒來後會感到疲勞，做夢還是持續刺激著我的創造力。

### 詞彙

inspiration 靈感
artistic 藝術的
fatigue 疲勞
intense 強烈的
fuel 激發

# Do your dreams reflect your real life?
你的夢會反映真實生活嗎？

Prologue

46 自我激勵

47 偶像與榜樣

48 夢

49 信念

50 佳節團聚

Epilogue

**你可以這樣回答**

Sometimes my dreams feel like a mirror of my real life.
有時我的夢感覺像是真實世界的鏡子。

My dreams are usually surreal and unpredictable.
我的夢通常是超現實而不可預測的。

**參考範例**

What I dream at night is usually a reflection of my thoughts during the day. When I'm concerned about work, my dreams often involve stressful tasks. Conversely, after a delightful and relaxing day, I tend to have carefree and pleasant dreams.

我晚上夢到的事物，通常反映我白天所想的事情。當我擔心工作的時候，我的夢常常會有壓力很大的任務。相反地，在高興而放鬆的一天之後，我通常會做無憂無慮而愉快的夢。

**詞彙**

reflection 反映
be concerned about 擔心…
stressful 壓力大的
delightful 令人愉快的，令人高興的
carefree 無憂無慮的

# Do you think it is meaningful to analyze or interpret your dreams?

你認為分析或解讀你的夢是有意義的嗎？

Prologue

46 自我激勵

47 偶像與榜樣

48 夢

49 信念

50 佳節團聚

Epilogue

### 你可以這樣回答

I think dream analysis can reveal our subconscious thoughts.
我認為夢的解析可以揭露我們潛意識的想法。

I am skeptical about the accuracy of dream analysis.
我懷疑解夢的正確性。

### 參考範例

Yes, I like to analyze my dreams and examine them in detail to find their hidden messages. There are books and websites dedicated to explaining the symbols in dreams, and I use them to gain a deeper self-understanding and insights into my future.

是的，我喜歡分析我的夢，並且詳細檢視，以求找到它們隱藏的訊息。有一些書和網站專門解釋夢中的象徵，而我會用它們來獲得對自己更深的了解，以及對未來的洞見。

### 詞彙

in detail 詳細地

be dedicated to
奉獻於…；專門從事…

symbol 象徵；符號

insight 洞察力，洞見

# Do you believe some dreams can predict the future?

你相信有些夢可以預測未來嗎？

Prologue

46 自我激勵

47 偶像與榜樣

48 夢

49 信念

50 佳節團聚

Epilogue

...........................................................................

...........................................................................

...........................................................................

...........................................................................

### 你可以這樣回答

I'm open to the idea that some dreams might reveal the future.
我對於一些夢可能揭露未來的想法持開放的態度。

I doubt that dreams can hint at something in the future.
我不相信夢可以暗示未來的事。

### 參考範例

I don't really believe that dreams can predict the future. From my viewpoint, dreams tend to reflect the past rather than the future, and those who claim to have prophetic dreams often fail to provide concrete evidence to support their assertions.

我不是很相信夢可以預測未來。從我的觀點來看，夢通常反映過去而不是未來，而聲稱有預知夢的人常常無法提供具體的證據來支持他們的主張。

### 詞彙

viewpoint 觀點
prophetic 預言的
concrete 具體的，實在的
assertion 斷言，主張

# Have you ever experienced déjà-vu? Do you think it is real or just a feeling?

你曾經有過既視感嗎？你認為那是真的，或者只是感覺而已？

......................................................................................

......................................................................................

......................................................................................

......................................................................................

### 你可以這樣回答

I've had déjà-vu a few times, and it always feels very real.
我有過幾次既視感，而且總是感覺非常真實。

Déjà-vu rarely happens to me, and I think it's nothing more than a feeling. 既視感很少發生在我身上，而我認為那只是感覺而已。

### 參考範例

Based on my experiences, I believe déjà-vu is more than a feeling. I often dream of or envision a situation and later experience it in reality. These occurrences have made me wonder about the mysterious connection between our subconscious mind and real life.

根據我的經驗，我相信既視感不只是感覺而已。我常常夢到或者想像某個狀況，然後在現實中經歷到這個狀況。這些發生的事讓我想知道我們的潛意識與真實生活之間的神祕連結。

### 詞彙

déjà-vu 既視感（似乎經歷過某個場景的感覺）

envision 想像

occurrence 發生的事

mysterious 神祕的

# Have you ever dreamed to live a different life?
你曾經夢想過著不同的人生嗎？

Prologue

46 自我激勵

47 偶像與榜樣

48 夢

49 信念

50 佳節團聚

Epilogue

. . . . . . . . . . . . . . . . . . . . . . . . . . . . . . . . . . . . . . . . . . . . . . . . . . . . . . . . . . . .

. . . . . . . . . . . . . . . . . . . . . . . . . . . . . . . . . . . . . . . . . . . . . . . . . . . . . . . . . . . .

. . . . . . . . . . . . . . . . . . . . . . . . . . . . . . . . . . . . . . . . . . . . . . . . . . . . . . . . . . . .

. . . . . . . . . . . . . . . . . . . . . . . . . . . . . . . . . . . . . . . . . . . . . . . . . . . . . . . . . . . .

### 你可以這樣回答

I have dreamed of living a different life where I'm a…
我曾經夢想過著當…的不同人生。

No, I'm quite happy with my current life.
不，我對自己目前的人生很滿意。

### 參考範例

Yes. In real life, I am a software engineer, but I often find myself daydreaming about living a different life, such as being a writer or a bookstore owner. I believe this happens because reading and writing are my favorite hobbies.

是的。在現實生活中，我是軟體工程師，但我常常發現自己在做過著不同人生的白日夢，例如當作家或者書店店主。我相信是因為閱讀與寫作是我最愛的嗜好，才會發生這種情況。

### 詞彙

software engineer
軟體工程師

daydream 做白日夢

hobby 嗜好

# What is your motto in life?

你人生的座右銘是什麼？

Prologue

46 自我激勵

47 偶像與榜樣

48 夢

49 信念

50 佳節團聚

Epilogue

### 你可以這樣回答

I live by the motto "Never give up."
我照著「永不放棄」這個座右銘生活。

I follow the motto "Treat others as you wish to be treated."
我遵循「想要別人怎麼對待你，就要怎樣對待別人」這個座右銘。

### 參考範例

My motto in life is "Life is too short to waste." Our time is limited and precious. Therefore, we should seize every opportunity to pursue our passions and dreams. By embracing this philosophy, I've learned to appreciate every moment and live with a sense of purpose.

我人生的座右銘是「人生太短了，不能浪費」。我們的時間是有限而珍貴的。所以，我們應該抓住每個機會來追求我們的愛好與夢想。藉由擁抱這樣的哲學，我學會感謝每一刻，並且帶著目的感生活。

### 詞彙

motto 座右銘

seize 抓住

passion 熱愛；（強烈的）愛好

embrace 擁抱

philosophy 哲學

# Do you believe in the saying "Action speaks louder than words?"

你相信「行為勝於言語」這個說法嗎？

Prologue

46 自我激勵

47 偶像與榜樣

48 夢

49 信念

50 佳節團聚

Epilogue

**你可以這樣回答**

What people do tells you more about their character.
人們做的事比較能讓你知道他們的性格。

I don't think so. Words can be more influential sometimes.
我不認為。言語有時候可能比較有影響力。

**參考範例**

Yes, I believe that what a person does is more important than what they say. For example, a leader's words might inspire people. However, they would never earn people's respect or realize their visions if they fail to embody their words through concrete actions.

是的，我相信一個人所做的事比所說的話重要。舉例來說，領導者的話語可能會激勵人們。然而，如果他們無法透過實際的行為來體現他們所說的話，就永遠不會贏得人們的尊敬或者實現他們的願景。

**詞彙**

inspire 激勵
vision 想像；願景
embody 體現
concrete 實在的，具體的

Prologue

46 自我激勵

47 偶像與榜樣

48 夢

49 信念

50 佳節團聚

Epilogue

# Do you think love is the fundamental value that underlies life?

你認為愛是人生底層的根本價值嗎？

...................................................................

...................................................................

...................................................................

...................................................................

**你可以這樣回答**

In my experience, love does guide my actions and relationships.
在我的經驗中，愛的確引導我的行為與關係。

While love is important, I think knowledge is even more crucial to us.
雖然愛很重要，但我認為知識對我們而言是更加必要的。

**參考範例**

Yes, I believe that love is the driving force of life. It can connect us and cultivate meaningful relationships. Even when we are alone, we need to love ourselves to recognize our inherent worth and the meaning of our existence.

是的，我相信愛是人生的驅動力。它能將我們連結在一起，並且培養有意義的關係。即使在我們一個人的時候，我們也需要愛自己，才能認出我們內在固有的價值，以及我們存在的意義。

**詞彙**

driving force 驅動力

inherent 內在的，固有的

existence 存在

# Do you have a religion? Why or why not?

你有宗教信仰嗎?為什麼?

Prologue

46 自我激勵

47 偶像與榜樣

48 夢

49 信念

50 佳節團聚

Epilogue

## 你可以這樣回答

I have a religion because it gives me a sense of belonging.
我有宗教信仰,因為它帶給我歸屬感。

No, I haven't found a religion that resonates with me.
不,我沒發現讓我有共鳴的宗教。

## 參考範例

I'm a Christian, and I follow the teachings and principles of the Bible. Christianity provides me with comfort and hope during times of difficulty. Moreover, it teaches me compassion and forgiveness, guiding me toward a meaningful life.

我是基督徒,我跟隨聖經的教導與原則。在困難的時候,基督教提供我安慰與希望。而且,它也教導我同情與寬恕,帶領我走向有意義的人生。

## 詞彙

principle 原則

Christianity
基督教,基督信仰

comfort 安慰

compassion 同情

forgiveness 寬恕

# Do you think it is necessary for people to have a religion?

你認為人們必須要有宗教信仰嗎？

......................................................................................

......................................................................................

......................................................................................

......................................................................................

Prologue / 46 自我激勵 / 47 偶像與榜樣 / 48 夢 / 49 信念 / 50 佳節團聚 / Epilogue

### 你可以這樣回答

I believe that religion is vital for those seeking a deeper understanding of life.

我認為宗教信仰對於尋求對生命更深層了解的人是必要的。

I think it's a personal choice whether people have a religion or not.

我認為是否有宗教信仰是個人選擇。

### 參考範例

I don't think people must have a religion. I believe that people can foster their values and morality through introspection. They can also find the meaning of their life through their personal experiences without following any specific religious belief.

我不認為人們必須要有宗教信仰。我相信人們可以透過內省來培養自己的價值觀與道德。他們也可以透過個人經驗找到自己生命意義，而不用跟隨特定的宗教信仰。

### 詞彙

foster 培養

morality 道德

introspection 內省

# Do you think that joining a religious group is a good way to make new friends?

你認為加入宗教團體是交新朋友的好方法嗎？

Prologue

46 自我激勵

47 偶像與榜樣

48 夢

49 信念

50 佳節團聚

Epilogue

........................................

........................................

........................................

........................................

### 你可以這樣回答

Joining a religious group can be rewarding for those seeking friendships.
加入宗教團體對於尋求友誼的人而言可能是值得的。

I think there are more flexible ways to make friends than joining a religious group.
我認為有比加入宗教團體來得有彈性的交友方法。

### 參考範例

I believe that joining a religious group can be an effective way to expand one's social circle. These groups often attract like-minded individuals, making it easier for people to connect, share their thoughts, and build meaningful friendships.

我相信加入宗教團體可以是拓展社交圈的有效方法。這些團體往往吸引志趣相投的人，使得人們比較容易連結、分享想法，並且建立有意義的友誼。

### 詞彙

effective 有效的
expand 拓展
like-minded 志趣相投的
friendship 友誼

# Do you believe in the afterlife?

你相信死後（靈魂）的生活嗎？

........................................................................................

........................................................................................

........................................................................................

........................................................................................

### 你可以這樣回答

I have faith in the spiritual existence beyond our physical life.
我相信在我們的肉體生命之外有靈魂的存在。

I'm open to the possibility of an afterlife.
我對於死後生活的可能性持開放的態度。

### 參考範例

I don't believe in the afterlife because there is no compelling evidence for its existence. When we die, our physical body ceases to function, leaving nowhere for consciousness to exist. Therefore, I think this life is all we have, and we should make the most of it.

我不相信死後的生活，因為並沒有令人信服的證據證明它的存在。當我們死的時候，我們的肉體停止運作，使得意識沒有地方可以存在。所以，我認為這一生就是我們擁有的一切，而我們應該充分利用它。

### 詞彙

compelling 令人信服的

physical 肉體的；物質的

cease to V
停止⋯，不再⋯

consciousness 意識

make the most of
充分利用⋯

# Does your family hold a reunion on Christmas Eve or other holidays?

你家會在聖誕夜或其他節日團聚嗎？

........................................................................

........................................................................

........................................................................

........................................................................

**你可以這樣回答**

Yes, my family has a tradition of holding a Christmas Eve reunion.
是的，我家有舉行聖誕夜團聚的傳統。

Christmas Eve isn't a family reunion day for us.
聖誕夜對我們而言不是家人團聚的日子。

**參考範例**

My family doesn't gather for Christmas because we are not Christian. Instead, we come together during Lunar New Year. We enjoy delicious traditional food, exchange blessings, and give red envelopes to celebrate. The time spent with loved ones creates precious memories that last a lifetime.

我家不會為了聖誕節團聚，因為我們不是基督徒。取而代之的是，我們在陰曆新年團聚。我們會享受美味的傳統食物、給彼此祝福，並且送紅包來慶祝。與所愛的人共度的時間，會創造出維持一輩子的珍貴回憶。

**詞彙**

exchange 交換

blessing 祝福

lifetime 一生，一輩子

# What do you enjoy about Lunar New Year?

你喜歡陰曆新年的什麼地方？

你可以這樣回答

I enjoy the vibrant atmosphere of celebration during Lunar New Year.
我喜歡陰曆新年期間有活力的慶祝氣氛。

I enjoy observing the customs and traditions associated with Lunar New Year. 我喜歡觀察與陰曆新年有關的習俗與傳統。

參考範例

When I was younger, I was always excited about receiving red envelopes. Now I've grown older, and I find joy in reuniting with my siblings, who work and study in different cities. Most importantly, seeing my parents happy during our reunion brings me immense joy and fulfillment.

在我比較小的時候，我總是對於收紅包感到興奮。現在我長大了，就對於和在不同城市工作、求學的兄弟／姊妹團聚感到喜悅。最要的是，在團聚時看到我的父母很快樂，我很大的喜悅與滿足。

詞彙

reunite 重聚
sibling(s) 兄弟姊妹
immense 巨大的
fulfillment 滿足

# On Lunar New Year's Eve, does your family dine at a restaurant or eat at home?

在除夕那天，你家會在餐廳還是家裡吃飯？

Prologue

46 自我激勵

47 偶像與榜樣

48 夢

49 信念

50 佳節團聚

Epilogue

**你可以這樣回答**

We usually eat at home on Lunar New Year's Eve.
我們除夕通常在家吃飯。

My family prefers to dine at a restaurant on Lunar New Year's Eve.
我的家族偏好除夕在餐廳用餐。

**參考範例**

My family used to dine at restaurants on Lunar New Year's Eve due to our large family size of over 30 members, but after the passing of my great grandfather, we no longer have big family gatherings and have shifted to celebrating the day in a smaller scale by cooking at home.

因為我們超過 30 人的龐大家族規模，我們以前除夕都在餐廳用餐，但我的曾祖父過世之後，我們就不再舉辦大型的家族聚會，而轉變為在家煮（年夜飯），以比較小的規模慶祝這一天。

**詞彙**

dine 用餐
gathering 聚會
scale 規模

# Do you feel at ease when meeting unfamiliar family members during family gatherings?

在家族聚會時，你見到不熟的家族成員感覺自在嗎？

........................................................................................

........................................................................................

........................................................................................

........................................................................................

## 你可以這樣回答

I generally feel comfortable meeting family members, no matter they're familiar or not. 我和家族成員見面時通常感覺自在，不管他們熟悉與否。

It depends on the way they interact with me.
取決於他們和我互動的方式。

## 參考範例

Like many people, I don't feel at ease when meeting unfamiliar family members during gatherings, especially when they inquire about my personal life and make comparisons with other relatives. I find it awkward to have my life and choices judged by individuals who feel entitled to do so.

和許多人一樣，我在家族聚會見到不熟的家族成員時感覺不自在，尤其是他們詢問我的個人生活、和其他親戚做比較的時候。我覺得自己的生活和選擇被那些感覺自己有資格（評判）的人評判，是很尷尬的事。

## 詞彙

inquire 詢問

comparison 比較

awkward 令人尷尬的

judge 評判

entitled 有資格的

# Do you enjoy eating rice dumplings during the Dragon Boat Festival?

你在端午節時喜歡吃粽子嗎？

....................................................................................

....................................................................................

....................................................................................

....................................................................................

Prologue

46 自我激勵

47 偶像與榜樣

48 夢

49 信念

50 佳節團聚

Epilogue

### 你可以這樣回答

Rice dumplings are a must for me during the Dragon Boat Festival.
粽子是我在端午節時一定要吃的東西。

I've never been a fan of rice dumplings, even during the Dragon Boat Festival. 我一向不怎麼喜歡粽子，即使在端午節的時候。

### 參考範例

I enjoy eating rice dumplings during the Dragon Boat Festival. The regional variations in their forms, flavors, and ingredients lead to debates every year. Personally, I love the variety and enjoy all flavors of rice dumplings, except for those with peanuts inside.

我在端午節時喜歡吃粽子。它們在形狀、口味與材料方面的區域性差異，每年都會引發辯論。我個人喜愛這種多樣性，也喜歡所有的肉粽口味，除了裡面有花生的以外。

### 詞彙

regional 區域的
variation 變異，差異
lead to 導致…
debate 辯論
variety 多樣性

Prologue

46
自我激勵

47
偶像與榜樣

48
夢

49
信念

50
佳節團聚

Epilogue

# Do you believe that having a barbecue is essential during the Moon Festival?

你認為烤肉是中秋節不可或缺的活動嗎？

....................................................................................

....................................................................................

....................................................................................

....................................................................................

### 你可以這樣回答

I believe that having a barbecue adds a special flavor to the celebration of the Moon Festival.
我認為烤肉為中秋節的慶祝增添特別的風味。

I think it's a matter of personal preference.
我認為這是個人偏好的問題。

### 參考範例

I agree that having a barbecue is a fun way to celebrate the Moon Festival, but it is not necessary. My family seldom celebrates the Moon Festival by having a barbecue because grilled food is not ideal for health. We prefer to take a leisurely walk to admire the moon.

我同意烤肉是很有趣的中秋節慶祝方式，但那不是必要的。我家很少用烤肉的方式慶祝中秋節，因為燒烤的食物對健康不理想。我比較喜歡進行悠閒的散步來欣賞月亮。

### 詞彙

grill 燒烤
leisurely 悠閒的
admire 欣賞

# What is your opinion on setting off firecrackers as a way to celebrate?

你對於放鞭炮慶祝的意見是什麼？

Prologue

46 自我激勵

47 偶像與榜樣

48 夢

49 信念

50 佳節團聚

Epilogue

### 你可以這樣回答

I appreciate the tradition of using firecrackers in celebrations.
我欣賞在慶祝時使用鞭炮的傳統。

I find firecrackers are noisy and bothersome.
我覺得鞭炮很吵，而且讓人討厭。

### 參考範例

In my opinion, setting off firecrackers can be a lively way to celebrate, adding excitement and a festive atmosphere to special events. Nonetheless, firecrackers also come with safety issues and have a notable impact on the environment, so it's essential to use them responsibly.

在我看來，放鞭炮可以是熱鬧的慶祝方式，為特別的活動增添刺激與節慶氛圍。儘管如此，鞭炮也伴隨著安全問題，而且對環境有顯著的影響，所以負責任地使用它們是必要的。

### 詞彙

lively 充滿活力的，熱鬧的
excitement 興奮，刺激
festive 節日的
notable 顯著的
responsibly 負責地

# Epilogue

## 回顧與感謝

## Q.358

# Have you learned any new skills in the past year?

你在過去一年學了什麼新技能嗎？

你可以這樣回答

In the past year, I've learned to V… / I've been Ving…
在過去一年，我學習…／我在學…

Unfortunately, I didn't have the opportunity to acquire new skills due to my busy schedule.
很遺憾，因為我忙碌的行程，我沒有機會學習新技能。

**參考範例**

I have been minoring in interpretation since last semester, and I am starting to get the hang of it. It is challenging to listen to the speaker, take notes, and interpret simultaneously. However, the more I practice, the more confident I become in my ability to interpret effectively.

我從上學期開始副修口譯（一直到現在），而我開始掌握其中的訣竅了。同時聆聽說話者、做筆記、口譯很困難。不過，我練習得越多，就對自己有效口譯的能力越有信心。

**詞彙**

minor 副修
（ ⟷ major 主修）

interpretation 口譯

get the hang of
掌握…的訣竅

simultaneously 同時地

# Looking back at the past year, what was your happiest moment?

回顧過去一年，你最快樂的時刻是什麼？

................................................................

................................................................

................................................................

................................................................

### 你可以這樣回答

My happiest moment in the past year was when…
我在過去一年最快樂的時刻，是…的時候

I felt the happiest when…
我在…的時候感覺最快樂

### 參考範例

My happiest moment in the past year was when I learned that my brother had recovered from cancer. Since his diagnosis, he quit his job, underwent chemotherapy, and endured six challenging years. I was overjoyed to hear about his recovery after all the struggles and pain.

我在過去一年最快樂的時刻，是得知我的哥哥從癌症康復的時候。自從他被診斷出癌症，他辭掉工作、接受化療，並且忍受了辛苦的六年。得知他在這些奮鬥與痛苦之後康復，我非常高興。

### 詞彙

diagnosis 診斷

chemotherapy
（癌症的）化學療法

endure 忍受

overjoyed 極度高興的

## Q.360

# What is your biggest achievement so far?
到目前為止，你最大的成就是什麼？

..........................................................................................................

..........................................................................................................

..........................................................................................................

..........................................................................................................

你可以這樣回答

I consider finishing my master's degree to be my most significant achievement so far.
我認為完成碩士學位是我目前為止最大的成就。

I'm particularly proud of having completed a marathon.
我對於自己曾經完成馬拉松感到特別自豪。

參考範例

My biggest achievement so far is raising funds for a documentary about turtles endangered by marine pollution. The project spanned ten years, covering five countries and two oceans. Despite many challenges, it's been an incredibly rewarding journey for me.

我目前為止最大的成就，是為了關於因海洋污染而瀕危的海龜的紀錄片募資。這個計畫長達十年，涵蓋五個國家與兩大洋。儘管有許多挑戰，這對我而言還是很值得的旅程。

詞彙

raise funds 募資
endanger
使瀕臨（絕種的）危險
marine 海洋的
span 跨越；持續（時間）
incredibly 極為…

# Who has been the most important person to you these days?

這陣子對你而言最重要的人是誰？

..............................................................................................................

..............................................................................................................

..............................................................................................................

..............................................................................................................

**你可以這樣回答**

… has been incredibly important to me recently.
…最近對我而言非常重要。

… is the person who matters the most to me these days.
…是最近對我而言最重要的人。

**參考範例**

My fiancée, Lisa, is and will always be the most important person in my life. She is my constant source of encouragement, just like the light in the darkness that brightens my days. I feel safe and completely at ease around her, which allows me to be vulnerable sometimes.

我的未婚妻 Lisa 現在和以後都會是我生命中最重要的人。她是我持續的鼓勵來源，就像黑暗中的光一樣照亮我的每一天。我在她身旁感覺安全，而且徹底地自在，這讓我可以稍表現出脆弱。

**詞彙**

fiancée 未婚妻
（⟷ fiancé 未婚夫）
constant 持續的
encouragement 鼓勵
brighten 使明亮
vulnerable
容易受傷的，脆弱的

## Q.362

# Is there any unexpected opportunity that came your way this year?

這一年有什麼出乎意料的機會找上你嗎？

.........................................................................

.........................................................................

.........................................................................

.........................................................................

### 你可以這樣回答

This year, I was unexpectedly offered a promotion at work.
這一年，我在工作上意外獲得升職。

This year was quite routine and didn't bring me any unusual opportunities.
這一年很平淡，沒有為我帶來任何不尋常的機會。

### 參考範例

Yes, I received a job offer for dubbing work. It appeared that the producer had come across my vlog on the Internet and liked my voice, which led to the invitation. However, I had to decline the opportunity due to my lack of experience and confidence in the field.

是的，我獲得了配音工作的提案。那位製作人似乎是在網路上偶然發現我的 vlog（生活紀錄影片），而且喜歡我的聲音，而有了這次邀約。不過，我不得不拒絕這個機會，因為我在配音的領域缺乏經驗與自信。

### 詞彙

dubbing 配音
come across 偶然遇到…
invitation 邀請
decline 拒絕
confidence 信心，自信

# Is there any challenge you have faced that ultimately led to personal growth?

有什麼你面臨的挑戰最終促成了個人成長嗎？

...................................................................................................

...................................................................................................

...................................................................................................

...................................................................................................

## 你可以這樣回答

After months of practice, I finally overcame my fear of public speaking.
在幾個月的練習之後，我終於克服了對公開演說的恐懼。

The challenges I faced when traveling solo in Europe pushed me out of my comfort zone.
我在歐洲單獨旅行時遇到的困難，迫使我走出舒適圈。

## 參考範例

Last year, I took part in a one-year exchange program in Paris. Initially, communicating in an unfamiliar language was challenging, making me work hard to improve my French skills. As time went on, I became more fluent and felt increasingly at ease in my new environment.

去年我在巴黎當了一年的交換學生。一開始，用不熟悉的語言溝通很困難，這使得我努力增進自己的法語能力。隨著時間過去，我的法語變得比較流利了，也覺得在新環境越來越自在。

## 詞彙

take part in 參加⋯
initially 最初
fluent 流暢的
increasingly 越來越⋯

## Q.364

# Have you developed any new hobbies during the past year?

你在過去一年培養了什麼新的嗜好嗎？

### 你可以這樣回答

I took up painting/gardening/jogging as a new hobby.
我開始畫畫／園藝／慢跑當作新的嗜好。

I've been learning photography / yoga / magic tricks recently.
我最近在學攝影／瑜伽／魔術。

### 參考範例

A few months ago, my colleagues and I started to play badminton. We joined a club, signed up for classes, and now play badminton regularly after work. I have noticed improvements in both my physical and mental well-being, and I feel much more confident overall.

幾個月前，我的同事們和我開始打羽毛球。我們加入了羽毛球俱樂部、報名上課，現在會定期在下班後打羽毛球。我已經注意到自己的身體與心理健康都有改善，也覺得整體而言有自信多了。

### 詞彙

improvement 改善
physical 身體的
mental 精神方面的，心理的
well-being （身心的）健康
overall 整體上

# Do you think you are a better person than a year ago?

你認為自己現在比一年前更好嗎？

**你可以這樣回答**

Yes, I think I've become more… over the past year.
是的，我認為自己在過去一年變得比較…

No, I think I still need to V…
不，我認為自己還需要…

**參考範例**

I believe that I have made significant progress in self-improvement in the past year. I have developed better problem-solving skills and enhanced my ability to collaborate within a team. Moreover, the experience of starting to live independently has also fostered my maturity.

我認為自己過去一年在自我改善方面有很顯著的進步。我發展了更好的問題解決技能，也提升了自己在團隊中合作的能力。而且，開始獨立生活的經驗也使我更加成熟。

**詞彙**

make progress 進步
improvement 改善
enhance 提升
collaborate 合作
maturity 成熟

# 台灣廣廈 國際出版集團
Taiwan Mansion International Group

國家圖書館出版品預行編目（CIP）資料

英文寫作練習365/國際語言中心委員會著. -- 初版. -- 新北市：
國際學村, 2023.12
　　面；　公分
ISBN 978-986-454-318-2（平裝）
1.CST: 英語　2.CST: 寫作法

805.17　　　　　　　　　　　　　　　　　112018963

## 🌐 國際學村

# 英文寫作練習365

作　　　者／國際語言中心委員會　　　編輯中心編輯長／伍峻宏・編輯／賴敬宗
撰 稿 協 力／莊硯翔、李護、張子瑄　　封面設計／何偉凱・內頁排版／菩薩蠻數位文化有限公司
　　　　　　　　　　　　　　　　　　製版・印刷・裝訂／皇甫・秉成

行企研發中心總監／陳冠蒨　　　　　線上學習中心總監／陳冠蒨
媒體公關組／陳柔彣　　　　　　　　數位營運組／顏佑婷
綜合業務組／何欣穎　　　　　　　　企製開發組／江季珊、張哲剛

發 行 人／江媛珍
法 律 顧 問／第一國際法律事務所 余淑杏律師・北辰著作權事務所 蕭雄淋律師
出　　版／國際學村
發　　行／台灣廣廈有聲圖書有限公司
　　　　　地址：新北市235中和區中山路二段359巷7號2樓
　　　　　電話：（886）2-2225-5777・傳真：（886）2-2225-8052
讀者服務信箱／cs@booknews.com.tw

代理印務・全球總經銷／知遠文化事業有限公司
　　　　　地址：新北市222深坑區北深路三段155巷25號5樓
　　　　　電話：（886）2-2664-8800・傳真：（886）2-2664-8801
郵 政 劃 撥／劃撥帳號：18836722
　　　　　劃撥戶名：知遠文化事業有限公司（※單次購書金額未達1000元，請另付70元郵資。）

■ 出版日期：2023年12月初版　　　ISBN：978-986-454-318-2